"Okay, fine, so we'll all apply," Debbie said, starting down the hallway toward the cafeteria. "Besides, it's not like we have anything to worry about. Mandy's never gonna make it through the deadline without having sex."

Her friends laughed and Mandy tried to smile, but it took some effort. She hadn't told Eric about this scholarship thing yet, and she had no idea how she was going to deal with the whole purity issue. If she went ahead and made love with him on her birthday, would that really make her impure? And if the guidance office decided that actual virginity was the deciding factor, did that mean she'd *have* to tell them she'd done it? It all seemed so fundamentally *wrong*. Her sex life was nobody's business, right?

"Aw, we're just kidding." Debbie wrapped her arm around Mandy's shoulders and gave her a squeeze. "You've been a pillar of virtue this long. What's another couple of months gonna do to ya?"

Mandy pushed through the doors of the cafeteria and caught sight of Eric emerging from the lunch line across the room. Her heart skipped, then thumped extra hard. She pushed her hands through her bangs to wipe up the beads of sweat along her hairline and took a deep breath.

Another couple of months? By then they might have to mop her up off the floor.

Also by Kate Brian:

The Princess & the Pauper

Lucky T

The
Virginity
Club

KATE BRIAN

Simon Pulse
New York   London   Toronto   Sydney

Previously published as *The V Club*

If you purchased this book without a cover, you should be aware that this book is stolen property. It was reported as "unsold and destroyed" to the publisher, and neither the author nor the publisher has received any payment for this "stripped book."

This book is a work of fiction. Any references to historical events, real people, or real locales are used fictitiously. Other names, characters, places, and incidents are the product of the author's imagination, and any resemblance to actual events or locales or persons, living or dead, is entirely coincidental.

ALLOY ENTERTAINMENT

Produced by Alloy Entertainment
151 West 26th Street
New York, New York 10001

SIMON PULSE
An imprint of Simon & Schuster Children's Publishing Division
1230 Avenue of the Americas, New York, NY 10020
Text copyright © 2004 by Alloy Entertainment
All rights reserved, including the right of reproduction in whole or in part in any form.
SIMON PULSE and colophon are registered trademarks of Simon & Schuster, Inc.
Also available in a Simon & Schuster Books for Young Readers hardcover edition titled *The V Club*.
The text of this book was set in Baskerville.
Manufactured in the United States of America
First Simon Pulse edition June 2005
10 9 8 7 6 5 4 3 2 1
Library of Congress Control Number 2005920083
ISBN 1-4169-0346-1

For M. V.

one

EVA FARRELL DREADED MEETING WITH HER GUIDANCE counselor more than she dreaded dental appointments and final exams and even those evil mock trials she was forced to participate in for history class. Mrs. Labella was everything Eva was not. She was big, she was pushy, she was loud. She constantly smelled of cigarettes and cinnamon gum—enough to make a girl dry heave. But somewhere along the way she had adopted Eva as her very own charity case. She was constantly telling Eva how smart she was, how intuitive she was, how she could have anything she wanted if she would just come out of her shell already and reach for the stars! (She also had a whole problem with mixing metaphors.)

Reach for the stars. Yeah. Eva couldn't even reach for the salt and pepper.

Going to see Mrs. Labella was right up there on Eva's personal torture list with oral reports and peer critique days in creative-writing class. So that morning when she walked into homeroom to find

1

the little blue slip on her desk telling her to go directly to the guidance office, she knew instantly it was going to be a bad day. No good day started out with one of Labella's pep talks.

Eva sat back into the vinyl couch in the waiting room, her knees pressed together and her ankles separated. She hugged her backpack to her chest and watched the clock. She'd already missed ten minutes of first-period chemistry. Maybe by the time she got back to class, they would be done going over the homework. At least she would miss the waiting-to-get-called-on sweats (number four on her personal torture list).

The perky guidance secretary looked over at her and gave her one of those I-haven't-forgotten-you're-here smiles. Eva looked away quickly. Eye contact was not one of her talents.

"Eva!" Mrs. Labella's voice boomed through the office. "There you are, girl! I have fabulous news! Mrs. Treemont kicked the bucket last night!"

Everyone in the outer office looked over at Mrs. Labella, standing there in her cubicle doorway in her purple flowered blouse with the huge bow splayed out over her sizable breasts. Her glasses were suspended from a beaded string around her neck, and they hung right off the edge of her bosom shelf, swaying back and forth. It took a lot for the other members of the guidance office to look at Labella in shock or wonder. They were used to her. But she'd just announced that the oldest, most revered, most mysterious resident of Ardsmore, Pennsylvania, had died. And she'd done it with a gleeful grin.

Eva scrambled out of her seat and slid past Labella into her office, figuring that it was the only way to break the uncomfortable silence. Labella closed the door after her and lowered herself into her chair. Eva clutched her backpack and waited.

"It's your lucky day, Eva Farrell," Mrs. Labella said, slapping Eva's knee. "That Treemont lady didn't seem like she had much while she was alive, but it looks like she was just sitting on her wad up in that old house, waiting to surprise us all."

Oooookay, Eva thought. *What'd she do before she died—give birth to twin baby aliens or something? Of course, I don't know how that would make this my lucky day. . . .*

Mrs. Labella took a gulp of her coffee and looked at Eva expectantly. Eva got that sinking feeling in her stomach that it was her turn to say something. Her mouth went dry.

"Well, aren't you going to ask me *why* it's your lucky day?"

Oh, how Eva hated this game. Mrs. Labella was always trying to trick her into talking by asking Eva to ask her questions. If only Labella could see Eva with her friends, she'd realize it was only teachers who intimidated her. Well, most adults, actually. And guys. And girls who were older. Or more confident.

"Why is it my lucky day?" Eva asked finally. Mrs. Labella grinned, triumphant.

"*Because* Mrs. Treemont has set up a scholarship, and I *know* that you are going to win it," Mrs. Labella said. "Her people faxed this over within an hour of her passing. It was waiting in our machine this morning." She picked up a piece of paper from her desk and cleared her throat before beginning to read. "The Victoria A. Treemont scholarship will be awarded to a student in the senior class at Ardsmore High School who meets the following requirements: He or she must have a grade point average of 3.2 or higher; he or she must have demonstrated commitment to school and community; he or she must submit three recommendations from faculty, community members, and peers; he or she must submit an essay demonstrating his or her qualifications for this scholarship; and he or she must exemplify purity of soul and body."

Eva blinked. As Labella had ticked off the requirements, Eva had been growing more and more intrigued. But purity of soul and body?

Shouldn't this scholarship have been earmarked for a nunnery?

Mrs. Labella placed the paper down on the desk and turned a beaming smile on Eva.

"Now, you can take that last part any way you want, but I know you'll have no trouble as long as you've kept the rabbit out of the henhouse, if you know what I mean." Eva covered her eyes with her hand. Someone outside the fogged-glass door snickered.

Omigod. She's the devil, Eva thought. *I am sitting in Satan's cubicle.*

Eva sank lower in her chair, turning ten shades of purple. The subject of sex seemed to be coming up a lot lately, even with her friends. It was like there was a sudden dearth of worthy topics in the world and they'd been left to gab endlessly about the one thing Eva knew nothing about.

"I . . . uh . . ."

"I don't know how they're going to prove whether or not you are a virgin, mind you, but I believe that's what old Treemont was getting at with that last line. And besides, you meet all the other requirements and then some," Labella continued. "Sweetie, this scholarship is for forty thousand dollars a year for four years. You could go to *Wesleyan.* You could go wherever you *want.*"

Suddenly every last disturbed thought in Eva's head was replaced by a vision of her in a heather gray Wesleyan sweatshirt, walking across campus, chatting with other students—students who understood poetry and writing and didn't think that recounting their latest baseball victory and making it rhyme qualified as literary magazine material.

"There's an informational session at the beginning of fifth period tomorrow, and I expect you to be there," Mrs. Labella told her. "You got it?"

Eva sat up straight and gingerly held out her hand. Mrs. Labella laid the scholarship information on Eva's outstretched palm.

An unfamiliar fluttering of hope danced around inside Eva's chest. She had a 3.6 GPA at least. And she volunteered three times a week at 4-H. And she could probably find three people who would recommend her. And an essay? No problem. Plus she was probably the only senior at Ardsmore who hadn't even been *kissed* yet. You couldn't get much purer than that. She could do this.

She looked up at Mrs. Labella's beaming face, took a deep breath, and asked the ever important question. "There's no interview . . . is there?"

"I can't believe she gave me a C-plus! I've never gotten a C-anything in my entire life!" Debbie Patel said, shaking her history paper in front of Mandy's and Kai's faces. "This is insane! The woman is insane!!"

Mandy Walters and Kai Parker exchanged a

smile. "Well, maybe Ms. Russo just didn't agree with your hypothesis that the Allies' more functional uniforms helped them win World War II," Mandy suggested helpfully.

"What? You don't think that function versus form in military uniforms is a factor?" Debbie asked. "You really think our guys would have done as well if they'd had to be sitting in those trenches with those tight German pants riding up their butt cracks? No. Soldiers need to be able to *move*. Whoever designed our uniforms helped us win the war."

"Oookay, Vera Wang. Whatever you say." Kai shoved her hands in the pockets of her baggy cargo pants and headed toward her locker.

Debbie didn't know why she was surprised by Kai's lack of appreciation for her cutting-edge history paper. The girl dressed more like a guy than most of the guys in this school. Still, somehow she made it work for her. Debbie had to appreciate *that* miracle.

"Hey, guys!" Eva said, pushing away from the wall where she'd been waiting for them. "You're not going to believe this. There's this new scholarship and—"

"We know," Debbie said. "Everyone's talking about it. Forty g's a year. Fashion institute, here I come."

"Uh, *no*. Cornell, here *I* come," Kai put in. "Or wherever I decide to go."

"Oh, you guys are applying too?" Eva said, her face falling.

"I'm not," Mandy said, tucking her blond hair behind her ears.

Debbie glanced at Mandy, who, as always, had a serene, content smile playing about her lips. Debbie so envied her. If there was one thing Mandy Walters did not have to worry about, it was money. In fact, there were a lot of things Mandy Walters didn't have to worry about. Her college applications, finding a boyfriend, her hair, her skin . . . Debbie shrugged this all off. *If I weren't such a babe myself, I'd probably have to kill her,* she thought, smirking.

"Thank God for that," Kai said. "If Miss All-American here applied, we'd all be screwed."

Eva leaned back against the wall again, looking deflated. "Well, if you guys are going to do it—"

"Don't even finish that sentence, Eva Farrell," Mandy said. "You have just as much of a shot as anyone."

"More so if that whole purity thing turns out to *not* be a joke." Kai popped open her locker and, as always, a mess of tangled clothes, CD cases, and notebooks spilled out onto the floor. Kai used the side of her leg to push it all back in as Debbie flattened the door back against the wall so she could check her hair in Kai's locker mirror.

"If that turns out not to be a joke, I'm in trouble," Debbie said.

"You're not even going to *need* Treemont's money," Mandy told her. "You're gonna win that FIT scholarship."

Debbie's stomach turned. At that very moment her mailbox at home might contain an envelope from FIT. *The* envelope. She had sent her scholarship application in weeks ago, along with her audition piece—a red, backless, Asian-inspired prom dress with a tulle lining and a mandarin collar. Some days she was sure it was going to snag her a spot in the freshman class on her way to Parisian runway shows and sipping fruity cocktails with Gwyneth. Other days she could just as easily envision her creation in the admissions office on the bottom of a pile marked *To be burned*.

"It's always good to have a backup plan," Debbie said, sounding a bit too much like her father for her own comfort. She brushed the thought aside and tugged at one of her springy black curls.

"Yeah, but I thought the Math and Science competition was your backup plan," Mandy said.

"Luckily that can now be my *backup* backup," Debbie said. She took a silver Clinique tube out of her makeup bag and applied a new coat of Black Honey lip gloss. "It'll be the fashion design scholarship," Debbie said, smiling at her reflection in the mirror. "Then if that doesn't work out, the Treemont, and if *that* doesn't work out, *maybe* the Math and Science competition."

Her father might be counting on Debbie's winning the statewide Math and Science competition and getting a full ride to Penn State for the science major of her choice, but Debbie had other plans. Like never cracking a science textbook again for the rest of her natural life.

"Um . . . Debbie? Didn't you hook up with Sam Crispo on Friday night?" Mandy asked, looking off down the hall.

Debbie turned around to follow her gaze. "Yeah, why?"

"I think he's showing those guys your bra," Mandy pointed out. Sure enough, a large group of salivating dorks were jostling around Sam's locker and Debbie saw a flash of black lace. She snapped her lipstick shut and shook her head.

"Never hook up with a junior," she said with a sigh, and rolled her eyes. She stalked off down the hall to deal with her latest guy's indiscretion. The lemmings at the back of the pack noticed her coming and wisely moved out of the way.

"Hi, Sam!" she said. A four-alarm flush rose to his face as he clumsily attempted to hide the bra behind his back. *You are so snagged,* Debbie thought. She held out her hand.

"I'll take that back if you're done practicing," she said.

Sam's mouth opened and a pained noise came out. He placed the bra in her hand and Debbie started to walk away slowly, knowing one of the Neanderthals would have to ask.

"Practice?" someone said.

Debbie stopped, smiled at her friends, who were watching the proceedings, and turned to face the guys.

"Oh, yeah. I let Sam borrow this after it took him half an hour to get it off me on Friday night. I guess he hasn't had much experience," Debbie said. She tilted her head and in a high sweet voice added, "So Sammy, was it any easier when it was wrapped around a pillow?"

The guys all cracked up laughing and Sam sputtered. Debbie returned to her friends.

"Too bad," she said, shoving the bra into her bag. "He was a hottie."

"What was that in the scholarship material about purity of soul and body?" Kai joked, bringing a fingertip to her chin, blinking her dark eyes rapidly, and looking up at the ceiling.

"Ha, ha," Debbie said.

"Hey, as long as they draw the line at virginity, Debbie will have no problem," Mandy said.

Kai's jaw dropped. "Oh, wait a minute. You're not telling me you're actually a *virgin*."

"Why is everyone always so surprised by that?" Debbie asked, widening her eyes innocently.

"It's the tattoo rule!" Eva and Mandy called out in unison.

"What the hell is the tattoo rule?" Kai shook her head, confused.

"All right. We've been hanging out a lot since you moved here, and you seem like a trustworthy girl. But you should be very honored. It's not just anyone who gets to join Club Tattoo," Debbie said.

"Sounds pretty intense," Kai joked.

Debbie looked around to make sure the coast was clear, then tilted her head toward the doorway to the nearest darkened classroom. Obviously intrigued, Kai followed, and Mandy and Eva stood shoulder to shoulder to block them from view. Debbie opened the button on her denim skirt and pulled the waistband down to reveal the small honeybee tattoo on the skin near her hip bone.

"Hey, that's really cool," Kai said, leaning down to inspect it.

"Thanks. I designed it myself," Debbie told her.

"Why a bee?" Kai touched the bee cautiously with her fingertip, as if she expected it to move.

"*Deborah* means 'honeybee' in Hebrew," Debbie said, zipping up her skirt. "Why the Patels of

Mumbai, India, went for a Hebrew name is still cause for speculation. But there ya go!"

"Okay, but I still don't get it. What's the tattoo rule?" Kai asked as the four of them moved back into the hall.

"This tattoo got me banned from watching TV for six months last year," Debbie said, frowning. "If I'm ever gonna reveal this tattoo to a guy, he'll have to be someone really special."

Debbie didn't see why everyone always seemed to be in such a rush to go all the way. She had plenty of fun doing everything else with her many boy toys, so she figured she might as well save the big deflowering for a guy who was really worth it.

If such a guy exists, she thought.

"Well, I'm honored to be admitted into the club," Kai said reverently as she sifted through her books. "So, then, I guess you've never been in love?"

"Have you *seen* the guys in this town?" Debbie smirked. *"Please."*

"Point taken," Kai replied.

"Have *you* ever been in love?" Mandy asked. Kai had only moved to Ardsmore, from Lake Tahoe, Nevada, just before the beginning of the school year. There were still some vital details her new friends had yet to uncover.

"Once. At least I thought I was," Kai said.

"What was it like?" Eva asked.

"In a word? Disastrous," Kai said matter-of-factly.

Kai looked really sad for a second and then cleared her throat. Her eyes flicked toward Mandy and she smirked. "Well, we know one of us around here is a lost cause."

Mandy's brow knitted in confusion, but a second later she giggled when a pair of arms circled her waist.

"Can I walk a beautiful lady to her next class?" Eric Travers, Mandy's Mr. Perfect, said, nuzzling her neck.

Debbie looked at Eva and stuck her finger into her mouth, fake gagging. Mandy whacked her arm.

"See you guys later," she said.

"I'll come with," Eva said, scurrying to catch up.

Kai followed Eric and Mandy with her eyes. "Have they always been that gross?"

"It was even worse when they first got together," Debbie said. "They went through this whole baby-talk phase? I couldn't be around them and food at the same time. It gave me the heaves." She returned to her reflection. "So anyway, you're definitely going to go out for the scholarship, right? Because your parents are boho do-gooders who can't be bothered with money . . ."

"And *you're* going to go out for the scholarship because there's no scratch left in the college pot now that all three Patel brothers have cashed in," Kai added. "Well, that and the whole exerting-your-independence thing."

"Exactly. I have to get money from *somewhere*," Debbie said, snapping the lipstick shut. "I mean, how the hell did Ravi Junior end up at Penn State? We all had him pegged for a life in and out of rehab, jail, and mental hospitals."

"It's just proof of the extent to which your father can put the fear of God into a person," Kai said.

Debbie nodded. There wasn't a single soul who'd come in contact with stoic, larger-than-life Mr. Patel who wasn't mortally scared of him. Not even Kai was immune to his icy glare. Debbie shuddered just thinking about it.

"You got that right," she said.

Eva's locker was closest to the cafeteria, so she always got there before her friends and saved their usual table. This time alone, watching the rest of the students in fifth-period lunch stream through the doors, was her favorite part of the day. Eva sat back with her creative-writing notebook open on her lap and jotted down various details about her classmates.

Tisha Morales continues her antishaving protest. Day 13. Leg hair is beginning to braid itself. . . .

15

Ryan Gibraltor has a hard-on again. Must've fallen asleep in AP bio . . .

Does Michelle Horowitz really not notice that her foundation is ten shades darker than the skin on her neck?

And then she saw him—just a glimpse of his shaggy blond hair through the slim window in the wooden door—and she stopped breathing. Riley Marx. He was laughing as he entered the caf, glancing over his shoulders at his buddies. Eva would have killed to know what they were laughing about.

He's wearing his Mr. Bubbles T-shirt today, she wrote, her hand suddenly shaky. *You've gotta love a guy in a Mr. Bubbles T-shirt.*

Actually, Eva had to love this particular guy no matter which of his myriad pop culture tees he was sporting. He didn't care what the other guys thought of him, even though his social position had yet to be defined at Ardsmore High. Unlike the rest of the male population of this school, Riley Marx was undoubtedly human.

And Eva had been fantasizing about him regularly ever since he'd arrived. There was the fantasy where he first spoke to her—when he came up to her in the hallway after classes and told her that he'd read her latest poem in the lit magazine and it had touched a chord deep within him. There was the one about their first kiss, sitting at the edge of the water at Huff Lake with champagne and candle-light. . . .

Even her friends knew about that one—the fantasy first kiss—but she never told them who the guy was. That part of the daydream was all hers. Besides, she knew it was never going to happen. Eva could hardly ever get up the guts to talk to *any* guy, let alone a man of perfection like Riley Marx. But the fact that it was impossible didn't make the crush any less intense.

"Hey."

Eva blinked. Riley and his friends had just walked by her table and Riley had lifted his chin and said "hey." Had he been talking to her? Was that even possible?

Oh God. What if he was talking to me and I didn't say anything and I was just sitting here staring into space like a complete wastoid? Eva blinked. *Did I just use the word* wastoid?

Eva flipped to a new page in her notebook and started to write frantically. Riley Marx had potentially just spoken his first word to her. At least ten pages of rambling were definitely in order.

"So, any special requests for your birthday, sweetness?" Eric asked as he pulled to a stop in front of Mandy's sprawling house that night. They'd met up after their respective team practices—football for him, volleyball for her—so Eric could drive her home. Mandy's VW Bug had been in the shop that morning getting the oil changed and the tires rotated, but it was back now, parked in the driveway, gleaming in the waning sun.

"You don't have to get me anything," Mandy said.

"Yeah, like that's gonna happen," Eric replied.

"Well . . . whatever," Mandy said happily. "If it's coming from you, it'll be perfect."

Eric put the car in park and turned to look at her, his blue eyes mischievous.

"Speaking of . . ."

Eric pulled his backpack out of the backseat and Mandy smiled. It was October 15.

"You know what today is," Eric said, fishing a small gray box out of his bag.

"Eric, you really don't have to keep doing this," Mandy said, even though she loved it. Eric grinned as she opened the box to find a tiny crystal penguin with black eyes and a tiny nose looking up at her.

"Oh! It's so sweet!" she said.

Ever since their first-month "anniversary" Eric had been giving her one Swarovski crystal animal on the fifteenth of every month like clockwork. Mandy had started collecting them when she was nine, but thanks to Eric that collection was now beyond impressive.

Mandy still remembered how touched and surprised she'd been when he'd given her the first one—a tiny sparkling turtle. He'd only been in her room once at that point and had asked her about the collection casually. But that was Eric. He was pretty much the most thoughtful guy she'd ever known.

She closed the box and kissed him on the cheek. "You are the best boyfriend ever," she added.

"What can I say?" Eric joked.

"Now you *really* don't need to get me anything for my birthday," Mandy said.

"Well, I was thinking, my parents are going to be away, and since we've been talking about it a lot lately . . ."

Mandy's heart thumped and she felt a stirring in that place she was still surprised could be stirred by mere words.

"Nothing's been *decided* decided," she said. Little did Eric know, Mandy *had* decided. She'd decided that this was it. Eric was going to be her first. She loved him; that was the most important thing. But furthermore, if they kept doing all the things they'd been doing and *not* having actual sex, she was fairly certain she was going to spontaneously combust.

She bit her bottom lip as Eric leaned toward her. His brown bangs fell over his eyes and her breath caught in her throat as his lips touched hers. For a few blissful minutes Mandy forgot that they were sitting right in front of her house, where anyone could see them. When Eric finally pulled away, his breath was warm and quick on her face.

"Just say you'll think about it," he said.

"Oh, I will," Mandy said. "A *lot.*"

She gave him a special sort of smile and felt naughty. Deliciously naughty. It was a nice change.

two

THE NEXT MORNING MANDY SAT AT THE KITCHEN TABLE, munching on her usual breakfast of Cheerios and bananas. She flipped through the pages of the new Princeton course catalog that had come in the mail the day before, but as she flipped through classes like Philosophy of the Modern Mind and Race, Racism, and the American Experience, all she could think about was Eric.

Eric unabashedly grabbing her hand at lunch, risking some serious ribbing from the rest of the guys, who were so anti-PDA. Eric calling her up on Sunday morning to let her know whether or not the comics were worth reading. Eric telling everyone at his last family barbecue how his girl was going to make the All State volleyball team for the third year in a row.

Mandy giggled, then sighed. *No wonder Debbie is always gagging in front of us. Maybe I should tell him,* she thought, imagining Eric's face when he learned that she did, in fact, want to have sex with him on her birthday.

Maybe I'll tell him before gym. That way if he gets all worked up, he can take it out on the soccer field, Mandy thought, blushing. *Or better yet, I'll tell him before football practice.*

The swinging door to the kitchen opened and Mandy focused her attention on the catalog, hoping her mother wouldn't ask her why she was all red in the face. She had a spoonful of Cheerios and banana slices halfway to her lips when her mom sat down across the Formica table from her.

"Mandy . . . ," she said, rubbing her palms together. "We should talk."

Mandy put her spoon down again as a knot of foreboding formed in her stomach.

To the casual observer her mother would have looked just as put together as always. She was wearing a pair of tan silk slacks and a black silk top, her hair was smooth and sprayed down, and her gold jewelry was all in place. But Mandy could see the dark circles under her eyes that her makeup was unable to hide. Something was definitely wrong.

"What's going on?" Mandy heard herself ask. Her voice sounded strange.

"Well, I don't want you to worry, but . . . it's about your father," her mother said, looking her in the eye.

Mandy went numb. "Is he sick?"

"No, no, no. Nothing like that. He's . . . well . . .

he's . . . Honey, he's being investigated for tax fraud."

Mandy clasped her hands together under the table. Where the hell was this coming from?

"Tax fraud?"

"Everything is going to be just fine," her mother said quickly. "But things just may be a little tight around here for a while. Maybe a long while."

Mandy forced herself to breathe in and out.

"Did he . . . I mean . . . he didn't—" Mandy couldn't even bring herself to ask.

"Of course not," her mother said firmly.

Right. Of course not.

"But sweetie, they may freeze some of our accounts, and this kind of thing could drag on. . . ."

Her mother's eyes traveled toward the Princeton catalog. Mandy's heart thumped.

"You may want to start thinking about looking into state schools," her mother said finally, looking ill.

"But Mom—"

"Penn State is a great school," her mother interrupted.

Mandy bit back the protestations that were bubbling up in her throat. The very idea of going to Penn State instead of Princeton made her sick to her stomach. Princeton was where she had always wanted her to go—it was her parents' alma mater, the place they had met. They had made yearly visits to the school every homecoming. She had never thought of going anywhere else, had always imagined herself on Princeton's lush, historic campus. Could all that be taken away?

"Mandy, really, it's going to be okay," her mother said firmly. "I'm sure everything will get back to normal . . . eventually. We're just going to have to pull together here and support each other."

Mandy closed the Princeton catalog, feeling a tightness in her chest. She couldn't not go to Princeton. How could they be taking away her college fund when her father hadn't done anything wrong? It just didn't seem fair.

"You can do that, right, sweetie?" her mother said.

Mandy nodded, not even sure what the question had been. Her mind was too busy. *The scholarship. The Treemont scholarship.* She had never even considered applying for financial aid before, but before, she'd never thought she would need it.

My friends will die if I go for it, she thought. *No. They'll kill me.*

"Mandy?"

Mandy took a deep breath and tried to focus. "Is Dad okay?"

"He's fine. Just a little stressed," her mother told her. "He should be home for dinner tonight."

"Okay."

"And Mandy, when you see him? Just . . . tell him you love him."

Mandy nodded resolutely and sat up straight. Her parents needed her to be strong and handle this like, well, like an adult.

"Okay, Mom. Whatever you say."

"That's my girl," her mother said with a smile. She walked around the table and kissed the top of Mandy's head.

Mandy felt herself relax. She could handle this. Her father was no criminal. The charges would eventually be dropped, and until then Mandy was going to blow her parents away with her ability to be mature. And she was going to look into this Treemont thing. What would it hurt to just look into it?

Her mother went about preparing her coffee and Mandy forced a spoonful of food into her mouth. *Poor Dad.* she could just imagine him sitting in his office at Marcel Corp, where he was the CEO, frowning and tap-tap-tapping his silver pen against his desk in frustration. She wished he had told her about this himself so that she could have hugged him right away and told him she knew everything was going to be all right.

Later. I'll tell him later. The next time I see him, she promised herself.

In the meantime she had a math quiz to think about, then volleyball practice, then a quick SADD meeting, and then tonight—Eric. She had to focus on reality and forget about this craziness for now. There was just too much to do. Mandy got up from the table and grabbed her things.

"I gotta go, Mom," she called out. "I'll see you tonight!"

Here he comes, here he comes, here he comes, Eva thought, watching as Mr. Greenleaf shuffled along the aisle at the end of English class, slapping papers down onto her classmates' desks. Eva's stomach hurt—on her personal torture list, waiting for papers and tests to be handed back was number five.

She took a deep breath. *Okay, just let me get a B,* she begged silently. *I'll be fine with a B.*

Mr. Greenleaf paused next to Eva's desk. She could smell that acrid, unplaceable scent that clung to every one of his heavy, elbow-padded blazers. Eva stopped breathing. He didn't move. She looked up and caught a glimpse of the white stubble under his chin. Greenleaf smiled.

"Ms. Farrell," he said in his pseudo–English accent. "Nice work."

He held out her paper and Eva gingerly took it out of his hands. There, at the top of the first page, was a little blue A with a circle around it. Eva's body temperature skyrocketed. Rob Garner leaned over, straining his neck to see her grade, then pursed his lips and eyed her, impressed.

"If anyone wants to see what I expect in a paper on Shakespeare, please ask Ms. Farrell to lend you hers," Mr. Greenleaf announced.

Everyone around Eva shifted in their seats, staring down at their own grades, and Eva wished, as she did so often, for the ability to disappear. Luckily, a few moments later the bell rang and everyone rushed for the door.

"Lemme see, lemme see!" Debbie called out, catching up with Eva at the front of the room. Eva handed over her paper as she shrugged into her backpack. Debbie's mouth fell open. "You are *so lucky*. That guy never gives out A's! Greenleaf will definitely write you a recommendation for the Treemont thing."

Eva's skin reddened and she looked at the floor as she walked. "I don't even know if I'm gonna apply."

"If I hear you say that one more time, I'm going to pants you right here in the middle of this hallway," Debbie said, pointing a warning finger at Eva. "Don't test me. Do you want the entire school to see you in your pink Hanes Her Way?"

Eva rolled her eyes, smiling. "They're not *pink*," she said, brushing by her friend. *They're purple.*

Eva paused at her locker, and before Debbie could say anything else, Danny Brown appeared out of nowhere, grabbed Debbie's arm, and crushed her against his chest.

"Debbie, Debbie, Debbie!" he growled, tightening his grip until Debbie bulged her eyes comically. Eva shook her head and looked away. Danny was Deb's most frequent hook-up partner, but something about him icked Eva out. He was always grabbing her and tossing her around like she was a football. He seemed to take it for granted that he could have anything he wanted from Debbie, anytime he wanted it. And they weren't even boyfriend and girlfriend. Eva didn't understand how her friend could be attracted to the guy. He was so . . . *slimy.*

"So, you comin' over tonight?" Danny put her back on the ground and Eva saw him brush Debbie's chest with his hand as he reached up to straighten his backward baseball cap. There was a distinct leer on his face. Debbie giggled and shoved his arm, but Eva felt a lump rising in her throat.

"Sure," Debbie said, flipping her curly hair over her shoulder. "I'll be there around eight."

"Sweet," Danny said. He hooked his thumb through his belt loop and eyed Debbie up and down in a way that made Eva squirm. "See you then." He winked before loping off down the hall.

"Wait a second, Danny *again*? What about Sam?" Eva asked.

"Sam was Friday night," Debbie said with a shrug.

"I don't know how you keep them all straight."

"That, my friend, is what the kiss list is for!" Debbie announced, producing a well-worn journal from her bag. It was black velvet with a pair of hot-pink lips on the cover: the book in which Debbie kept her infamous kiss list—a rundown of the guys she'd fooled around with, how far they'd gone, and even how good they were.

"You brought it to *school*?" Eva asked.

"I figured I'd show it to Kai," Debbie said. "Now that she's in Club Tattoo, she might as well know all my secrets."

Debbie opened the book to the latest entry. "Check it out. I had to knock Sam down a few stars for the bra incident." Next to Sam Crispo's name were four stars, but three of them were scratched out.

In blue ink it read: *Sam is a master of the slow, sexy kiss. It took him forever to get up the guts to go for the bra clasp, but I let him take it off. He's just too yummy!* Then in black, obviously added later: *He brought my bra to school. This merits immediate removal from the Circle of Trust.*

"You're insane," Eva said.

"I like to think of it as organized and self-aware," Debbie said.

Eva laughed. "How many guys are in that thing now?"

"Um . . . *a lot*," Debbie said.

Eva raised her eyebrows.

"What? They're not relationships. It's not like I'm breaking any hearts," Debbie said. "I'm just . . . kissing my frogs."

Eva sighed and slammed her locker. She had no idea why she was still shocked by Debbie's cavalier attitude toward guys. *I should be used to this by now. Maybe if I had that many guys wanting to kiss me, I'd suddenly be a kissing bandit, too.*

Eva instantly felt bad for thinking that way. *She's just popular. There's nothing wrong with it. Right?*

"Seriously, Eva." Debbie shook her head. "You have no idea what you're missing."

"Yeah. Maybe," Eva said. But she wasn't so sure. As far as she could tell, there was only one frog around here worth kissing, and she knew *that* wasn't going to happen anytime soon.

Eva sat at the second-to-last desk in the semicircle of seats in one of the English classrooms, which afforded her a view of everyone else in the room— all the better if she happened to notice anything worthy of her creative-writing notebook. She sighed and glanced at the clock as Mr. Simon, the head of the guidance department, went over the requirements for the Treemont.

They had to have this meeting during fifth period, she thought. *Right now Riley might be walking to the cafeteria, and I'm missing him!*

The door to the classroom opened and Eva's heart stopped beating.

Apparently not, she thought. Riley Marx was, in fact, stepping into *this* room. His brown T-shirt had a Hershey bar on it and read, I Live for Chocolate.

Eva's skin tingled all over as an image popped into her head—his hands in her hair, the total love in his Caribbean blue eyes as he pulled her toward him. Oh God. Last night the daydream had gone further than ever before—all the way until he'd leaned her back on the warm picnic blanket, deepening the kiss. . . .

"That kid has balls for walking in here," Kai said, leaning toward Eva from the desk to her left.

Riley wiped his hand against the back of his baggy jeans, cracked a heart-melting smile, and looked around.

"Sorry I'm late," he said, with that easy confidence that never ceased to amaze Eva. If she'd walked in late, she would have ducked her head, fallen into the nearest chair, and been mortified for at least ten minutes. Riley simply sidestepped into the room, looking around for a good seat.

"Are you sure you're in the right place, Mr. Marx?" Mr. Simon asked, his bushy eyebrows coming together behind his glasses.

"Is this for the Treemont scholarship?" Riley asked.

"Yes, it is," Mr. Simon replied.

Riley's smile widened. "Then I'm in the right place."

A few girls in Eva's vicinity giggled, eyeing Riley as he continued to scan the room. His gaze fell on the empty chair next to Eva's and her pulse quickened.

Riley took a step toward the center of the room and Eva held her breath. He was heading toward her. He was going to sit next to her.

Oh God. Oh God. Oh God.

"Riley! Over here!" a voice called. Eva turned around to see Debbie waving at him from her perch on the wide shelf that ran along the back of the classroom, where she sat. Riley lifted his chin in Debbie's direction and turned sideways to slide along the wall. As he approached, Debbie pushed her hair forward and rubbed at the back of her head. Eva knew this was Debbie's patented move.

"It looks like I just have an itch, but what I'm really doing is fluffing my curls," she'd told Eva a few months ago.

As Riley sat down next to Debbie, she crossed her legs at the ankle, bit her lip, and smiled coyly up at him.

Ugh. She's like a peacock flashing her feathers, Eva thought. *Except only male peacocks do that, I think. Or something.*

Eva wanted to hurl. Her skin burned with a sudden flash of anger toward her best friend. So far, Riley had somehow escaped Debbie's seemingly inescapable claws, but if Eva knew Debbie, all that was about to change. She'd fooled around with Sam on Friday, was going to Danny's tonight, and Riley was next. One more frog in the boy-crazed marsh of Debbie Patel's existence.

Eva pulled out a pen and started to vent into her notebook, crooking her arm to hide her work from Kai. Couldn't Debbie leave just one guy for the rest of the world?

three

THERE WAS JUST SOMETHING ABOUT RILEY MARX THAT Debbie liked. Ever since the first day of junior year when she'd seen him—the new guy—unabashedly playing his guitar out on the steps to the parking lot in front of the school, she'd known there was something different about him.

Tall and lean, with perfectly scruffy blond hair and a heart-melting smile, Riley Marx was an enigma. Plus he was totally sexy, with those unbelievable eyes, those guitar-calloused fingertips, and that tiny mysterious scar to the left of his mouth.

He was also one of the very few guys at this school who had never come on to Debbie—never even flirted with her. So she was pretty sure he was gay.

Up at the front of the room Mr. Simon was just finishing up his Treemont speech, which, like most of his speeches, contained no information that everyone in the room didn't already know. "So, I think that covers everything. I'd like to have everyone fill out this form, and then if you have any questions, I'll open the floor. Now, this is just a preliminary form so we can get an idea of who's applying. You'll get the actual application in homeroom later this week."

Debbie grabbed two forms when Liana Hull passed them back. Liana eyed her and Riley, then leaned across the aisle to her friend Melissa Bonny and whispered just loud enough so Debbie could overhear.

"I guess *some* people didn't realize that the Sexaholics Anonymous meeting is being held down the hall."

Debbie rolled her eyes. Liana was just pissed that Debbie was hooking up with Danny, Liana's ex. But so what? Debbie didn't care. Let Liana and Melissa say what they wanted to about her. Debbie knew that she didn't have sex, and so did all the guys she hooked up with. That was all that mattered.

Debbie smiled at Liana and then waved and blew her a kiss. Liana made a disgusted face and turned around again. To Debbie's left, Riley was patiently filling out his own form, completely oblivious to anything else. Left-handed, Debbie noticed. That meant he was artistic. Not surprising.

Debbie flipped her hair so it brushed against his arm. He looked up.

"So," Debbie said, smiling. "Pretty *thrilling* meeting, no?"

"Yeah, totally," Riley said with a smirk. "Hey, are you going out for this *and* that Math and Science competition thing?" He tapped his pencil against the biology textbook that Debbie was leaning on and raised his eyebrows.

"Not if I can avoid it," Debbie replied. "Science isn't exactly my thing."

"Could've fooled me," Riley said.

"What do you mean?"

"You get A's on everything," Riley said.

Debbie, to her surprise, flushed. "How do you know that?"

"Everybody knows it," Riley said, lifting his shoulders. "The Science Club has spun off a radical we-hate-Debbie-Patel faction because you're always throwing off the curve. They have T-shirts and everything."

"Shut up. You're not serious."

"Okay, fine, I'm not. But they'll definitely be psyched if you don't compete. They'll probably throw a party."

"Well, then I'm happy for them," Debbie said.

"So what *is* your thing?"

Debbie's heart unexpectedly skipped a beat. She couldn't remember the last time a guy had asked her a question about herself other than, "Got a pen?" "Are you busy tonight?" and her all-time favorite, "When girls change together after gym, do they ever, y'know, shower together, too?"

"Fashion," she said, the word sounding foreign to her. "Fashion is my thing." She was fairly certain she'd never mentioned her true passion to anyone other than her closest friends. It felt good to say it.

"Cool," Riley said. "Not that I know much about clothes or anything, but you certainly seem to have a unique thing going on." He motioned to her outfit—a black T-shirt she'd cut up and resewn into a halter top and a flouncy knee-length skirt covered in multicolored diagonal stripes.

"Thanks."

Debbie was glad when Riley went back to his application, because she felt herself blushing. And Debbie never blushed.

Riley tapped his pen against his form. "See, this is where I run into trouble. I haven't volunteered at anything since I moved here. I helped with the spring cleanup at my church last year, but that's not gonna cut it."

"My mom makes me go with her to this soup kitchen in Harrisburg every Saturday," Debbie said. "I guess it looks like it's about to pay off."

"Ah, the grand benefits of do-gooding." He smirked. "Too bad my parents never felt so compelled."

Debbie smiled. Riley talked like an adult and it

wasn't even irritating. How the hell did he pull these things off?

"You should talk to Eva Farrell," Debbie said. "She's like a goddess down at 4-H. Maybe she can get you a job there."

"Oh, yeah?" Riley asked. Debbie glanced across the room at Eva, who was hunched over her own form, scribbling away. Her clothes were baggy and her hair was in bad need of a brushing.

What am I going to do with her?

"Yeah. She's a little shy, but she'll definitely help you out," Debbie told him.

"Thanks," Riley said, gracing her with one of his incredible smiles. "Good thing I sat next to you then, huh?"

Debbie's heart did that weird skipping thing again—something it only ever did when she was kissing somebody for the first time. But she and Riley weren't even touching. Weird. "Yeah," she said, smiling back. "Good thing."

Debbie went up to the front of the room and turned in her form. Just then Mandy walked in. *What the . . . ?* Debbie and Eva exchanged a look. What the hell was Mandy doing here? She needed a scholarship like she needed another brand-new VW.

"Hey, Mr. Simon. Sorry I'm late," Mandy said.

"Well, knowing you, I'm sure you had a good reason, Mandy. Just complete this application." He handed her a form and pulled her aside to fill her in. Soon Mandy slipped into a desk and Debbie waited for her to turn around and make eye contact, but she didn't.

Well, that's odd.

Mandy kept her head down and started filling out the paperwork. Debbie bit her lip. Mandy was *really* doing this. And if she was really doing this, she was definitely going to win—just like she always won everything else.

Suddenly Debbie couldn't wait for the meeting to be over. Someone had some explaining to do.

Okay, this is so not good, Kai thought as she stared down at her nearly empty form. She'd done a lot in her seventeen years, but in print she looked like the underachiever of the century. Her family had only moved to Ardsmore a couple of months ago. There was simply no way she could have racked up all the activities and hours of community service this scholarship required. Plus it had just occurred to her that her intense lack of class participation probably wasn't going to help when it came to asking teachers for recommendations. She was going to have to do some *major* butt kissing to fix this.

Better stock up on lip balm.

"So! Any questions?" Mr. Simon asked, clapping.

Kai's hand shot up.

"Yes, Kai," Mr. Simon said, his expression amused. He crossed his arms over his chest and leaned back against the large metal desk at the front of the room. Simon was Kai's guidance counselor, and he seemed to find everything she said to be knee-slappingly hysterical.

"Yeah, I was just wondering how, exactly, they're going to decide how pure we all are," Kai said.

Right on cue, Simon laughed uncomfortably. As did most of the other people in the room. Kai simply raised her eyebrows and looked around. All she'd done was ask the question the rest of them were dying to ask.

"Yes, purity was one of Mrs. Treemont's more, well, *interesting* requirements," Mr. Simon said. "In fact, we're still trying to decide exactly how to handle that one, Kai. But we'll let you know as soon as we do."

He stood up straight and looked around, waiting for more raised hands. "Well, if that's it, just hand me your forms on the way out and we'll keep you posted about interviews. Thank you, everyone, for coming."

Mandy quickly slipped out the door, followed by a clearly blood-seeking Debbie.

Kai gathered up her things and handed her form to Simon, wishing he had given her a better answer to her question. But as long as they didn't subject everyone to an invasive gynecological exam, which just *had* to be illegal, she would be fine.

I have to join a few more clubs and volunteer somewhere ASAP, Kai thought. Especially now that Mandy appeared to be in the running. Kai needed this scholarship, and she would do whatever it took to win.

"Mandy! Wait up!" Debbie called out.

Mandy stopped, her stomach churning, wondering how she ever could have thought she was going to get away with this without an explanation. When she turned around, Debbie, Kai, and Eva were all rushing to catch up with her.

Here goes nothing. "Hey, guys," she said brightly.

"Hey," Debbie said, pausing in front of her. "So, you're applying?"

"Yeah." Mandy forced herself to shrug. "It's open to everyone, right?"

"Well, yeah, but some of us actually need it," Debbie said.

Mandy swallowed hard.

"You're definitely going to win," Eva said quietly. "Look at the qualifications. They might as well have been written specifically for you."

Mandy felt a hotness prickling the back of her neck. She knew how this must look to them. Here she was living in one of the biggest houses in

Ardsmore and driving around in her own car.

If only they knew.

"Mandy, what's going on?" Kai asked suddenly, almost gently. "Is everything okay?"

Mandy gazed into the faces of her three best friends, all looking so concerned. Maybe she *could* tell them. After all, it wasn't like her father was guilty. Maybe they could all have a big laugh about it.

But then, if he wasn't guilty and it was all going to blow over, why spill it and leave it up to speculation? The whole thing was just so . . . embarrassing. Poor little rich girl's father is being investigated by the government.

"Okay, there's a reason I'm doing this, and . . ." Mandy closed her mouth. She paused. And then opened it again. "I just . . . can't tell you what it is." She looked Debbie in the eye. "I'm sorry, I just can't." Mandy's heart was pounding in her chest.

"Since when do you not tell us stuff?" Debbie asked, sounding almost more offended than before.

Mandy looked away, wishing this part of the drama could just be over already. It wasn't like she *wanted* to have to apply for this thing.

"Look, you guys, Mandy has her reasons. We all have our reasons. Let's just drop it," Kai said. Her voice had adopted a commanding tone that no one would argue with. Mandy felt a sudden warmth toward Kai. Clearly Kai understood that there was something here that shouldn't be pried into. Kai had her back. Mandy could have kissed her.

Mandy exchanged a look with Debbie and lifted her eyebrows hopefully.

"All right, Walters," Debbie said with a sigh. "But sooner or later you've got some serious explaining to do."

"I know," Mandy said. "I will."

"Okay, fine, so we'll all apply," Debbie said, starting down the hallway toward the cafeteria. "Besides, it's not like we have anything to worry about. Mandy's never gonna make it through the deadline without having sex."

Her friends laughed and Mandy tried to smile, but it took some effort. She hadn't told Eric about this scholarship thing yet, and she had no idea how she was going to deal with the whole purity issue. If she went ahead and made love with him on her birthday, would that really make her impure? And if the guidance office decided that actual virginity was the deciding factor, did that mean she'd *have* to tell them she'd done it? It all seemed so fundamentally *wrong*. Her sex life was nobody's business, right?

"Aw, we're just kidding." Debbie wrapped her arm around Mandy's shoulders and gave her a squeeze. "You've been a pillar of virtue this long. What's another couple of months gonna do to ya?"

Mandy pushed through the doors of the cafeteria

and caught sight of Eric emerging from the lunch line across the room. Her heart skipped, then thumped extra hard. His blue eyes found hers as he smiled that special smile that was only for her. For a split second her vision actually went hazy. She pushed her hands through her bangs to wipe up the beads of sweat along her hairline and took a deep breath.

Another couple of months? By then they might have to mop her up off the floor.

four

"HEY, EVA! EVA! WAIT UP!"

Eva's toe hit a bump in the sidewalk the second she heard a male voice calling her name. She tripped forward, stumbled a few graceless steps, and then, thank God, caught herself before she could hit the ground.

"Hey, are you all right?" Riley Marx asked. He put a warm, steadying hand on her arm.

Omigod, I just tripped in front of Riley Marx. Omigod, Riley Marx is talking to me. Omigod, Riley Marx is touching me. Her mind swam. Her ears pounded.

"I'm okay," Eva said. Was this what a person felt like before they fainted? She really, really hoped not.

"I'm Riley," he said.

"I know," Eva said, blushing.

"Oh . . . well . . . good," Riley said. "So, listen, Debbie told me you work at 4-H and—"

He's talking to me. Riley Marx is talking to me, Eva thought fuzzily. *And now he's looking at me like I'm a lunatic.*

"So would that be okay?" he asked.

Oh. There must have been a question in there somewhere. "Uh . . ."

"My working at 4-H?" he prompted.

"No. I mean . . . yes. I mean . . . they're always looking for people, so I'm sure you could . . . you know . . . be one of those . . . people."

Yep. There I go. Might as well be talking Portuguese.

"Great! So when are you working there next?"

I know the answer to this one. I do.

"Uh . . . tomorrow afternoon?"

"Cool. So I'll meet you there?" he said with a hopeful smile.

"Yeah."

Holy crap.

Riley Marx was going to meet her somewhere.

Riley Marx had jogged to catch up with her right in front of the school. He'd shouted her name in front of dozens of people. And smiled at her and put his hand on her arm. And it was all thanks to Debbie! Where was that girl when Eva needed to offer to be her slave for life?

"Oh, hey, and I wanted to tell you that I read that poem you had in the last literary magazine. It was intense," Riley said, his blue-green eyes sparkling. "The bubbles were a metaphor for us, right?"

Us. He said the word us.

"Like, people in high school . . . fighting to get

46

to the top?" Riley prompted. "And then when they get to the top they always burst?"

He actually understands my poetry. Daydream number one is coming true, right here, right now!

"Um . . . yeah," she said.

"You're really good," Riley told her.

"Really?" Eva blurted, then flushed over the squeaking sound of her voice. "I mean, that's so cool that you get me. I mean, got . . . *it.* The poem."

Okay, this was *not* what she said in the daydream.

"I didn't think anybody read the lit magazine," she rambled against her will. "Except the people who are in it, you know, and our parents, of course. I mean sometimes my nana reads it too—"

Shut up shut up shut up.

Riley's smile widened. "Yeah, well, there are *some* intelligent people at this school."

"Yo, Marx!"

A pack of Riley's friends trudged down the pathway toward him and Eva. They walked in almost a perfect triangular formation with Scot Gibbins front and center. He was the biggest, richest, most self-satisfied one of the crowd. Eva wondered if they practiced moving together like that or if it just happened naturally.

"Dude, Melissa just told me that you went to the Treemont scholarship thing," Scot said, drawing to a stop next to them as the other guys settled into place around him.

"Yeah, I did," Riley said, looking amused.

Scot let out a snorting laugh and glanced at his friends, who all laughed in suit. The sun reflected off his close-shaven head. "Don't you have to be el virgino to apply for that thing?"

"That's what the requirements say, Scot," Riley replied. "Why? You thinking of throwing your name in?"

"Dude, *please*. I'm no virgin," he said. "Just ask Melissa." Scot waggled his eyebrows repulsively. "She'll tell you how it is. The Gibber can do it *all night lo-ong*." Scot did a weird slow-motion thrusting dance and then high-fived one of his little gang.

"Yeah, I'll get right on that. Thanks," Riley said coolly before returning his attention to Eva.

"You do that, Boy Scout," Scot teased, earning another round of laughter from his followers. "See ya later, Marx."

The guys loped away, their red-and-gray varsity jackets blending together. None of them had even glanced in Eva's direction. Riley shook his head.

"Like I said, there are *some* intelligent people in this school, but not many," he joked.

Eva nodded.

"So, I'll see you tomorrow, after school, at 4-H," he said, backing up a few steps.

"Okay," Eva said.

"Awesome. Thanks, Eva!"

Eva stood there dumbfounded, watching as Riley jogged away.

Mandy ran her laps along the wall of the gym next to Kai, trying to think of a way to phrase the question she wanted to ask without sounding like the prim and proper priss she was widely acknowledged to be. Part of her wanted to just let it go, but a much larger part was dying of curiosity. She looked up at her friend's focused expression and opened her mouth to speak.

Of course Coach Davis picked that exact moment to blow her whistle.

"Okay, ladies, let's pair off and do some bumping drills," she called across the gym as the volleyball team lumbered to a stop, their sneakers squeaking and squealing on the polished hardwood floor. "I don't want to see any more wild passes like we had at the last game."

Mandy jogged over to the ball bin, grabbed one, and rejoined Kai, who had snagged a spot at the far corner of the gym. She bent at the waist and hung her arms down, watching the ball and waiting as Mandy bumped it to her.

"Thank God Simon didn't answer your question about the purity thing," Mandy said. "I really don't think I want to hear a detailed description of what my guidance counselor considers to be impure."

"Oh, please. The guy's probably a closet porn freak," Kai replied. "He probably sits alone every night and—"

"Ew, Kai! Make me vomit!" Mandy said, missing the ball completely as it hurtled past her shoulder.

"But come on, can't you totally picture it?" Kai called as she ran to retrieve the ball.

"Okay. I'm totally going to have nightmares tonight," Mandy said, covering her eyes. "Thanks a lot, Kai."

"I do what I can." Kai grinned.

"So," Mandy said, fielding the pass when Kai served the ball to her, "what made you ask him?" *Casual enough. Just making conversation.*

Kai narrowed her eyes as the ball arced toward her and bumped it expertly back. "Just curious," she said. "Aren't you?"

"Yeah, sure," Mandy replied, shrugging as she hit the ball. Her heart started to flutter nervously. Or maybe it was just normalizing after the thirty laps. "I just mean . . . you're not . . . *concerned* about it or anything, are you?"

"Nope," Kai said before slamming the ball back with a direct trajectory toward Mandy's head.

Mandy raised her arms and blocked the ball just seconds before it would have rearranged her nose.

Her wrists stung and the ball bounced back toward Kai, who stopped it with her foot and then kicked it up to her hands.

"Sorry," Kai said nonchalantly. "Your pass was too high."

"Right. No problem," Mandy said. But she knew her pass had been fine.

O-kay, clearly this is not a good topic for Kai, Mandy thought as they started to volley again. But that didn't seem fair. Her *own* sex life was open forum whenever she and her friends got together. Why couldn't she ask one little innocent question without Kai trying to knock her on the head?

"So, listen, you know that if there's ever anything . . . you know . . . that you want to talk about . . . ," Kai said.

Mandy flushed slightly. "Oh, yeah. I know. Thanks."

"Do you know who you're going to ask for recommendations yet?" Kai asked.

"Not sure," Mandy replied, relieved. "Maybe Ms. Russo, maybe Davis, I don't know. You?"

"No idea. But you shouldn't have any problem getting them," Kai said, popping the ball back to Mandy. "You're, like, universally worshiped around here."

Mandy smiled and bumped the ball back, her negative feelings erased. Kai had been nothing but

KATE BRIAN

supportive when her friends had found out she was going to apply for the Treemont scholarship—she was the one person who hadn't looked shocked or suspicious. The least she could do was grant Kai the same favor and not pry into *her* personal life.

No matter how weird she was acting.

Kai tossed her purple-and-blue volleyball up and down as she cut across her front lawn toward the mailbox. Practice had just ended, and she was feeling good and loose and definitely ready for a shower. Mandy's little inquiry at the beginning of drills had pissed her off, but she'd taken it out on the volleyball court for two hours and now she was feeling much better.

It wasn't that Kai didn't want to confide in Mandy. After being bumped all over the world her entire life, Kai was a pretty good judge of character. And of all the friends Kai had made in all the places she'd lived over the last few years, Mandy was definitely one of the most trustworthy and open-minded. It was just that Kai didn't like to divulge much to new people, since she never knew how long she was actually going to know them. The idea of leaving a string of acquaintances with intimate knowledge of her personal life scattered across the greater USA was pretty creepy, actually.

But Kai forgot about all of this as soon as she

52

opened the mailbox and saw that it was crammed full of thick packages. "Yes!" she whispered under her breath. She dropped her volleyball on the grass, jimmied the stack of white and brown envelopes out, and cradled them in her arms so she could flip through them.

"Cornell . . . Michigan . . . Colorado . . . Stanford . . . Miami . . . UCLA . . ." She slapped the packages together and jogged inside, her duffel bag whacking against her thigh. She couldn't wait to tear into this latest horde of application materials. While the rest of her class seemed stressed beyond belief about filling out their college apps, Kai couldn't wait to get started. Just the idea of going somewhere that would definitely be home *for four whole years in a row* made her kind of giddy.

Kai bounded into the house and hurled everything onto the island in the center of the kitchen. The applications fanned out and knocked over a box of cereal that was still sitting there from that morning. She grabbed a bottle of raspberry iced tea out of the fridge and popped it open.

"Kai!" her mother called out, walking into the kitchen with Kai's baby brother, Yukio, cradled in her arms. She paused in the middle of the kitchen, clucked her tongue, and shook her head. "You leave the kitchen a mess in the morning, and you come home in the afternoon and make it even more of a mess."

Kai put down her iced tea and gathered Yukio from her mother's arms, smothering him with kisses. Yukio squirmed and giggled and pressed his pudgy palm against her face.

"More applications?" Kai's mother asked, gathering the envelopes into a neat pile. "How many schools do you plan to apply to?"

"At least fifteen or twenty, Ma," Kai said, scrunching up her nose and rubbing it against Yukio's. "You guys always said I should keep my options open."

"Yes, but it costs so much money just to apply," Kai's mother said, pulling the wooden clip out of her bun and letting her long hair tumble down her back. "We are not made of money, Kai."

"*Oh,* so *that* explains why the maid hasn't been here yet today!" Kai joked. Her mother was a photographer and her father was a lawyer who had moved them across the country, landing them in this state or that to help the helpless before moving on to someplace new. It had never been a secret that the 'rents weren't exactly down with financial planning. As far as Kai knew, they didn't even have a savings account.

"Well, have you been looking into scholarships? Loans?" her mother asked.

"As a matter of fact, I'm applying for this big

scholarship at school," she said, putting down her bottle again and rubbing at a sudden knot in her shoulder.

"Good," her mother said with a nod. "It's never too early to plan."

Kai leveled her mother with the patented wry Kai stare. "This from a woman who never has a job in place before moving to a new town and doesn't own a calendar. Do you even know the order of the months?"

"Very funny. But we're not talking about me. We're talking about you," her mother replied.

"Okay! Okay! Don't get all parental on me now," Kai said, handing Yukio back to her. She and her parents often acted more like friends than parents and child. But lately, ever since Yukio had been born, they'd been asking questions they'd never asked before, like when she would be home, who she was going out with, when her report card was coming. It was like welcoming the new baby had awakened some long-dormant protective hormones in them. And Kai wasn't quite sure what to make of it.

The front door opened and closed, and Kai looked at her mother. It was a bit early for her dad to be home, and when she saw the excited expression on her mom's face, she instantly knew something was up.

"Huroyo? Kai?" her father called out.

"In here!" her mother said giddily.

Her father stepped into the doorway. As always, the blond tuft of his hair was sticking straight up, and his glasses were resting atop his forehead like a headband. He grinned at Kai as if he was about to present her with a lifetime supply of Oreos.

Kai's stomach clenched. *Oh, no. I hope this isn't what I think it is. Please don't let us be moving again.*

"Kai." Her father smiled mysteriously.

Please. Please. Please. Please. Please.

"Kai, you remember Andres, don't you?"

Kai blinked. Once. Twice.

There he was—Andres Cortez. Andres Cortez of Toledo, Spain, with his sun-darkened skin and his long black hair and that cleft in the center of his chin, standing in the middle of her house in Ardsmore, Pennsylvania, like it was the most normal thing in the world.

"Surprise!" Kai's mother and father called out.

Kai's jaw dropped open. And she froze.

"Hello, Kai," Andres said, stepping forward and taking her hands in his. He leaned in and kissed the side of her face, sending a thrill of excitement down the entire left side of her body—a reaction that made her sick with herself. "How wonderful it is to see you."

"What are you doing here?" Kai said, barely able to speak.

"Andres is going to be staying with us for a while," her father explained, walking up and laying his arm companionably over Andres's shoulders. Kai cringed.

"I have to go shower!" she announced. Then she turned abruptly and ran for her basement bedroom. Maybe her parents' protective instincts hadn't been honed *quite* enough yet—otherwise they never would've brought *this* guy home.

Mandy parked her car next to her father's BMW. She wondered if this was a bad sign or a good sign. Her father almost never made it home before dinner, let alone before she got home from practice.

He probably just wants to spend some extra time with Mom and me because of all the stuff that's going on, she told herself. *Stop being so pessimistic!* Mandy jumped out of the car and ran inside. She was going to shower, change, and head over to Eric's to have some pizza and "study." And maybe, if everything felt right, she would tell him about her decision about her birthday.

Screw Mrs. Treemont and her scholarship. They're never going to find out anyway, she thought as she opened the front door. *I am a sexual being! I cannot be denied!*

Mandy was giggling to herself when she heard something that made her stomach turn. There was yelling coming from inside the house, her father's baritone coming through clenched teeth, her mother's voice high-pitched and on the verge of losing it.

"When were you going to tell me about this? On my first trip to the . . . ?"

Leaving the door open, Mandy took a tentative step into the parlor so she could hear more clearly.

"Now, Shirley, no need to be dramatic," her father replied. "Don't you think I feel bad enough that you and Mandy have to go through this?"

Mandy's heart pounded double time in her chest. She took another few steps across the parlor, feeling like she'd regressed to the seventh grade— probably the last time she'd heard her parents fight. A sudden door slam made her jump.

"Don't you walk away from me, Charles!" Her mother's voice came more clearly this time. Her parents had entered the sunroom just off the parlor. Mandy instinctively ducked next to the door so they wouldn't see her.

"How can you be so blasé about this?" her mother demanded. "You tell me I'm going to be dragged in for questioning and—"

"You're not going to be *dragged* anywhere," Mandy's father replied. "Calm down."

"I will not calm down! What's next!? Are they going to want to question Mandy?" her mother shouted. "Are they going to make her explain every bottle of nail polish she's ever bought? How could you do this to us?"

Mandy swallowed against a dry throat, her mind reeling. *How could you do this to us?* That didn't sound like the type of thing you said to a person who was innocent. *But no, they're just fighting,* Mandy told herself. *Everyone says stuff they don't mean when they fight.*

"Charles—"

"I'm done with this conversation, Shirley," her father said.

"But I—"

"No more!" he roared. "Not tonight!"

Mandy could hear them coming in her direction. She rushed back to the foyer on the toes of her sneakers and slammed the front door so that they would think she'd just arrived—that she hadn't heard a thing. Moments later both her parents entered the foyer, carefree smiles plastered on their faces. The only evidence that anything had transpired was the pallid quality of her mother's skin.

"Hi, pumpkin!" her father said, wrapping her up in a bear hug. "How was your day?"

"Fine," Mandy managed to say. *This is too weird.*

"Did you get back that history paper?" her mother asked brightly.

History paper? Is she kidding?

"I got it back yesterday, actually," Mandy said. "I got an A."

"Oh, that's wonderful, sweetheart. You were so stressed about that!"

"I think we should celebrate," her father said, his arm wrapped around her shoulders like a vise. "Ice cream for dinner, Shirley?"

Her mother laughed lightly and Mandy just wanted to scream. *What the hell are they doing?*

"Actually, I promised Eric I'd go over there for pizza tonight," Mandy told them. "We're gonna study for calculus."

"Well, then, we'll celebrate another time," her father said, his smile never faltering. He leaned down and kissed her on the forehead. "I'm very proud of you, Mandy."

"Thanks," she replied.

It wasn't until she was halfway up the stairs that she remembered her promise to tell her dad she loved him the next time she saw him. She almost went back down again, but the very idea made her cringe.

For now, all she wanted to do was escape.

five

DEBBIE LEANED BACK FROM HER SEWING MACHINE, looking over the seam she'd just finished off. She tugged at the silky fabric and smiled. Her father was going to love this traditional sherwani suit. He would wear it to her cousin's wedding next month, and everyone would ask if he'd bought it when he went to India last summer, and he would smile proudly and say, "No. My daughter made it with her own two hands. She is very talented."

There was a sharp rap on her door and Debbie had just enough time to shove her work in progress into her hamper before her father walked in.

"Mail call!" he said, dropping a couple of envelopes on her bed. Debbie's breath caught in her throat and she had to concentrate to keep from lunging across the room. There was something fat and white in the pile. Could it be?

"Deborah . . . sewing? Again?" His already lined face sprouted even more wrinkles. "Did I tell you Bob Schneider got you a list of topics to study for the Math and Science competition? He's on the advisory board for the competition, you know."

"I know, Dad," Debbie said. Her father acted like having a friend who worked in the chemistry department at Penn State was as noteworthy as being butt buddies with J.Lo.

"Debbie, watch your tone," her mother scolded, bustling in with a clean load of laundry.

"Sorry," Debbie replied.

"I'll go and get the list," her father said, shuffling out.

"Super," Debbie said under her breath.

Ugh. Another math and science talk with Dad. They were her two least favorite subjects and, in a wacky twist of fate, they were also her two best subjects. Back in middle school, Debbie had loved math and science, and she and her father, a physics professor at Lock Haven University, had bonded over the shared interest. But in the past few years she'd become bored with proofs and equations and theorems and hypotheses. Now whenever her father brought it up, all it did was remind her of how far apart they'd grown and how he didn't understand her at all anymore. How he didn't even try.

"I looked over the paperwork for the Treemont scholarship," Debbie's mother said.

"Oh, yeah?" Debbie tried to be nonchalant.

"Yes. But you won't need it if you win the Math

and Science scholarship," her mother said as she sorted the laundry into piles on Debbie's bed.

"Yeah, but if I win the Treemont, I don't have to go to Penn State. I can go wherever I want."

"Did you have someplace particular in mind?" her mother asked. Debbie knew from her tone that it was more of a warning than a question. Her mother might as well have said, *"You better not have someplace particular in mind, because if you go anywhere other than Penn State and study science, it will be akin to ripping out your father's and my hearts and jumping up and down on them."* Her mother was queen of the passive-aggressive.

"No, not really," Debbie said.

"Don't give me that look, Deborah. The Math and Science scholarship is a great opportunity, and Penn State is a very good school. Do you think we would have sent Ravi Junior there if it wasn't a very good school?"

Debbie rolled her eyes, sat down on the bed, and lifted her T-shirts into her lap to refold them. Her mother always folded them up the middle— like Debbie wanted to go to school with a big crease down her front.

"I know Mom, but say I do the Math and Science competition and say I win, then I *have* to go there and I *have* to major in science or math. It's kind of restricting. . . ."

She widened her dark eyes and looked up at her mother, begging her silently to get it. Debbie didn't *want* to sit in a basement all day and run equations surrounded by pasty-faced guys named Alvin.

How could her mother look at the girl sitting in front of her in her handmade denim-and-silk skirt and lace-sleeve T-shirt and think, *Yes, this girl is a lab rat. Let's fit her for some Bunsen burners. And all just to make her father happy.*

How come no one ever seemed to think about what might make *Debbie* happy?

"All you have to do is take the test," her mother said. "See what happens."

"I'll think about it," Debbie told her. She glanced at the clock on her nightstand and stood. "I'm late. I'm going to study at Danielle's."

"Okay," her mother said as she walked to the door. "Say hi to Danielle and her parents for me."

"I will," Debbie said, but she knew she wouldn't. In fact, she *couldn't*, because *Danielle did not exist.* Debbie had made her up to cover her many trips to Danny's house—trips her parents would never approve of. Debbie always felt awful when her mother sent messages for imaginary Danielle's imaginary parents, but the awfulness usually passed pretty quickly. She grabbed her book bag for good measure and jogged out of the room.

"Where are you off to?" her father asked, intercepting her at the bottom of the stairs.

"Studying with a friend," Debbie said.

"I was hoping we could go over the topics for the competition."

Debbie stopped with her fingers curled on the doorknob and instantly tensed up. Couldn't her father think about anything else? And why was it that the second her dad mentioned it, she wanted to break something?

"Another time, Dad," she said. She pulled out a pot of strawberry lip balm and applied a shimmery coat to her lips. "I have plans."

She headed out the door before she could get a good look at the disappointment on his face.

"So," Kai said.

"So," Andres repeated.

She and Andres were supposed to be setting up the pullout couch for him in her dad's office, a task that would have been a lot easier if Kai could have found the will to move.

"You're . . . here," she said.

"Yes. That is true."

Kai snapped her fingers and punched one hand against the other over and over. "Why is that again?"

Andres cracked a smile that almost made Kai take a seat in her father's creaky old desk chair.

How was it possible that after all this time, he could still affect her like that?

And why did he seem completely unfazed? Had he totally forgotten everything that had happened between them that summer two years ago? Their hours of languishing together in the hot Spanish sun, the midnight talks that had lasted until dawn, that one night they'd spent together camping alone in the desert. That one night when friendship and innocent kisses had led to . . . ?

Because if he *hadn't* spaced on all of that and he was still able to act this normal, then he was an even bigger jerk than she'd originally thought.

"I want to come to school here . . . in the States," Andres told her, even though her parents had explained all this just moments ago. "I came to look at schools and maybe try out for the soccer teams."

"Yes, but why are you staying *here?*" Kai asked, pointing at the shag carpet with both hands.

"Your mother and my mother made an agreement," Andres said, taking the brown cushions off the couch and stacking them in the corner. "They are very old friends."

"I *know* our mothers are very old friends, but that doesn't explain why you have to stay with us," Kai said, taking a step back as he pulled out the bed. "We barely have enough room in this house for ourselves."

Andres lowered the bed until the legs dug into the shag carpet, then turned around and looked at her. With the small room made smaller by the presence of a queen-size mattress, the only space they had to stand in was about three feet square. Kai was staring right at that cleft in his chin. She picked up the sheets from the desk and held them to her chest.

"You are afraid to be so close to me," Andres said with a cocky smile. "That is why you protest so much."

She saw his hand reaching up and moving toward her face and suddenly she was practically burning with anticipation. But the second before his fingers touched her, she slammed the sheets into his chest and backed out the door.

"I'm not afraid of anything," Kai said, which was the truth—usually. Except right about then she was petrified. Ever since she'd found herself in Andres's presence again, it was like every single cell in her being was pulling her to him.

"You're not going to help?" Andres said, looking down at the pink-flowered sheets.

"You're a big boy. I think you can make your own bed," Kai replied, narrowing her eyes. She turned to go.

"Good night, *bonita*!" he called after her. Kai shook her head and slammed the door behind her.

* * *

Eva flicked the burner on under the pot of Campbell's tomato soup, then grabbed her Wesleyan catalog and settled back into one of the wooden kitchen chairs. It creaked and shifted under her weight, and Eva was careful not to lean back on the weak third rung. She pulled one foot up onto the seat, rested her chin on her knee, and flattened the catalog on the table. She'd been through it so many times, the spine had already given. It cracked welcomingly as she pressed her hands over the smooth pages.

Eva stared down at her favorite photograph of the campus, the one depicting three students walking across a brick path, the trees glowing in brilliant shades of orange and yellow and red.

Why are you doing this to yourself? Eva thought, sighing. She knew there was no way she was ever going to Wesleyan University. If she went to college at all, it was going to be Ardsmore Community—a school she could walk to from home—a school that put up hot pink registration flyers on the lampposts outside her building every fall and spring. A school where all the burnouts and druggies and other low-income kids from Ardsmore High were going to go, if they went anywhere.

But she couldn't help herself. As the soup bubbled on the stove and the pipes in the ceiling began their nightly clang fest, Eva let herself go.

She let herself imagine what it would be like to live on that beautiful campus and go to classes in those ancient, airy buildings, to sit on the lush green lawn, discussing writing and poetry with other students who understood themes and rhythms and depth. She saw herself at Wesleyan.

Maybe, just maybe . . . If she could win that scholarship somehow—beat out all those other people by some miracle—then it could actually happen. She could get out of here. She could have the life she'd always wanted for herself.

After all, Riley Marx had spoken to her that afternoon. Apparently anything could happen.

Eva heard the jangle of her mother's keys at the apartment door and jumped out of her chair. She shoved the catalog into the nearest cabinet and started to butter the bread for the grilled cheese sandwiches.

"Hey, sweetie." Her mother pulled off her old gray trench and piled it onto the chair Eva had vacated along with her pocketbook and keys. "Sorry I'm late. The car wouldn't start again."

"No problem," Eva said. Her mother placed her hands on her shoulders and kissed the back of her head.

Then she watched from the corner of her eye as her mother walked right over to Eva's cabinet for a glass. When she opened the door, the catalog fell out and fluttered to the floor. *Of course,* Eva thought. *The one night she doesn't sit right down and put her feet up.*

"What's this?" Eva's mother asked, bending to pick up the colorful book. Her brow creased as she looked at Eva. "Wesleyan? Did you order this?"

"Yeah," Eva said, her face burning red.

"Eva, we could never afford this," her mother said, dropping the catalog on the counter in a little puddle of tomato soup that Eva hadn't had a chance to wipe up. As her mom shoved her glass under the faucet, Eva picked up her catalog and toweled it dry.

"I know, but there's this new scholarship—"

"People like us don't win scholarships," Eva's mother said bitterly. Eva snapped her mouth shut and turned back to the stove.

Just because you didn't go to college doesn't mean I can't . . . , Eva thought. But she could never say it. She knew her mom hadn't gone to school because her dad had gone first, saying only one of them could go at a time while the other worked. And then he'd graduated, and Eva had been born, and he had disappeared. It was something they never talked about.

"I just don't want you to get your hopes up, honey," her mother said, softening her tone as she lowered herself into a chair. "You need to face reality. Dreams are well and good, but they don't put food on the table, they don't heat the house on a cold night, and they don't pay for doctors' appointments."

"I know," Eva said. "Forget I said anything."

Her mother gave her a sympathetic look, then leaned her head back and groaned, twisting her neck from side to side.

"You wouldn't believe the day I had," she said, leaning her cheek into her hand. Her brown hair hung in clumps from its bun as she began her nightly rundown about her job at Urgent Care—a twenty-four-hour emergency medical center where she worked as the receptionist. She told Eva about the addicts that came in every day, the kids who needed fifteen stitches, and the evil woman at one of the insurance companies who always talked down to her like she was some kind of moron.

Eva didn't begrudge her mother her half hour of venting. After all, her mom spent at least twelve hours a day getting abused. Eva always listened and offered the responses her mother was looking for. . . .

"Jerk!"

"Unbelievable!"

"That sucks!"

Her mother was all the family she had, and that

was what family did for each other—supported each other—listened.

Yep. This is enough reality for me, she thought as she slid a sandwich from a spatula onto her mother's plate. *More than enough.*

six

Danny yanked Debbie's shirt off over her head, then grabbed the back of her neck and pulled her to him. Debbie gasped. If there was one great thing about fooling around with Danny Brown, it was that he was very self-assured. Not like those guys who were so afraid to go in for the kiss, they bumped noses with you awkwardly before finally mauling you with their tongue. No. Danny definitely knew what he was doing. No wonder Liana Hull was still so tweaked that he'd broken up with her.

They fell back on his bed together and Danny moved in on top of her. She was kissing his neck when she felt his hand sliding toward the zipper on her skirt.

"Danny . . . no," she said firmly, pushing his fingers away.

"Come on, Deb," he said in her ear. "I've got condoms."

"Goody for you. Maybe you can make some water balloons or something. Because I'm still not going to do it with you." Debbie kissed him on the shoulder. "How many times are we going to go through this?"

"All right, fine. But one of these days I'm going to break you down," Danny said, nuzzling her neck.

In your dreams, she thought.

"God, you're so hot," Danny whispered. In the dark his voice and his touch sent even greater waves of pleasure through her.

Danny moved down her neck and started kissing her shoulders and chest, giving Debbie a perfect view of the digital clock on the dresser at the foot of his bed. The red numbers read 9:55.

"Damn! I gotta go!" she said, sitting up straight and knocking Danny right off her.

"Seriously?" he asked, his breath ragged and loud in the darkness. "Now?"

"I'm supposed to be home by ten," Debbie said, groping around for her T-shirt.

She felt the weight of the bed shift as Danny got up and crossed the room. The overhead light flicked on and Debbie found the light blue cotton shirt balled up at her feet. She grabbed it and yanked it on.

"Sorry I have to run," she said, shoving her foot into her boot.

"Whatever," Danny said. "I promised my dad I'd work on my Penn State application tonight anyway." He pulled a form over to him and opened to the first page, scratching at the back of his blond crew cut.

"You're applying there?" Debbie asked as she twisted her skirt around.

"Yeah. It's my first choice," Danny said. "Plus I might be able to walk onto the soccer team."

Debbie glimpsed a fat blue Penn State catalog on the corner of his desk and leaned over him to pick it up. It couldn't hurt to look through the thing, right? See what other majors they did have— just in case. As much as she didn't like to think about it, FIT was by no means a sure thing. It might not even be a possibility, what with the stiff competition for the Treemont scholarship. Maybe Penn State *could* still be her backup plan. As her mother had said, it would make her father happy, and even though she changed her mind every five minutes as to whether or not that was important, she might as well consider the possibility.

"Mind if I borrow this?" Debbie asked, flipping through the pages.

"Knock yourself out," Danny said with a shrug.

"Thanks." Debbie shoved the thick book into her bag. "I'll see you tomorrow."

"Later."

Debbie rushed down the stairs and out to the car. If she made all the lights, she would only be five minutes late. When it came to Debbie Patel's parents, it was all about keeping them just happy enough and just enough in the dark.

Eric leaned Mandy back against the arm of the couch as he kissed her, shifting until he was lying next to her with one leg hooked around hers. He slipped his hand up under her sweater, tickling her skin. Mandy tried to concentrate on him. On his lips and his hands and his gentle touch, but she kept feeling herself going rigid. Her fingers were flat on the couch instead of clutching his shoulders or pulling his shirt out from his jeans so she could touch his back. She couldn't stop thinking about that argument she'd overheard her parents having. And if there was one thing that could kill her libido dead, it was her parents' faces looming across her mind's eye while Eric's hands were cupping her breasts.

Ew.

Eric slid his lips along her jaw and down to her neck and Mandy sat up. Eric fell half off the couch in surprise.

"Hey, baby. What's wrong?" He pushed a tendril of hair behind her ear and looked at her with concern.

"Nothing," Mandy said as she pulled her French notebook onto her lap. "I just . . . I'm kind of distracted."

"A big French test tomorrow or something?" Eric asked. He pushed himself up next to her on the couch and looked down at her notes.

"Not tomorrow," she said. "It's Friday, but this chapter is impossible. So I guess I kind of want to work on it."

"Oh. Okay," Eric said. He cleared his throat and smiled. "I'll just work on this, then." He grabbed his copy of *Hamlet* before settling back into the couch.

Mandy leaned in next to him and stared at her French book. The truth was, she knew the French chapter inside out and backward, but she just couldn't stop thinking about everything she had overheard. Was it possible? Could her father have done what they said he'd done? And if so, what did that mean for her family?

"Hey, listen," Eric said suddenly. He turned toward her. "Did you think any more about your birthday?"

"Um, not really."

"Oh, okay," he said, forcing a smile. Mandy took a deep breath. She had planned to tell him today—tell him that she was ready and willing. But she hadn't said it before gym. She hadn't said it before practice. Now was the perfect time, yet something was still stopping her. She just wanted their first time to be perfect. And with everything else that was going on right now . . . she just felt like *nothing* could feel perfect. Not with this IRS thing looming and her parents fighting and the fact that she was going to have to find another way to pay for Princeton. It was just too much.

Well, there is one easy out, she thought. The perfect temporary excuse.

Mandy looked at Eric. God, he was so beautiful. And she wanted him so much. She hated that she *needed* an out.

"What?" Eric noticed her staring. "What's up?"

"Well, it's just. You know that scholarship? That Treemont thing?"

"Yeah. What about it?"

"I'm going to apply for it."

"Why?" Eric asked, sliding backward on the couch for a better look at her face.

"I don't know, I just figured—"

"It's not like you need it."

"I know," Mandy said, looking away. Why did everyone feel the need to point that out? "But it's . . . it's open to everyone, so I thought I would try for it."

"Okay," Eric said slowly. "But I'm not sure I understand. What does that have to do with your birthday?"

"Well . . . apparently the Treemont woman only wanted the scholarship to be awarded to a virgin."

"Yeah, I heard something about that. But how are they going to know whether you are or not?" Eric asked.

"I don't know, but we've been together so long . . . ," Mandy said. "People probably assume we've already done it."

"And oh, how wrong they are," Eric said.

"Eric," Mandy pleaded.

"Sorry." He tossed his book aside and turned to face her fully. "It's just, if they already think we have, then you're screwed anyway, so we might as well just do it, right?"

Mandy suddenly felt sick to her stomach.

"Um. Wow. Okay, *that* was romantic," she said, standing up and taking a few steps away. She felt momentarily dizzy and had to shut her eyes to steady herself.

"I'm sorry, sweetness," Eric said, getting up and walking over to her. He slipped his strong arms around her from behind and kissed her cheek. "You know I only want us to be together when you're ready. It's just . . . if you *are* ready, we shouldn't let this scholarship get in the way. Especially since you don't really *need* it. . . ."

Mandy opened her eyes and took a deep breath. "I know," she made herself say. "And you know I want to. Just . . . I don't know, just let me think about it."

"Not a problem," Eric said. He turned her around and touched his forehead to hers. "I love you."

"I love you too." Then her stomach lurched in a way that she couldn't ignore. "I'll be right back," she said, her eyes burning. She rushed to the bathroom and sat down on top of the toilet bowl lid, leaning forward with her head between her knees. Breathing in and out slowly, Mandy told herself to calm down. She just wasn't used to hiding things from Eric. Mandy held her hand over her abdomen. She hadn't eaten much today because of the nervousness in her stomach, which only seemed to be getting worse. And now she had yet another layer of stress, the scholarship. Because even though she'd brought the scholarship up as an excuse, the fact remained that what Eric had said about the scholarship was right. How was she going to convince a panel of faculty members that she—a person who had been caught making out with Eric in the auditorium, in the stairwell, even in the girls' locker room—was pure in body and in spirit?

Just breathe. Just breathe. Mandy carefully started to stand. She felt weak but was able to hold herself up fine. As she turned around, a headline on one of the old magazines that Eric's mom kept in a basket by the toilet bowl caught her eye. She sat back down and grabbed the wrinkled issue of *Newsweek,* barely believing what she was seeing.

The words *Teen Virgins* were spelled out in huge letters next to a picture of five kids her age, all grinning out at her. Intrigued, Mandy flipped to the article and started to read.

"Saving themselves . . . pure by choice . . . healthy decisions . . . Support clubs raise self-awareness. . . . Virginity clubs are somewhat of a trend. . . ."

Slowly Mandy smiled. She had an idea.

seven

"I'D LIKE TO WELCOME EVERYONE TO THE FIRST MEETING of the Ardsmore High School Virginity Club!" Mandy announced. "Although in order to keep anyone from being embarrassed, we're just going to call it the V Club."

The fifteen students in the classroom—fourteen girls and Riley Marx—applauded her politely as she stood before them. Mandy smiled at Debbie, Kai, and Eva, who were front and center in the first row of desks, ready to support her.

I totally pulled it off, Mandy thought, feeling quite proud of herself.

She'd gone to Principal Shreever's office that morning, gotten her personal approval for the club before homeroom, and rushed a typed statement to the tech office about ten seconds before morning announcements. Leo Katz had snorted a laugh when he read the word *virginity* over the PA, and everyone in Mandy's homeroom had cracked up, but she didn't care. This was one of the best ideas she'd ever had.

"Okay, I know a lot of you are wondering what brought this idea about, and if you're thinking it has something to do with the Treemont scholarship, you're not wrong," Mandy continued. "The guidance office has yet to decide exactly how they're going to handle the purity requirement Ms. Treemont stipulated, so I figured we might as well get ahead of the game. If you're a member of this club, you're clearly embracing your choice not to have sex.

"This club will act as a support system—a place where you can talk about your beliefs and your experiences, but we'll also act as a civic service organization," Mandy continued, pacing the front of the room. "We are going to get our name out there by volunteering and helping out in the community, so any suggestions for club activities will be considered. I've already lined up an activity for this weekend. We'll be meeting at the assisted living facility on Vincent at twelve o'clock on Saturday afternoon to run their Scrabble tournament. I know it's short notice, but come if you can." Mandy paused for breath. "Any questions so far?"

Liana Hull raised her hand. "Are we gonna have to take a vow of abstinence or something? I read about that somewhere, and I think it's kind of archaic."

A few people giggled.

"Some clubs come up with their own honor code for everyone to sign instead of just making it like a ritualistic vow of abstinence," Mandy said.

She picked up the *Newsweek* magazine from her desk. "Does anyone want to try writing one for us?"

Liana's hand shot up again and Mandy handed her the magazine to help her with ideas. "See what you can come up with by our next meeting."

"Cool," Liana said.

Mandy walked over to Madame Kopec's desk, where the teacher was lounging back, eating bite-size Snickers and apparently not stressing too much about her role as faculty adviser. Mandy picked up her notes and they slipped from her fingers. When she stood up after grabbing them from the floor, her mind swam. She had to close her eyes to get her balance.

Okay, no one noticed, she told herself, flushing as she looked out at the expectant crowd. *Mental note: Eat something after practice.* All the stress was doing nothing for her appetite, but she was going to have to try to force something down. She'd been dizzy all day.

"Now, the first thing I think we should do is nominate members for various administrative positions," Mandy said, turning slowly toward the blackboard. She picked up a piece of chalk and swallowed against the nausea. "Our officers will be responsible for drafting a mission statement, and they'll really decide the direction of the club. We'll vote on the nominations next week. Any nominations for president?"

Eva raised her hand as prearranged by her and Mandy at lunch that day.

"Eva?" Mandy said with a smile.

"I'd like to nominate Mandy Walters."

"Thank you, Eva," Mandy said, turning to write her own name on the board. When she turned back, Kai's hand was up.

"Kai?"

Kai stared her straight in the eye. "I'd like to nominate myself."

Debbie and Eva looked at Kai, surprised.

"You . . . what?"

"I can do that, can't I?" Kai said with a shrug.

"Uh . . . yeah, I guess," Mandy said. "I mean, sure."

She turned and wrote Kai's name under hers, trying to keep her hand from shaking. What the hell was Kai doing?

"Anybody else?" Mandy asked, trying her best to sound normal. No one moved. "Then we'll move on to nominations for vice president."

As Mandy took down the names of the other nominees, her mind was reeling. This club was

Mandy's idea—Mandy's club. Why would her friend try to take it away from her?

"What's up with Mandy?" Kai asked, swinging her backpack over her shoulder as the meeting broke up. Kai could have sworn Mandy's hands were trembling as she packed up her bag. "She looks kind of . . . I don't know, *iffy*."

"Yeah. I agree. Before, when she dropped her notes, I sorta thought she was gonna faint," Eva said. "All the color went out of her face."

"She's probably just pissed that Kai nominated herself," Debbie said.

"Ya think?" Kai asked.

"Dude, you do not mess with Mandy's upward mobility," Debbie replied. "She'll kill ya dead."

"Whatever," Kai said. "It's just one club. I need it for my application, and Mandy's president of, like, everything."

"This is true," Eva said.

Mandy was now wrapped up in a conversation with Liana, so Kai headed for the door to wait.

"So Kai, when do we get to meet this hot Spanish guy of yours?" Debbie asked, leaning back against the wall to let a few club members pass.

"He's not really that interesting."

"Please! He's Spanish. From *Spain*," Debbie said emphatically. "Who cares if he's interesting? Or even good looking! I bet he has *the* sexiest accent."

Kai looked away, suddenly recalling the little encounter she'd had with Andres that morning in the hallway outside the bathroom. He'd just gotten out of the shower, and apparently they didn't know how to dry off in Spain, because his whole body was glistening with moisture. He was holding a towel around his waist but it barely concealed a thing. Kai had frozen in place, experiencing a momentary lapse of logic, and Andres had said, "Good morning," flirtatiously. His eyes had danced like he just *knew* that she wanted him. And at that very second Kai *had* wanted him. She'd wanted to jump his very sexy bones. And she hated herself for it.

"Okay, fine. If you're not gonna spill, then I gotta get to lacrosse," Debbie said.

"Yeah, Coach Davis is probably gonna hit me with extra laps," Kai said.

She shot one last glance at Mandy, hoping to catch her gaze and smile. But Mandy wouldn't even look in her direction.

Mandy let her eyes unfocus on the checkerboard squares of the volleyball net. On the other side of the court Cheryl Christiansen was getting ready to serve, but Mandy was paying no attention.

"Mandy! Yours!"

She looked up just in time to see the ball arcing

over her head toward the net from behind. Mandy jumped up to spike it and missed the mark, sending the ball careening off the side of her hand into the bleachers. Her teammates groaned and stared at her, annoyed.

"Water break!" Coach Davis shouted, blowing her whistle. Mandy started to jog off the court with the rest of the team, but Davis stopped her with a hand to the arm.

"All right, Walters, what's going on with you lately?" Coach asked, dropping the whistle against her flat chest. "Your head hasn't been in the game these last two days."

"Sorry, Coach," Mandy said automatically. She looked down at the floor.

"I don't want 'sorry,'" Coach said firmly. "I want you to tell me that you'll shape up, and then I want you to do it. We've got state semis next week. This is no time for my star player to crack."

I know we have state semis next week! Mandy wanted to snap. *Haven't I been playing in them for the past three years? Haven't I won the MVP award for the past two? Get off my back already!*

Her anger surprised her.

"You got anything you want to tell me, Walters?" Coach asked.

"I'll shape up, Coach," Mandy said.

"That's what I like to hear," Coach said, whacking her on the back. "Now go get a drink and get back here for cooldown."

Mandy jogged out into the hallway, averting her eyes as she passed Kai, who was walking back in, swiping at her mouth with the back of her hand. Between her father's disappearing act, Eric's sex pressure, Davis's little lecture, and Kai stabbing her in the back, she felt like she was on the verge of a nervous breakdown.

Twenty-eight more minutes, Mandy thought as she bent over the water fountain. *Just twenty-eight more minutes and you can get out of here.*

Unfortunately, she couldn't think of a single place she wanted to go.

eight

"THIS IS THE LAST STOP ON THE TOUR," EVA SAID, pausing with her back to the day-care room at 4-H. Riley looked at her expectantly and pushed his hands into the front pockets of his jeans. He was wearing a black Atari T-shirt that was somehow totally sexy.

Eva was so proud of herself. She'd been showing him around for half an hour, and she was actually starting to sound like a functional human being—an intelligent one, even. She hadn't said a single stupid thing since they'd passed the janitor's closet where the middle school kids were constantly getting caught playing Seven Minutes in Heaven and she'd said something about how she would show it to him, "except then people would expect us to make out."

She shuddered now just thinking about it.

"Don't keep me in suspense," Riley said, flashing his dimple.

"Oh, right. This is where I spend my time," Eva

said, opening the door and letting the noise of little-kid chatter fill the hallway. "This is the day-care center."

Riley stepped past her into the room and paused. Eva watched him take it all in. The couple dozen kids seated at four low tables, the huge reams of paper covered in bright splotches and smears of thick paint, the little vats of primary-colored blobs the tiny Picassos were dipping their fingers into.

Eva absolutely loved it in there, but she knew that to some people, it could be a little overwhelming.

Slowly Riley turned to her and raised his eyebrows. "Where do I get my smock?"

Eva leaned back against the cinder-block wall behind her. Everything he said was completely perfect.

Sharon Bates, the always-chipper day-care supervisor, was walking around the room, encouraging the kids along. When she spotted Eva, her face lit up.

"Well, look who it is!" she called out. "Hey there!" She bustled over, her long skirt flowing behind her, her silver bangles all a-jangle. "Eva, I'm so glad you're here." She pushed a paint-caked strand of hair behind her ear. "I have a meeting upstairs I have to get to. Would you mind taking over here for a bit?"

"No problem," Eva said. "Sharon, this is a new volunteer, Riley Marx."

"Well, hello there, Riley Marx," Sharon said, turning her infectious grin on him. "Hope you don't mind getting messy."

"I live to get messy," Riley replied.

"I *like* this one," Sharon said to Eva.

Ditto, Eva thought as Riley headed for a bin of old paint-spattered shirts.

Sharon leaned in to Eva's ear to whisper, "Now, Hayden's been acting up a bit today—too much sugar, I'm afraid. Little bugger snuck an extra cupcake when I wasn't looking. Just keep an eye on him."

"Sure," Eva said.

Riley buttoned on a huge blue shirt with a bright yellow splotch of paint on the front and joined one of the tables. He sat down next to a little boy named Mesach.

"Hey, man. Whatcha got there?" Riley asked, pointing at Mesach's painting.

Eva tried to hide her smile behind her hand. Riley Marx in person was even better than her dreams.

The door behind her opened and Eva turned to see Mandy walking into the room in a pair of mesh shorts and a T-shirt.

"Hey!" Eva said, surprised. "What're you doing here?"

"I went to help out in the gym, but they've actually got too many volunteers," Mandy said, pulling her ponytail holder out of her hair, then gathering it all up again to retie it. She paused, hands to head, when she spotted Riley.

"Am I imagining things or is that Riley Marx sitting over there bonding with a five-year-old?" Mandy asked.

Just then Riley dipped his finger in red paint and swiped it across a little girl's nose, sending her into a fit of giggles. "Nope. It's really him."

"Okay, not that I don't appreciate a guy who has the guts to basically declare himself a virgin and then hang out with toddlers the same day, but is he *trying* to get the other guys to beat him to death?" Mandy joked as she refastened her ponytail.

"Hey!" a little girl named Lisa shouted.

Tow-haired, sugar-hyped Hayden was reaching toward Lisa with a tiny paint-covered hand. Before Eva could jump into action, Hayden had swiped a giant maroon stripe across Lisa's nose.

"Hey! Don't do that!" Riley said, standing up.

"Why not?" Hayden snapped. "You did it!"

"Because . . . ," Riley started to explain, but just then Lisa retaliated by dumping a little cup of blue paint right on Hayden's head.

"Lisa, no!"

But it was too late. Mesach laughed and flicked

a wad of black paint at the boy across from him. The little boy shoved his hand into some yellow and launched it at Mesach but ended up with his hand in little Tina's red hair instead. Suddenly every kid in the room was flinging paint, laughing, and giggling. Eva, Riley, and Mandy tried to intervene, but before they knew it, they looked like a set of walking Jackson Pollack paintings.

"It's anarchy!" Riley called out as three little ones ran around his legs, trying to catch each other. Eva wrangled kids into separate corners, but whenever she turned her back, they escaped and jumped each other again. Mandy finally just sat down and took it, letting herself get spattered from every angle. Pretty soon she was laughing uncontrollably.

Eva looked at Riley, who dropped his arms at his sides in submission.

"What are we going to do?" Eva asked as the mayhem increased.

Riley picked up a cup of blue paint and walked across the room to Eva. "Well," he said. "You know the old saying." He dipped his finger in the blue paint and looked at her mischievously.

"What're you going to do with that?" Eva asked, backing up a step.

"If you can't beat 'em," Riley said as a screech filled the air. "Paint 'em!"

He reached out and painted a blue streak right across Eva's forehead. Her mouth dropped open at the cool stickiness and she laughed. She looked Riley in the eye and suddenly forgot who she was and who he was. All she could see at that moment was revenge.

Exhausted and achy, her skin tightening thanks to the impromptu body painting she'd just been subjected to, Mandy dragged herself up to the front door. She paused to close her eyes and wish for an uneventful evening. Her father's car was in the driveway again, and the last thing she wanted to deal with right now was more drama.

Mandy walked in and closed the door behind her, listened, and waited. Sweet silence. Maybe the fighting had officially ended. At the very least, a cease-fire had been called.

Mandy started up the stairs, thinking of how fabulous the hot water of the shower was going to feel on her body. She'd only made it halfway when she heard her father's heavy footsteps approaching the foyer. Mandy's pulse started to race. She swallowed hard, her hand on the banister. Since when was she afraid to see her father?

"Hey, pumpkin!" her dad said as she turned around. He made a mock shocked face and laughed. "What happened to you?"

"Finger-paint war," Mandy said, cracking a small smile.

"Aren't you a little old for finger paints?" her father teased. Mandy studied his face, his clear blue eyes, his posture and clothing. He looked normal. Like nothing was going on. Was it possible that everything had, in fact, blown over?

"Apparently I'm not," Mandy replied. She came down a few steps until she was at eye level with her father. Then she steeled herself and took the plunge. This was her dad. He'd never hidden anything from her in the past. She didn't want him to start now. "So, how're you doing, Dad?" she asked.

Her father blinked. "Fine," he said with a smile. "Everything's fine."

"Really?" Mandy asked hopefully. "So you're not being, you know . . . ?"

Her father was just staring at her now, that smile frozen on his face. But it was beginning to look strained.

"Investigated anymore?" Mandy finished weakly.

"Your mother told you about that, huh?" her father said, pushing his hands into the pockets of his gray slacks. He shifted his feet and Mandy felt like she'd just done something very, very wrong.

"Well, she . . . I mean, yeah," Mandy admitted. "Shouldn't she have?"

"Of course," her father said, looking down at his highly polished shoes. "Of course. But Mandy, I don't want you to worry," he added, meeting her eyes again, the smile in place. "Everything is going to be fine. This is not something you should be concerned about."

"Okay, but Dad, I—"

"Why don't you go upstairs and get cleaned up and then you can tell me all about this finger-paint war over dinner?" her father said.

"Okay," Mandy said, her stomach twisting. She jogged upstairs to her room and closed the door behind her. It took about fifteen seconds for the shouting to start on the other side of the house. Mandy couldn't make out the words, but she didn't need to.

A shiver ran over Mandy's skin. This was her father. And her father wouldn't break the law and, more important, her father wouldn't lie to her. He was just . . . stressed. And he wanted to protect her. Right?

Mandy couldn't think about it anymore. She sat down on her bed and hit the play button on her answering machine. "Hey, it's me." Eric's voice sounded less gentle than usual. "Just wanted to see how the whole V Club thing went. The guys were all over me about it at practice. But . . . well, whatever. Call me back."

Mandy closed her eyes as a door slammed downstairs and the machine beeped.

"Mandy, it's Kai. I think we should talk. Call me back."

Another beep. Mandy lay back on her bed and pulled her comforter out from under her pillows, folding it over her paint-caked body.

"Hey, it's me again," Eric said. "I tried your cell. Where are you?"

The tape beeped and rewound as her parents continued to wage World War III down below. Mandy turned over onto her side and hugged the comforter to her.

When the phone rang, Mandy was suddenly filled with anger so fierce she bolted up and yanked the phone cord out of the wall, then scrounged her cell out of her backpack and shut that off too, ignoring the message icon. She locked her bedroom door and turned out the lights.

She was not going to call Eric back and apologize for his friends' Neanderthal reaction to the V Club, and she was not going to call Kai and let her explain why she thought Mandy was being so unreasonable. She was not going to go downstairs and sit at the table with her parents, pretending everything was okay.

Mandy crawled into bed and bundled up the covers around her, listening to her own ragged breathing and the beating of her heart. As the fighting escalated, she squeezed her eyes shut and clutched her comforter.

Just stop, she thought. *Stop, stop, stop, stop, stop.*

"Those of you who are applying for the Treemont scholarship, I have the final application materials here," Ms. Russo told her homeroom class on Thursday morning. "Come on down."

"The moment of truth," Kai whispered to Debbie as they both got up from their seats and approached Ms. Russo's desk. She smiled and handed them each a packet. Kai flipped through it quickly as she walked back to her desk.

Recommendations . . . interview . . . grades . . .

She finally found what she was looking for on the last page.

"'Please submit an essay of no fewer than 2,000 words explaining your definition of purity and how you exemplify that purity in your daily *life*'?" Debbie read aloud.

"They have to be kidding," Kai said, slumping back in her chair.

"Another essay?" Debbie grumbled.

"Oh, don't worry, Debbie. I'm sure they'll *love* your essay," Marni Raab said, pausing by Debbie's desk. "Let's see, 'I haven't gotten any diseases yet, so I *must* be pure.'"

Kai's mouth dropped open as she glanced at Debbie.

"At least I'm not terminally hideous," Debbie replied, smirking.

Marni narrowed her eyes but kept moving. Kai reached over and slapped hands with Debbie, then went back to staring at the essay page. At least it didn't say that you *had* to be a virgin in order to qualify. That was something. But what was her definition of purity?

I think I should be commended for not coming within five feet of Andres for the past few days, Kai thought. *If anyone knew how much self-control that took, they'd hand me the scholarship money on the spot. And probably throw me a parade.*

She knew this essay was going to have to be killer, but her personal definition of purity wasn't something Kai had ever really thought about.

The bell rang and Kai shoved the application into her bag. The essay could wait. For now, she had bigger eggs to fry. Like convincing her teachers to write her some recommendations and winning that V Club presidency. She could think about her purity, or lack thereof, later.

nine

DEBBIE PULLED HER CHAIR CLOSER TO THE PRIVATE cubicle desk in the library and leaned her head on her arm. The small type on the pages of the thick Penn State catalog blurred together before her eyes and she sighed. It didn't matter how many times she went through it—there was no mention of fashion anywhere in the hundreds of pages. Architecture, yes. Art history, yes. Theater arts, yes. Fashion arts, nada.

"Hey!" a male voice whispered as Riley Marx appeared at the top of her cubicle, his hands clutching the side wall. "I'm not entirely sure, but I don't think we're supposed to use study hall as nap time."

"I'm not napping," Debbie said, sitting up and shaking her hair back. "I'm considering my future, and it's taking a lot out of me."

"That's not a good sign."

Riley pulled up a chair and scrootched over until he and Debbie were both sharing the small cubicle space. His knee brushed hers and Debbie smiled.

"I thought you weren't going out for the Math and Science competition," he said.

"I'm not," she said. "Or I wasn't." She slapped the Penn State catalog closed. "I don't know."

"You sound very focused, Ms. Patel," Riley joked, lowering his voice to a responsible-sounding adult pitch.

"Oh, and I guess you're one of those people who knows exactly where you're going to be in five years?" Debbie challenged, pulling all of her hair over one shoulder and arching her eyebrows at him. She leaned in a bit closer, resting her elbow on the desk. Riley's eyes flicked toward her cleavage and Debbie tried to suppress a smile. *Maybe he's not gay after all. . . .*

"No, not exactly," he said. "But hopefully it'll be some med school or another. That's why I have to win one of these scholarships."

"Yeah? Well, if I go out for both, you're gonna be in big trouble," Debbie said coyly.

"Really?" Riley shot back. "Well, if you're such a science brain, maybe we should study together for the competition. Did you see all the subjects it's going to cover?"

He looked down at his hands and flushed slightly. She totally had this guy. "So?" he said. "Wanna study together?"

Yes, yes, yes!

She shrugged nonchalantly. "I guess," she said. "And who knows, if you're nice to me, maybe I'll just let you win."

Riley grinned and Debbie locked eyes with him. There was something about the way he was looking at her that made the hair on her arms stand on end, tickling her skin. He was going to ask her out. She could feel it.

"Hey, Boy Scout!" Danny said, coming over and slapping Riley on the back. "Be careful talking to this girl. She'll totally corrupt you."

"Ha, ha," Debbie said, mortified to feel her face burning. "Danny, shouldn't you be off, like, knocking rocks together, trying to make fire?"

"Just came for my catalog," Danny shot back. "You done?"

He reached over and grabbed it from her desk before she could answer, then sauntered away. Debbie shot eye daggers at his back as he left. Danny could be such a jerk sometimes.

"Boy Scout?" Debbie asked Riley, arching her brows.

"Just a little nickname I picked up since going out for the scholarship," Riley said. "I really thought they would have come up with something more creative, but I guess that's giving them too much credit."

"Major mistake," Debbie conceded. "I cringe

to think what they'd come up with for me. Miss Impure?"

"Miss Not-so-chaste?" Riley joked.

Debbie laughed. "How about Ms. Kissable?"

"Lady Has-sexalot," Riley put in.

There was a loaded silence as Debbie's heart shrank into a ball. "What did you just say?"

"Oh God, sorry," Riley said. "I'm sorry. I took that too far."

Suddenly Debbie felt like someone had just walked into the library and ripped off all her clothes and she was sitting in front of Riley Marx completely naked.

"But I don't even have—"

"No, really. I'm really sorry." Riley's face was turning bright red. "Please. You don't have to explain yourself to me."

"Where did you . . . I mean . . . who told you that I—?" She swallowed and looked at him. What was wrong with her? Why was she so thrown? It wasn't like she didn't know that people talked about her and her many conquests behind her back. But somehow hearing Riley say it, hearing *Riley* say it, just cut right through her.

"Debbie, please forget I said anything." Riley pressed his palms into his jeans and groaned. "God, it's none of my business anyway. Can we just forget this ever happened?"

"Yeah, sure," Debbie said, grabbing up her bag. She felt like a moron and all she wanted to do was get the heck out of there—get away from his clear, probing gaze.

He thinks you're a whore.

"Debbie," he said, reaching out and grabbing her hand as she stood. "Don't be mad. Really. I didn't mean to—"

"I know," Debbie said, somehow forcing a smile. "I just have to go. I'll . . . I'll see you in bio and we'll figure out when to study."

As she left the library, she walked past Danny and his friends and heard them snickering and slapping hands. Somehow she managed to maintain her pace and not run for the door.

The last of the rug rats had just fallen into a deep sleep when Riley opened the door to the day-care center. Eva held a finger up to her lips and Riley closed the door as quietly as possible before tiptoeing across the room to her. Eva's heart was slamming into her rib cage by the time he reached her side.

Okay, no reason to have a heart attack. He's just a guy. . . . The yummiest guy in Yum City.

"Hey," Riley whispered. "Guess there's not much to do here right now."

"Nope," Eva said. "You don't have to stay if you don't want to."

"Oh. You want me to go?" Riley asked, his brow creasing.

"No!" Eva blurted. Hayden stirred at her feet and Eva held her breath.

Sharon tiptoed over to them and placed one hand on each of their backs, leaning in between them. "Why don't you two kids go out back and get some fresh air?" she suggested. "I'll be fine here for the next little while."

Eva opened her mouth to protest. Before she could, Sharon pushed her and Riley toward the door to the playground.

Eva sat down in one of the two leather swings and Riley sat next to her, swinging in the opposite direction so he could face her. Eva looked down at her hands in her lap as an awkward silence fell between them. Well, at least it felt awkward to her.

"So, Eva, tell me the three most fascinating things about you," Riley said out of nowhere. "I will give you fifteen seconds to compose your answer."

"What?" Eva blurted with a laugh.

"They asked me that during my early admissions interview for Penn," Riley said. "Insane, right?"

"Totally."

"So?"

"What?"

"Three most fascinating things," Riley prompted.

"I thought you were kidding!" Eva protested, blushing.

"I was, sort of. But I seriously want to know," Riley said.

Eva eyed him. He was swinging back and forth but staring straight at her. "Um . . ." Eva clutched the chains that held her swing. "I don't know. I mean, I don't know if there's anything about me that anyone would describe as *fascinating.*"

"Not true." Riley shook his head. "You're a poet, that's one. Oh, and did you know that Mr. Greenleaf is telling *all* his classes about your *Hamlet* paper? The man worships the paper you write on. I think he's in love with you."

"Really?" Eva asked, floored.

"No, not really. Because that would be gross." They both laughed, and Riley continued. "So there, that's two fascinating things about you. Now you only have to tell me one."

Eva smiled, looking up at the sky. "Okay, okay. One thing. I . . . uh . . . I can't stand peanut butter and jelly sandwiches."

"Whoa. But I thought *everyone* liked peanut butter and jelly," Riley said.

"Ick," Eva said. "The smell of them alone disgusts me. I threw up on the bus in third grade once just because the kid next to me was eating one."

"That *is* fascinating. I mean, PB&Js are the world's perfect sandwich."

Eva swung a little higher, feeling the breeze in her hair. "Well, that's fascinating, too. Is that what you told the Penn interviewer?" she joked.

"Nah, I didn't think he could handle it. I just told him that I play a mean blues guitar. I'm going to school for pre-med, but I secretly want to be a movie critic, and I'm saving myself until I get married."

Eva stuck her feet into the sand to stop her swing and almost tumbled off headfirst. She gaped at Riley. "*That's* what you told him?" she asked.

"Yeah. And I think I freaked him out a little bit. He drank, like, half a glass of water before continuing," Riley replied. He straddled his swing and leaned back into the chain. "It's okay, though. I didn't really want to go to Penn."

Eva stared down at her sneakers, the toes turned in toward each other, and leaned forward on her swing, carefully mulling her next words.

"Can I ask you a question?" she said tentatively.

"Shoot," Riley said.

"Why? Are you saving yourself, I mean?"

"I figure, what better gift can you give the person you're gonna spend the rest of your life with than to tell her you've been waiting for her?"

Eva had never heard anyone say anything so perfect in her entire life.

"What about you?" he asked.

"What about me?" Eva asked back.

"You were at the V Club meeting; you're applying for the scholarship," Riley said. "What do you think about the whole sex thing?"

"I don't," Eva said automatically.

"You don't what?" Riley asked.

"I don't think about the sex thing," Eva said, starting to swing again. "Too many other things to think about."

Like that I should work on the first kiss first, she thought, gazing across at the trees as they bobbed up and down in front of her. Suddenly she felt giddy and light, like she could take off and fly right over them.

ten

EVA HOVERED NEAR THE CORNER OF MR. GREENLEAF'S desk, her heart pounding. He had to know she was standing there. Every other student had already left, and she felt as conspicuous as a yellow school bus sitting in the middle of his room. Still, he kept his head bent over the page he was writing on, his hand sweeping across the page.

Say something. You can't stand here forever, Eva told herself. But he was the adult. He was supposed to take pity on her. Was he really this evil?

"He worships the paper you write on," she heard Riley's voice say in her mind. A little spark fluttered to life in her chest.

"Mr. Greenleaf?" she said.

"Eva." He didn't even look up.

"Uh . . . okay. So. I'm applying for this Treemont scholarship and I was wondering if . . . you're not too busy, I mean . . . if you might consider . . . um . . . writing me a recommendation?" He glanced up from his work. "I mean, I totally understand if you don't want to. I'm sure it's a pain in the neck and if you don't have the time, I—"

"I would be honored to write a recommendation for you, Eva," he said. And then he did the most unexpected thing. He smiled. "Do you have the form?" he asked.

Eva held it out and he took it, looking down at it over his little half-moon glasses.

"I'll return it to you as soon as I'm finished," he said. Then he went right back to his work.

"Thank you," Eva said, not quite believing what she'd just done. "Really, thanks."

"See you tomorrow," Mr. Greenleaf said.

"Right." Eva was grinning from ear to ear. She turned and practically skipped out of the classroom. There were about six inches of fluffy air between her and the floor. She'd done it! She'd asked Greenleaf and he'd said yes! Eva came around the corner at the end of the hall, practically laughing from her giddiness, and stopped dead in her tracks. And she came crashing back to earth. There, not three feet away, were Riley and Debbie, laughing so hard Debbie was clutching his shoulders to keep from falling to the floor.

"Eva!" Debbie called out, noticing her before Eva could turn and flee. "Did you do it?"

"Do what?" Riley asked, his beautiful eyes turning to her.

"Uh . . . yeah, I did," Eva mumbled. She couldn't stop staring at Debbie's fingers, which were now resting on the chest area of Riley's Bad Religion tour T-shirt.

"He didn't say no," Debbie asked. "Did he?"

"No, he said yes."

"That's great!" Debbie said, grinning. "She got a recommendation from Greenleaf," Debbie told Riley, whose face lit up.

"See! I told you he would do it!" Riley said.

"Yeah . . . thanks," Eva said. "So . . . what're you guys doing?"

"Oh, we're just talking about my two favorite subjects, math and science!" Debbie said, nudging Riley with her shoulder. "We're going to cram for the Math and Science competition together."

Stop touching him, Eva thought. *God, can't you stop touching him for five seconds?*

"I thought you weren't going to do that competition thing," Eva said.

"I decided to keep my options open," Debbie said, winking.

Okay, I'm gonna hurl, hurl on her shoes, Eva thought. *That'll teach her a lesson.*

"I'd better go get my books before bio," Riley said. "I'll see you guys later. Congratulations, Eva. That's really cool about Greenleaf."

Eva flushed and hated herself for it. If Riley and

Debbie were going to be studying together, then Riley and Debbie were going to be hooking up by this time next week.

"Thanks," she said, looking away.

"He is *so* delicious," Debbie said the second Riley was out of earshot. "How could I have never realized how delicious he is? Can you even believe those eyes?"

He's going to be on her list. She's going to have details and a rating on Riley.

"I better get to class," Eva said, walking quickly down the hall. Eva had run away from a lot of people in her lifetime—guys she'd tongue-tied herself in front of and authority figures of all kinds. She'd just never thought she'd have to run away from Debbie.

"Do you think they're going to let us bring a list of the formulas?" Riley asked. He tossed his pencil onto his open physics book and rubbed his eyes. "They have to let us bring the formulas, right? No one can remember all this."

They were sitting together at a large round table at the Ardsmore Public Library. They were supposed to be concentrating on the test, but all Debbie could think about was how Riley was even cuter when he was stressing.

"Definitely," Debbie said, trying not to stare at

him. About fifteen minutes ago he had run his fingers up through his blond hair in a moment of velocity-versus-speed confusion, and it was still sticking up in front. She hadn't told him about it because she kind of liked it that way—Riley Marx, mad scientist.

But as hot as he looked, Debbie had decided she was going to control her flirtatiousness around him. She had no idea what, exactly, Riley had heard about her, but she felt the distinct desire to prove whatever it was wrong. She'd worn her most responsible outfit to the library—wide-leg jeans and a black polo shirt—and had gone a full hour without tossing her hair or licking her lips—a new individual record.

"I think I need a break," Riley said, reaching up with one hand and pushing his hair forward. He blew out a breath and looked around the deathly quiet periodical room. "I'm gonna get some M&M's. You want anything?"

"I'll come with you," Debbie whispered, pushing her seat back. Then she immediately wondered if that was wrong. Did following him out to the vending machines make her seem too clingy?

Argh, what am I doing? Since when do I have to work to impress a guy? And since when do I care what anyone thinks about me?

And then she stopped short when she realized

her answer. It wasn't just that she cared what *anyone* thought of her. It was that she cared what *Riley* thought of her. Somehow his opinion seemed important. And he was, after all, the Boy Scout. If she wanted him to like her, she was going to have to refute all those rumors—somehow.

So far neither one of them had brought up the dramatic scene from the school library, and Debbie was relieved that Riley seemed as determined to put it behind them as she was. The last couple of nights had been spent tossing and turning while she wondered what Riley had heard and if he was going to hold it against her. But it wasn't like she was ashamed of the things she'd done, so it shouldn't matter what Riley thought.

Unfortunately, it did.

"So how do you take your M&M's? Are you a plain, a peanut, or a crunchy?" Riley asked, shaking the change in his hand.

"Plain, definitely," Debbie replied. She stood with her hands behind her, concentrating hard to keep from playing with her hair.

"Well, you don't seem very plain to me," Riley joked.

Debbie flushed from the exertion of holding back about a thousand witty, cute responses.

No reason to fuel the I'm-a-slut fire.

"Thanks," she said instead.

Riley bent and grabbed the brown bag of candy from the dispenser. "You okay?" he asked, his brow furrowing as he stood up.

"I'm fine," Debbie said.

He shook a bunch of M&M's into his hand and held it out to her. "Listen, if it's about what happened in the library the other day—"

Debbie's heart thumped. "I thought we were forgetting about that," she said, holding her hands out in a cup so he could dump the candy in. Normally she would have stood there and opened her mouth so he'd have to place one of them on her tongue.

"Okay. Fair enough," Riley said. "As long as you forgive me for being such an idiot."

"I forgive you," Debbie said with a smile. A not too leading smile.

"Gladness," Riley said, popping an M&M in his mouth before opening the door for her. "Okay, we have an hour before we have to leave for the V Club thing. By then I plan to be a physics god."

"I'm sure the elderly folks will be very impressed," Debbie said.

She walked back into the library, making sure not to sway her hips or shake her hair out. Any other guy and she would have laid it on so thick they'd already be back in the ancient history section fogging up the windows. But Riley was different. She had to make him forget everything he'd heard about her. She had to make him realize she was not the slut of the century.

She was going to prove to Riley Marx that she was the type of girl he wanted. She was going to prove to herself that she was good enough—even for him.

Mandy watched through the bookshelves as Debbie and Riley returned to their table, hoping they wouldn't look up and see her. She sat in a big, cushy chair against the wall at the back of the library, and she'd been there all day, since well before her best friend and her study date had shown up. Normally she would have gone over and sat with them, but Mandy had come to the library specifically to be alone.

Once Debbie and Riley were bent over their books again, Mandy looked down at her own work, or lack thereof. She'd intended to write her speech for the V Club elections, but so far all she'd written in her notebook was, *Fellow members, I am running for V Club president because* . . .

Even in the silence, miles away from her house, which was clear on the other side of town, Mandy was having trouble concentrating. She'd barely slept at all last night, haunted by a recurring nightmare in which her parents were drowning in Huff Lake and she couldn't move her feet from the sand to swim out and help them. She had just watched her parents drown over and over and over again until 5 A.M., when she'd woken up in a cold sweat, turned on the television, and forced herself to stay awake.

And in less than an hour I have to go be chipper girl at the rest home. That should be fun.

There was a stirring over by Debbie's table and Mandy looked up. *Eric.* Her heart thumped at the mere sight of him. She heard her name whispered and saw Debbie and Riley glance around. They didn't see her, but Eric started walking in the direction of the stacks. Mandy held her breath as he came around the end of the bookshelf to her right.

"Hey, sweetness," he whispered when he saw her. His handsome face was lined with concern. As he approached, the vinyl of his jacket swished, the noise sounding insanely loud in the silence of the room.

There was no chair in the vicinity, so Eric crouched at Mandy's feet and put his hands on her knees as he reached up to kiss her. Mandy instantly felt calmer in his presence. Being with Eric was still the safest place she could think to be. How had she let herself forget that?

Just tell him what's going on, she thought. *You'll feel so much better if you just tell him.*

Maybe Eric could make everything okay.

"Your mom told me you were here," Eric whispered. He reached up and touched her face. "Why didn't you call me? I would've come with."

"You really want to study on a Saturday?" Mandy asked, smiling slightly.

"No. I really want to be with you on a Saturday," Eric replied, causing her smile to widen. "I feel like I haven't seen you all week."

"I know," Mandy said, looking down at her hands.

Eric studied her face, his eyes flicking back and forth slightly. "Is everything okay?" he asked. "I feel like . . . I don't know . . . maybe this is going to sound crazy, but I sort of thought maybe you were avoiding me?"

"No!" Mandy protested, even though it was somewhat true. "It was just a busy week."

"Yeah, but you didn't call me back the other night, and we never go to bed without talking first," Eric said. He inched a bit closer to her and leaned in. "You're not mad about all the sex talk, are you, 'cause I'll drop it right now."

"No, it's not that," she said.

If only it were just that, she thought. *If that was all I had to think about, we'd be doing it already.*

She looked into Eric's eyes. She loved him so much. Why had all this other stuff had to happen and get in the way of everything?

"Then what is it?" Eric pressed.

Mandy shook her head.

"What is it, Mandy?" Eric asked. "I'm not stupid. I know something's going on with you."

Mandy felt like her heart was swelling up and filling her chest. She looked at Eric and tried to keep the tears back. God, she wanted to tell him. She was practically dying to get it out of her, but when she opened her mouth to speak, it seemed to close itself right back up.

"Tell me," Eric said gently.

I can't, Mandy thought. *I can't tell you, because I think he's guilty.*

Suddenly she was filled with a sadness so all-encompassing she could barely breathe. This was the thought she'd been trying to keep at bay all along, but there was no denying it anymore. If she couldn't even tell Eric what was going on, if she couldn't tell him that her dad was being investigated but that it was nothing to worry about because it was all a big mistake, there was only one reason why. She suspected her father had done it. He'd committed tax fraud. Her father was a criminal.

"Mandy?" Eric said.

"Eric, I really need you to go right now," Mandy said.

"What?"

"I swear it's not you. I just . . . I really just need to be alone."

Suddenly his face changed. He pulled his hands away from her knees. He got up, his jacket swishing, and stood there for a second, looking at her like a stranger. Mandy wanted to say something to make him feel better, but there was nothing left in her to comfort him.

"Fine, call me when you feel like talking," he said finally and walked away.

Mandy pulled her legs up to her chest and rested her forehead on her knees, too upset to even cry.

Kai stood in the corner of the sun-drenched activity room at the Ardsmore Assisted Living Residence and watched as Mrs. Buerkle opened up a can of Scrabble whoop-ass on the rest of her table. The second she'd walked into the room, Kai had noticed Mrs. Buerkle and picked her out as the coolest in the bunch. For one thing, she was wearing a Pittsburgh Penguins hockey jersey and a pair of jeans instead of the muumuus and crocheted sweaters that abounded in this place. But it wasn't just her clothes; there was something about her that Kai identified with. Like *she* could be this woman in sixty-five years.

"Combover! Ha! Triple word score!" Mrs. Buerkle announced, placing her tiles carefully on the board.

"That's not a word," Mr. Consuelo, who had a quite awful combover himself, protested.

"I believe they added it to the official *Webster's* dictionary recently," Mrs. Buerkle protested. "Am I right, Kai?"

"I think she's got ya there," Kai said with a smirk. "Unless you want to challenge . . ."

Mr. Consuelo looked defiantly from Kai to Mrs. Buerkle and back, then deflated. "Eh, forget it. She always wins."

Kai smiled as Eva and Debbie walked over to join her from opposite sides of the room. Mandy was making her rounds, checking up on everyone like she was already in charge of the club, but she'd kept a good distance from Kai all afternoon.

I'm really going to have to talk to that girl and find out what's up her butt, Kai thought.

But for now, she was having too much fun to care. When she'd woken up that morning, Kai had felt that supervising a Scrabble tournament between old fogies was the last thing she would ever want to do. But it had gotten her out of touring Bucknell with Andres and her parents, and it was turning out to be more than a fair trade.

"How's everybody doing over here?" Debbie asked brightly.

"Fine, dear. Just fine," a large lady whom everyone called Babs replied. So far she'd racked up all of thirty-four points with words like *at, mad,* and *can.* But she seemed to be enjoying herself. "Now tell me, what kind of club is it that you girls belong to?"

This should be good, Kai thought.

"It's called a V Club," Debbie said.

Eva flushed and looked at the floor.

"A *what?*" Mr. Consuelo asked, blanching.

"Is that like a knitting circle?" Mrs. Hallstrom, the fourth player, asked, tipping her hearing-aided ear toward the girls.

Kai laughed. "Um . . . no. We're just a bunch of virgins celebrating our virginity."

"Well, now I've heard everything," Mr. Consuelo said, pulling off his glasses to pinch the top of his nose.

"So you're *all* virgins?" Mrs. Buerkle asked just as Mandy wandered over to the group.

Why does it feel like they're all looking at me? Kai thought, her skin overheating.

"Yeah, we all are," she said. "Every last one of us."

Mandy and Debbie exchanged a look that made it obvious they had been wondering about Kai. Kai was unsurprised. After all, Mandy had pretty much insinuated her suspicions already during volleyball practice. But it still irritated her that they had obviously talked about it behind her back.

"I think it's great," Babs said. She leaned over and grasped Eva's wrist. "You hold on to your flower, girl. Don't let just any old rake take it from ya."

Kai was certain that Eva was about to faint to the floor.

"I think it's insane!" Mrs. Buerkle put in, glaring at Kai like she had just betrayed a lifelong trust. "In this day and age? You girls have come so far! Why would you feel the need to restrict yourselves like that?"

Kai and Debbie looked at each other blankly. *Good question.*

"It's not a restriction," Mandy said, stepping into the fray. "It's a choice. A healthy choice."

"Damn straight," Babs said, shifting her large butt in her small chair. "I wish I'd had some friends to support me before I gave it up to that Richard kid."

Kai's eyes sparkled as she looked at her friends. "Richard?"

"Oh, yeah. Bad seed, that one," she said, clucking her tongue. "He acted like he was my friend, you know. Got all sensitive and pretended like he was interested in me and my family and everything I had to say. Then he takes my flower and heads for the hills. Never heard from him again."

"Men are worthless," Babs concluded.

'That's it. I don't have to listen to this!" Mr. Consuelo said, standing rather quickly for a man with a cane.

"Don't listen to Babs, girls," Mrs. Buerkle said,

turning in her seat. "Not all men are like that. Sex can be wonderful. You shouldn't close yourself off to the experience altogether."

"Who're you, Dr. Ruth?" Kai joked.

"Shoulda been," Mrs. Buerkle lamented. "You know how much money that woman has?"

"My Harold could go for hours!" Mrs. Hallstrom announced rather loudly, causing the entire room to fall silent.

"Well!" Mandy called out suddenly. "I think it's time for snacks! Debbie. Kai. Let's go!"

She grabbed Kai and Debbie's arms and pulled them toward the refreshment table as everyone around them resumed their games. Babs's words kept replaying in Kai's mind.

"He acted like he was my friend . . . then he takes my flower and heads for the hills."

Apparently Kai's life story wasn't all that original.

eleven

"THANKS FOR THE RIDE," DEBBIE CALLED OUT AS SHE
climbed out of Riley's car later that day. She couldn't
have been happier with her own self-control. A
whole day and no touching, no suggesting, no nothing. She was *good*.

Still, her nonflirtation hadn't prevented Riley
from flirting with *her*. Maybe whatever he'd heard
about her didn't actually bother him. Maybe
there was still a chance he wanted to go out with
her.

Debbie jogged into the house, her hair bouncing over her shoulders, and started right up the
stairs. Her father entered her room right behind
her and she jumped.

"Who was that, driving you home?" he asked
sternly.

"Oh, that was just Riley," Debbie answered. In
her excitement she forgot to come up with a girl's
name. The second she realized her mistake, she
headed her father off at the pass. "We're studying

together for the Math and Science competition," she announced.

Her father's face lit up with a rare smile. "So, you decided finally to take my advice," he said, crossing his arms over his polo shirt.

Debbie was irked by his obvious satisfaction, but she didn't let it affect her. She was in too good a mood. "Yes, I did," she said.

"I'm very proud of you, Deborah," he told her.

Debbie smiled. It was actually kind of nice when he said he was proud of her. It happened so infrequently lately. She was surprised by a sudden rush of warmth toward her father.

"Hey, Dad," she said, surprising herself. "I have a lacrosse game this Friday. . . . Do you think you might want to come?"

"This Friday? Yes. I think I can make that. I have been meaning to come see you play."

"Great! It's at five on the field behind the school."

"Good," her father said. "I look forward to it."

After he left, Debbie launched herself onto her bed, bouncing up and down as she reached for her phone. She dialed the voice mail number and hit the button to listen to her messages.

"Hey, sexy, it's Danny. I need my weekly Debbie fix, babe. Where ya been? If you're not doing anything tonight, I was thinking we could try out my parents' water bed—"

Ordinarily she would've *liked* a message like that, but somehow now it gave her a strange feeling she couldn't quite place. She erased the message before listening to the rest, then hung up the phone. She hadn't spoken to Danny since his little snicker fest with his friends at the library last week, and she wasn't about to start now.

If she had any real shot with Riley, she was going to have to avoid the likes of Danny Brown.

But what was he saying about me? Debbie wondered, unable to keep the thought from coming. *What has he been telling people?*

"It doesn't matter," she said out loud. Her father was coming to her game on Friday, and she and Riley and the rest of the club had had a lot of fun this afternoon. There were more important things to focus on than Danny Brown and his ego issues.

Debbie yanked open the drawer to her bedside table and pulled out her black velvet notebook. Danny had a whole section to himself at the back, where she kept a rundown of all their times together. She grabbed her red pen and wrote in big scrawling letters at the bottom of the last entry: I WILL NEVER FOOL AROUND WITH DANNY BROWN AGAIN. She underlined it three times. Then she tossed everything back in the drawer and slammed it shut.

Debbie got up from her bed and picked up her

book bag. She had a regular old calculus test coming up and she knew she should go over her notes, but the very thought of doing more math right then took her mood down yet another notch. There was always her purity essay to work on, but she was definitely not in a defending-her-chastity kind of mind-set. Not with Danny's voice still echoing in her head.

She glanced over at her sewing machine and the edge of her father's suit that was sticking out of her sock drawer.

Dropping her bag, Debbie sat down behind her sewing table and pulled out the silky fabric. If there was one thing she could get lost in, it was sewing, and if there was a moment to get lost, this was it.

"So, in conclusion," Mandy said, forcing herself to smile at the fifteen obviously bored faces before her, "I think I have a lot of great ideas, I *know* I have a lot of energy—"

Lies, lies, lies, Mandy chided herself.

"And if you elect me president of this V Club, I will do everything possible to make you proud. Thank you."

At least that's over, Mandy thought as everyone politely applauded her speech. She plopped down into the chair next to Eva's, feeling exhausted. Her entire day had been leading up to this moment, and now that it was over, all she wanted to do was pass out.

Eva smiled an encouraging smile at Mandy as Kai stood up to give her own speech. Mandy settled back and tried not to let her irritation show on her face. She wanted to appear happy, unconcerned, confident. Unfortunately, those traits that used to come so naturally to her were in short supply of late.

"I'll make this short and sweet," Kai was saying. "This club isn't about being a virgin, it's about making choices—choices that are right for us, choices that will shape our lives and the people we become. This club is about letting people know that there are things worth believing in, that we believe in ourselves."

An uncomfortable sensation of dread spread its way through Mandy's veins and she shifted in her seat. She saw Debbie flash an impressed glance in Riley's direction. Melissa Bonny was nodding and had a slight smile on her lips. Eva looked riveted.

The room burst into applause for Kai's speech—much more enthusiastic than their response to her own. Mandy found herself staring at the linoleum floor, blinking quickly to keep the unshed tears from spilling down her face.

Kai was on edge. Yukio had been put down for the night, and her parents were on their way out for their weekly alone-time dinner. Andres was in the kitchen, getting what must have been his seventh snack of the night, while Kai sat on the couch in the living room, dreading the moment the door closed behind her mom and dad. She and Andres, alone in the house together for the first time. The possibilities were endless.

Uncomfortable silence was one, a nice long talk about their past another—neither of them at all appealing right now. But Kai refused to retreat to her bedroom like a little girl. This was her house. She was going to sit her ass in front of the TV and watch *Friends* reruns, dammit.

"Good night, Kai," her mother said. She lifted her hair while Kai's dad slid her jacket up to her shoulders. "Be good."

"Aren't I always?" Kai replied.

Her mother and father both smirked as they walked out, closing the door firmly behind them.

"Do you want anything?" Andres called.

"No!" Kai shouted back.

Two seconds later Andres walked in, carrying an impossibly large sandwich, a bowl of chips, and a bag of Double Stuf Oreos. Kai lifted the remote and turned the TV up to an uncomfortably loud decibel. When Andres sat down on the couch again, he was a good foot closer to Kai than he had been before he got up.

Just keep yourself and your big stupid sandwich out of my personal space.

"I brought these for you—just in case," Andres said with a smile, holding out the bag of Oreos. "They are your favorite—yes?"

"Thanks," Kai said tersely. She grabbed the bag from him and dropped it on the coffee table.

"Did I do something?" he asked.

"Why are you trying to be nice to me?" Kai snapped. She hated how defensive she sounded, but she couldn't help it. Ever since Babs's little speech on Saturday, all the old wounds were reopened and felt fresh and painfully new.

"I thought we were friends," Andres said.

"That's a laugh," Kai told him. And then she scoffed for good measure.

"I do not understand you, *bonita*. If this is about my first night here, I am sorry if I made you uncomfortable. I will not touch you again."

Kai fumed silently, clenching her teeth. There were so many things she wanted to yell at him, she couldn't even get them straight. Her leg started to bounce up and down violently.

"Unless you want me to."

Andres reached out and touched her shoulder with the tips of his fingers and Kai jumped up from the couch, elbowing him in the nose.

"Are you kidding me?"

"What?" Andres looked baffled. "I don't understand what you want."

"I want you to leave me alone," she said.

"Where does this come from? You and I are old friends, Kai. We shared something very special. We should be able to cherish that."

Kai rolled her eyes. "What a load of crap. I can't believe I ever liked you!" she shouted, her anger bubbling over.

Andres, however, was clearly unaffected by this statement. He spread his arms across the top of the couch and looked back, his chin raised. Kai had once been attracted to that confidence. Now it just infuriated her.

"I recall that you did a bit more than like me," he said.

"Oh, really?" Kai said. She crossed her arms over her chest as her face burned.

"I recall that you made love with me," he said.

"Yeah, and then you never even wrote back to me."

Kai blinked. She hadn't just said that. She hadn't just said the one sentence she'd always promised herself she would never say. What was wrong with her tongue?

"Kai, I thought about writing back. I did. But we were in two different countries. Why fool ourselves? We could not have anything."

"I know this," Kai told him, scrambling for a way to save face. "Let's just drop it."

"No. I will not just drop it," Andres said, getting up and crossing the room to her. "We could not have anything then, but that does not mean that we can't have a little fun together now." He patted the seat next to him. "Come sit by me."

"Andres, go to hell," she said firmly, her heart pounding.

"What is wrong with you?" Andres asked, his frustration finally coming through.

She glared at Andres and set her jaw. "I want you to go," she said.

"What?" he blurted, his expression dumbfounded.

"This is my house, and I want to watch TV, and I don't want to be in the same room with you," Kai told him.

Andres just stared at her for a moment, confused. "Kai, please. I have no desire to be enemies with you."

He sounded so sincere, it caused a pang in Kai's heart, but she didn't let it affect her. She needed a victory here, even if it was just a tiny one. Finally Andres grabbed his food and trudged off to his temporary bedroom.

Kai sat down on the couch again, fuming, just as her show went to commercial. She couldn't believe the extent to which Andres was able to get under her skin. She wasn't going to let him make her regret her past. She'd learned from it. She'd moved on. Why did he have to come here and try to drag her back into those emotions, those sensations, those moments she had tried so hard to put behind her?

Okay, focus on something else. Don't let him get to you like this. Kai grabbed the phone off the coffee table and punched in Mandy's number. If she couldn't sort through all these Andres-related feelings at the moment, maybe she could at least rectify the Mandy situation. She had to take control of something in her life.

The call connected and Kai heard Mandy fumbling with the phone. "Hello?"

She was crying. Kai's heart twisted up tight.

"Mandy? What's wrong?"

"Kai, I'm gonna hafta call you back," Mandy said through her tears.

"No, wait. What's going on? Are you okay?"

"No. Not really," Mandy said. Then she hung up.

Kai hung up, too, then hit redial. She grabbed the TV remote and muted it, but it was a pointless move. The line was busy. She hung up again and tried Mandy's cell.

"Hi! This is Mandy! Here comes the beep!"

Kai leaned back, took a deep breath, and tried to think. Whatever was going on with Mandy, she obviously didn't want to talk about it right now, but Kai was not going to let this go. The V Club issue aside, something was going on with someone she genuinely cared about, and whether or not Mandy had been giving her the cold shoulder lately, she had to try to help her.

Kai picked up the phone and dialed again.

"Hello? Debbie's House of Couture!"

"Deb," Kai said flatly, "we have a situation."

twelve

MANDY PUSHED HER MACARONI AND CHEESE AROUND on her plate with her plastic fork, her head rested against her hand. As usual, the cafeteria buzzed with gossip. Only now everything she heard sounded so ridiculous.

"I called him on the phone, but he e-mailed me back. Does that count . . . ?"

"Are you going to go to Devon's party tonight? I want to go, but I'm worried my ex will be there. . . ."

"She's prancing around in that stupid jacket. Did you see that? God! She thinks she's just *so* . . ."

"Do you think my hair looks okay? Because I think I might have overconditioned it last night. . . ."

Mandy wished her life could be that simple again.

"Mandy?"

It was Eva's tentative voice. Mandy put her fork down and looked up. Her head felt heavy and she waited for the dizziness to pass.

"What?" she said.

Eva looked at Kai across the table and Kai looked at Debbie. Mandy's heart thumped with foreboding. There couldn't possibly be more bad news.

"What?" she said again.

Debbie lowered her voice. "Mandy, we're worried about you."

Mandy blinked against the spotlight that was now trained on her. This was so exactly what she didn't need right now. "What do you mean?" she asked, trying to sound nonchalant.

"You look so tired. And you haven't been eating," Debbie said, her eyes darting to Mandy's plate. "And Kai said that when she called you last night, you were crying. . . ."

Mandy scowled at Kai, who didn't even have the decency to look away.

"Plus everyone's noticed you've been off your game," Kai added.

Mandy suddenly felt her anger bubbling up again. "Oh, thanks a lot," she snapped. "It's good to know that *everyone's* noticed. What do you want to do, give me some pointers?"

Eva paled as if she'd just been slapped, and it only irritated Mandy more. What the hell? Couldn't she even vent a little without everyone getting all shocked? She was so sick of playing the goody-goody all the time.

"That's not what I meant," Kai answered, shaking her head. Something about it made Mandy feel like she was about four years old.

"We just want to know if everything's okay," Eva said gently. "If something's wrong, you can tell us."

"Is it Eric?" Debbie asked.

"Like you'd really care if it was. You'd love it if we broke up," Mandy said.

"Mandy, what is wrong with you?" Debbie asked. "You don't even sound like yourself."

"Maybe that's because everyone is ganging up on me!" Mandy felt a sob well up in her throat. "And, God! What does that even mean? What do I usually sound like?"

"Not like this," Kai said, staring at her plate.

"Oh, no, of course not!" Mandy said. "Because perfect little Mandy Walters never says anything negative. She never says how she *really* feels."

Eva shifted in her seat. Mandy was starting to attract attention from other tables. "Mandy—"

"Well, here's a news flash," Mandy said, standing. "*This* is how I really feel."

She grabbed her backpack off the back of her chair and headed for the side door of the cafeteria, her heart pounding so fast she was almost tempted to dial 911 on her cell. She didn't even know where she was going, and somewhere in the back of her mind she knew she could get in trouble for traipsing across the school grounds in the middle of a class period, but once again, Mandy didn't care. How could her friends have ambushed her like that? They had no idea what was going on in her life.

"Mandy!"

It was Eric. She kept walking. She didn't want to talk to him. She didn't want to talk to anyone.

"Mandy, come on!"

He jogged to catch up with her and held both her shoulders. He looked deep into her eyes, and suddenly the sobs exploded from her body. She could hardly breathe. She could hardly think straight.

Eric hugged her to him. He ran his hand gently over her hair as she sobbed uncontrollably into his chest, leaving a puddle right in the middle of his shirt.

"I . . . can't . . . take . . . it . . . anymore," Mandy heard herself say. "I just want everybody to leave me alone."

But even as she said it, she wrapped her arms around him and held him tight.

"Well, you're in trouble, then, 'cause I'm not going anywhere," Eric said softly. He kissed the top of her head, and the tightness in Mandy's chest lessened ever so slightly. "Everything's going to be okay," he said. "Whatever it is, it's going to be okay."

Mandy sniffled, squeezed her eyes closed, and wished she could believe him.

* * *

Eva's entire personal torture list was in upheaval. For the first time in years, she had two new tortures vying for number one: waiting to be interviewed and staging an unsuccessful intervention on a best friend.

Of course, once she got in there in front of the panel, they were both sure to be bumped for another contender: *being* interviewed.

"Are you okay?" Riley asked her. He leaned forward on the couch they were sharing, trying to get a better look at her face.

"No," Eva replied. The fewer syllables she uttered, the better. Her sweaty palms were pressed into the cotton fabric of her skirt. She was sitting on the edge of her seat, her spine ramrod straight, rocking forward and back ever so slightly. She couldn't stop thinking about the way Mandy had fled the cafeteria earlier that day. And whenever she tried to stop thinking about it, all she could think about was getting into the conference room and vomiting all over the panel.

There was a panic attack in her near future. She could tell.

"Okay, I think you need to breathe," Riley said, concerned.

"It's not like I'm not trying!"

And then the unthinkable happened. Riley put

his hand on her back and slowly started to rub circles into her gray sweater. Eva, if possible, became even more rigid.

"Breathe in . . . breathe out . . . breathe in . . . breathe out . . . ," Riley said in a low soothing voice.

Eva hazarded a glance in his direction and saw that his brow was knitted over his eyes and he was watching her very intently. She followed his directions, breathing in slowly and out slowly, and gradually she felt her back start to relax. Her heart rate went from extremely dangerous to only mildly alarming. Eva inched back slightly on the faux-leather couch in the guidance office waiting room.

"See? You're gonna be just fine," Riley said, removing his hand.

He was wearing a tie and jacket. He looked like a junior investment banker. Eva had never even imagined Riley in a suit. It was going to add a whole new layer to her daydreams.

Of course, those had been harder to dwell on now that Debbie always entered, unbidden, right before Riley kissed Eva. Before Eva could stop her brain, she was envisioning Debbie grabbing Riley and sticking her tongue down his throat.

Eva looked at Riley's profile. Did he like Debbie? Had he kissed her yet? Were they really studying together, or was his time with her spent doing the same things Debbie did on her other "study dates"? God she really wanted to know, but she knew she would never have the guts to ask.

"Maybe we should try talking about something else," Riley suggested. "Are you going to Devon's tonight?"

"Doubtful. You?"

"Yeah, I'll probably check it out. Let off some steam. You should show."

Eva stopped breathing again. Was Riley *asking* her to go?

Nah.

The door to the conference room in the corner opened and Liana Hull walked out, a secretive, confident little smile on her face. Eva's pulse accelerated all over again.

"Okay, you're next," Riley said, sitting forward on the couch, his feet flat on the floor, his knees jutting out at odd angles because of his legs' length. "Now, I want you to go in there and kick a little ass."

Eva scoffed. "Not in my current repertoire."

"What are you talking about?" Riley said, his blue-green eyes wide. "I don't know if you've realized this yet or not, but you are the person to beat on this scholarship thing."

"Please!" Eva reddened.

"I'm completely serious," Riley said, turning to face her better. "Yesterday I overheard Becca

Rabinowitz telling Melissa Bonny that she thought you were a lock. Then Elise West, Jennifer Shaloff, and Christina Sfekas overheard and they all agreed."

"Really?" Eva said, sitting up a little straighter. "*All* of them?"

"Yup. And I agree with them too," Riley said. "Look at the facts. You've been volunteering at 4-H for years, you're, like, a straight-A student, you're published in every issue of the lit magazine." He ticked off her attributes on his fingers as he spoke. "You got a recommendation from Greenleaf. Did you know that three other people asked him, and he turned every one of them down?"

"Really?" Eva said again, smiling.

"Yes, really," Riley said. "I should know. I was one of them. He said he'd already agreed to recommend you and that it would be hypocritical for him to write a letter for anyone else." Riley shook his head and pursed his lips comically. "Little fake English bastard."

"I'm so sorry," Eva said. "I had no idea he—"

"I'm just kidding," Riley told her. "All I'm trying to say is, stop stressing. There's nothing to stress about. You're golden."

Eva grinned. "Thanks."

"Eva Farrell?" Coach Davis called out from the doorway of the conference room. Eva's heart jumped, but it wasn't nearly as bad as it had been just moments ago. In fact, she felt a tiny bit . . . could it be . . . psyched?

"Now, like I said," Riley whispered, leaning in so close, her entire body shivered with uninhibited delight. "Go in there and kick a little ass."

Eva nodded once with determination, stood up, and straightened her skirt. Coach Davis smiled at Eva as she walked by and took her seat in front of the five-member panel. There was Mrs. Labella, who shot her a discreet thumbs-up; Mr. Simon, the coach; Vice Principal Stravinski; and Ms. Russo, one of the senior history teachers. For once in her life, Eva was thankful for Labella's presence. Every other person on the panel intimidated her to no end.

"Okay, Eva, make yourself comfortable," Mr. Stravinski began. "We want this to be as painless as possible."

"Painless. Yes. That sounds good," Eva said.

They all chuckled. She'd made them laugh. *Go, me!* Eva thought, blushing.

"Well, our first question is a general one," Mr. Simon said. "Why do you think we should award you this scholarship?"

Eva took a deep breath, saw Riley in her mind's eye, and said the first thing that popped into her head—a risk she'd never taken before in her life. "Well, I asked Mr. Greenleaf for a recommendation, which means I've already overcome my greatest fear for this scholarship, so that should show you how dedicated I am."

Did I really just say that?

More laughter. Eva, to her surprise, felt herself start to relax. Mrs. Labella looked so proud, Eva feared she was about to burst into song.

"But seriously," she said, a real answer forming in the back of her mind. A real answer that sounded *good.*

I can do this, she thought. *I can actually do this.*

Debbie tried not to look at the sidelines every five seconds. She tried to concentrate on the game at hand. But it was no use. While her *brain* knew her father was never going to show, her eyes kept darting over, checking the crowd, looking for him. Only three minutes were left in the game. Kai was there. Eva was there. Mandy, who had been avoiding her since the cafeteria meltdown, was not. And—surprise, surprise—her father was not there either.

"Patel! What're you doing!?" Coach Grenier shouted from the bench. "Get in the damn game already!"

Debbie gripped her lacrosse stick harder, honed in on the ball, and ran. Suddenly all she could see were the two girls on the opposing team, gunning for the net. Debbie raced, her pulse pounding, sensing the ball carrier's next move. When blondie shifted to pass the ball, Debbie was there. She snatched it right out of the air, turned, and was off.

She ran faster than she knew was possible, dodging every defender in her way like a girl possessed.

Right in front of the goal Debbie stopped short, throwing off the last defender. She pulled back and whipped the ball into the upper-left corner of the net. The crowd went wild; her teammates piled on top of her. It was the game-winning goal.

Debbie ran over to Kai and Eva, her smile slightly strained. Kai gave her a huge hug. "That was awesome!" she said. "I've never seen anything like it."

"Thanks," Debbie said, wiping her hand across her forehead. "Mandy didn't show, huh?"

"No," Eva said sadly.

"I think she kinda hates us," Kai said. "You guys wanna go grab some food? Maybe figure out if there's anything more we can do?"

Debbie knew it was pointless, but for some reason she really wanted to get home and see if her father had left a message for her. When he had told her he would come today, that he'd been *meaning* to come to one of her games, she had thought they might have actually found some common ground again—something to share that wasn't science related. Some part of her wasn't ready to give up on that yet. Debbie didn't want to care, but she did.

"Can't," she said, taking a couple of steps back toward her teammates, who were starting to huddle around Coach for the postgame talk. "But I'll see you guys tonight at Devon's."

Devon Randall was hosting tonight's football party after the Worthington game, and everyone Debbie knew was going to be there. Including Riley, hopefully. She might be miles away from breaking through with her dad, but she was *this close* to getting Riley to make a move—she could feel it. All she had to do was drop a few subtle signals and the Boy Scout would be all hers. Tonight was the night.

Getting Riley Marx to kiss her might be the one thing that could cheer her up.

thirteen

"THANK YOU SO MUCH FOR COMING OVER," EVA SAID, clutching her hands together and watching Kai as she attacked Eva's closet like the Tasmanian devil.

"No problem. I was psyched to get out of there anyway," she said, tossing a couple of blouses onto Eva's bed.

"Andres still playing personal space invader?" Eva asked, untwisting the shirts from the mass and flattening them out.

"Something like that," Kai said. She walked over to Eva's mirror, holding a pink T-shirt up over her chest, and eyed her reflection thoughtfully. "I'm surprised you didn't call Deb or Mandy."

"They're both going straight from the game," Eva said, perching on the end of her bed. "I finally talked to Mandy, though. She said she was sorry for freaking out."

"Did she tell you what her deal is?" Kai asked.

"No. We didn't get that far. She had to go pick up Eric," Eva told her.

"Ah," Kai said. She pawed through the piles of clothes on Eva's bed and pulled out an old pair of roughed-up jeans, which she shoved toward Eva along with the pink top. "This and this," she said.

"Really?" Eva asked, standing up. "I haven't worn these jeans since my ill-fated haiku phase."

Kai smirked. "Trust me. Just put them on."

Eva went into the bathroom and pulled the T-shirt on over her head. She was convinced the jeans would never fit, but the waistband, which used to stick out around her waist, now settled in perfectly on her hips. Eva looked at herself in the bathroom mirror. Not bad. Except for that sliver of her stomach that was exposed.

"I can't go out like this," she said, walking back into the room, her arms held over her tummy.

Kai rolled her eyes and pulled Eva's arms out like a pair of wings. "You look hot. You want to look hot, don't you?" Then she eyed Eva quizzically. "Are you ever going to tell me who you want to look hot for?"

Eva flushed and turned to the mirror. She really didn't look half bad. The white embroidery along the neckline of the pink tee was pretty, but it wasn't like it drew the eyes away from that stretch of skin down below. Could she really survive the night with her belly button showing?

"Okay, I'll wear it. But I reserve the right to bring a cardigan," Eva said, snagging her black sweater from her bed.

"Whatever," Kai said. "And don't think I didn't notice you ducking the question."

"Of course," Eva replied. "Thanks again, Kai."

"What are friends for?" Kai asked, grabbing her bag and keys. "Are we going?"

Eva's heart fluttered nervously as she gathered her stuff. It was the first time she'd ever actually dressed up for a party, and it was impossible to ignore the reason. She wanted Riley Marx to notice her. For the first time ever, Eva *wanted* to be noticed.

"Yeah, let's go," she said. She closed her bedroom door behind her, and then the phone rang.

Eva glanced at the phone that hung on the wall in the kitchen. *Don't answer it,* a rebellious little voice in the back of her head told her. *You know it can't be good.*

"Are you gonna get that?" Kai asked, her hand on the doorknob.

Eva swallowed and tromped into the kitchen, resigned. She wasn't in the least bit surprised to hear her mother's voice on the other end of the line.

"Eva, the car died. I'm at the Amoco on Sheridan Road. Do you think you could get one of your friends to swing by and pick me up?"

Sheridan Road. Of course. The one road that was at least a mile from any bus line in either direction. Eva took a deep breath, looked at Kai, and sighed.

"Yeah, Mom. We'll be there in twenty minutes."

"There are going to be some people here tomorrow. They're going to take some things, but I don't want you to worry. You don't have to be scared. . . ."

Mandy stood in Devon's kitchen on Friday night, holding a cup of soda in one hand, her other arm wrapped around her stomach as she stared at the flowered pattern on the tiled floor. Her father had stopped her just before she'd left for the game that evening, and his words kept replaying in her head as the party raged all around her.

"They're going to take some things. . . . You don't have to be scared. . . ."

How could she not be scared? She had no idea how this whole thing had started. Where it was going. Would there be a trial? Would they lose the house? Could her father end up in *jail*? Would her mother end up in jail? Would they have to go on welfare? Move in with her grandparents? Her father still hadn't explained *anything* to her. Both of her parents were too busy walking around like nothing was wrong. Pretending for the rest of the world. Just like Mandy was.

She knew she was going to have to give Eric an explanation and soon. She had been avoiding him since her cafeteria breakdown. But she wasn't ready for that particular drama yet. She was going to have to live through tomorrow's drama first.

"Stop fidgeting. You look great," Kai told Eva. Kai opened the front door at Devon's later that night, letting the pounding dance music spill out over the lawn. They had already picked up Eva's mother and dropped her at home, losing a full hour of party time.

What if Riley's already been here and gone home? Eva wondered.

Ever since Riley had mentioned Devon's party to her that afternoon, a new fantasy reel had started rolling in her head. One where her eyes would lock with Riley's from across the crowded room. He would see her in her stunning party outfit, make a beeline for her, and tell her how beautiful she was. It wasn't original, she knew, but it was knee-weakeningly good.

Of course, now that she was here, she remembered that she hated crowds, she wasn't so sure about her "stunning" outfit, and in the face of so many overly coiffed girls, she felt anything but beautiful.

Reality sucks.

Mitch Mascarenhas barreled through the doorway, fleeing from a couple of his friends who were bent on doing who knew what to him. He knocked into Eva, sending her slamming into Kai.

"Whoa, whoa," Kai said with a laugh, righting Eva. "You need to find your party legs."

Eva smiled, but inside she was terrified. What had she been *thinking*? She didn't do parties. She didn't do flirting. She didn't do dressing up for guys. Especially not after a night of helping her mother haggle with an overgrown mechanic named Lou and listening to her mom lament all the way home about what a rip-off the guy was. Now not only was Kai privy to her family's bleak financial situation, but Eva was quite sure she smelled like gasoline, and she was no longer quite as confident as she'd been when standing in the middle of her bedroom.

"I'm gonna go get us some drinks," Kai said.

Before Eva could grab her and demand that she never leave her side, Kai had already maneuvered halfway through the throng, weaving in and out like she'd done it a million times before.

I guess world traveling teaches you a few things, Eva thought.

When another passerby nearly sent her sprawling down the two steps into the living room, Eva flattened herself against the stucco partition behind her and did her best wallflower. She watched as Melissa and Scot ground to the music, clutching each other like a couple of wannabe porn stars. She rolled her eyes as half the football team engaged in a chug fest on the other side of the room. Nowhere did she see Riley Marx. She was just beginning to think that she had, in fact, missed him when she heard someone shout his name.

"Yo, Riley! Yeah, that's it! You go, Boy Scout!"

Eva found the shouter, Chris Chin, with her eyes, then followed his gaze to the staircase, where Riley Marx was following a girl upstairs. And not just any girl. He was following Debbie Patel.

"So much for that virgin scholarship," one of Chris's moronic friends shouted. A bunch of guys laughed and slapped hands. Riley and Debbie kept walking, either not hearing them or choosing to ignore them, but Eva had a feeling their voices would be echoing in her head for a long time to come.

Riley and Debbie. Debbie and Riley. Riley and Debbie. Upstairs. Together.

Eva pulled her cardigan on over her pink shirt and held it close to her, wishing she'd been born stupid so she wouldn't have to understand what Debbie and Riley were about to do. The question was, why had Eva even bothered coming here? Was her life lacking in teen angst drama in some way?

Had she not seen this coming from miles off? From every angle?

She lowered herself onto the step next to her and sighed, feeling sick to her stomach. Somehow she had allowed herself to imagine that she meant something to Riley. That their conversation on the swings and his support of her in the guidance office, even the crazy laughing paint fight, had affected him the same way they'd affected her. But clearly she'd been wrong.

Maybe she actually *had* been born stupid.

fourteen

DEBBIE LEANED AGAINST THE DOORJAMB TO DEVON'S upstairs guest room and waited for Riley. The second floor was empty, thankfully, so she didn't have an audience as she readied herself. She shook her hair over her shoulder, licked her lips, and arched her back slightly. Her heart pounded erratically in her chest, but she wasn't nervous. This was her moment.

She and Riley Marx had been hanging out all week, and Debbie was proud of the fact that she had yet to make a move, especially considering the many chances she'd had to jump his bones—in the library, in the car, after the V Club meeting when they'd walked out to the nearly deserted parking lot together. She'd been the picture of self-restraint and she felt she'd earned her dues.

And she just knew that he wanted to hook up with her too. He'd been so nice to her and had spent so much time with her. And besides, he wouldn't have come upstairs with her if he didn't want to.

Just don't forget, this is Riley, Debbie told herself. *Subtlety is key.*

The door to the bathroom opened and Riley stepped out. He looked at her and smiled.

"You didn't have to wait for me," he said.

Debbie hesitated. Of course she had to wait for him. He hadn't *actually* thought she'd come up here with him just to help him find the bathroom. Had he?

"Well, you know, I just thought we could hang out up here for a while," Debbie said, tilting her head toward the deserted bedroom behind her. Trying to suggest without being *too* suggestive.

Take the hint, she urged him silently. *Come on, Riley. Take the hint!*

"Why?" Riley asked, looking confused. "Everyone else is downstairs."

"I don't know," Debbie said, forcing a giggle. "It's just so much more relaxing up here, isn't it?"

"Yeah, but we're at a *party*. We can all relax when we're at our own houses going to *sleep*." Riley reached out and punched her lightly on the arm. Debbie could feel her face burning. She tried to smile, but it came out like a grimace.

"Come on," Riley said. "Let's go back down."

Debbie followed Riley down the stairs, but she had to clutch the banister to keep her hand from shaking. Was it possible that he hadn't recognized the signals she was sending? Or had he just turned her down flat without actually saying the words? She felt like something inside her was deflating.

Kai couldn't have been more surprised when she saw Mandy winding her way through the packed party toward her. At first she thought she must be coming to talk to Eva, who was slumped back into the couch to Kai's left, her cardigan buttoned all the way to the top. But instead Mandy sat down to Kai's right, laid her hands over her stomach, and sighed.

"Do you hate me?" Mandy asked, staring straight ahead.

"What? No!"

"Good," Mandy said. "I was just . . . really tired the other day and I didn't mean to explode like that. I'm sorry."

"Hey, that's okay," Kai told her. "We didn't mean to attack you. We just . . . we were worried about you."

"Well . . . like I told Eva," Mandy said, sitting up and looking past Kai at Eva, who lifted her hand in acknowledgment. "I just haven't been sleeping well lately, and it's got me all messed up."

"It's okay," Kai said again. She was about to pump Mandy for more information—see if she could get to the root of things—when someone by the front door caught her eye. Kai's heart dropped.

It couldn't be. But it was. As Eva launched into a rambling explanation of how they'd all been really tense and stressed lately, Kai could only focus on one thing. One big toothy grinning thing. Andres.

He was standing near the wall, sipping from a cup and laughing with Abby Alessi, doing that thing with his lips that he thought made him look like Antonio Banderas. Kai couldn't believe it.

"That little bastard," she said under her breath.

"Who?" Mandy and Eva said in unison.

They followed her gaze and she didn't have to answer. Andres stuck out like a sore European thumb with his slick hair and his silky shirt tucked into his acid-washed jeans.

"Omigod. Is that—?"

"You bet your ass it is," Kai said.

"Damn. He *is* beautiful," Mandy said, causing a little twist in Kai's stomach. "Did you bring him?"

"No. I didn't even tell him I was coming here," Kai said.

"Well, then how did he find you?" Eva asked, sounding disturbed.

"I'm about to find out."

Kai pushed herself up from the couch and stalked across the room, the crowd parting before her like the Red Sea.

"Bonita!" Andres stretched out his free arm to hug her.

"What're you, stalking me now?" Kai stopped and crossed her arms over her chest.

"Oh, please. Get over yourself," Abby said, tossing her long blond hair. "He's here with me."

Andres shrugged apologetically, and Kai gave Abby a look that could have melted glass. She grabbed Andres's wrist and yanked him away from Abby and out the door. Beer sloshed over the rim of Andres's cup and he protested, but Kai ignored him. Wasn't there anyplace she could go to escape this guy?

When Kai hadn't returned after five full minutes, Mandy started to wonder. Maybe it was just because she'd been so on edge in general lately, but something about this Andres thing didn't feel right. Kai had barely talked about the guy since he arrived, and whenever someone, usually Debbie, brought him up, she got all defensive and weird.

Kai had always seemed so fearless. Since the first time Mandy had seen her practicing spikes against the wall in the gym at a summer volleyball practice, she had admired and envied that spark in Kai. But there was something about this Andres guy that spooked her friend. And the fact that someone was able to spook Kai, well, *that* spooked *Mandy*.

"I'm gonna go check on them," Mandy said, pushing herself up.

"I'll save the couch," Eva said.

Mandy slid along the wall, hugging the furniture for the quickest route across Devon's increasingly crowded living room. She opened the front door carefully and peeked out, but Kai and Andres were nowhere in sight. The street at the edge of Devon's lawn was dark, and Mandy could see the outline of badly parked cars and SUVs. She listened hard and finally heard voices somewhere off to her left. They sounded angry.

Pulse racing, Mandy hustled toward the nearest corner. Maybe she hadn't been able to bust in on her parents' arguments, but this situation was different. She had to find out if everything was okay. At least here she could try to help. Mandy approached the side of the house, and as she got closer, she could make out what the voices were saying.

". . . Am not just going to sit in your house with nothing to do just because you are afraid for me to meet your friends," said a voice with a thick Spanish accent.

"Andres, just go home," Kai's voice said, sounding firm.

"What are you afraid of? Are you afraid I will tell them what we do together?" Andres asked. "Are you so ashamed of being with me? Is that what this is about? It's just sex, *bonita*! What is the great deal?"

Mandy felt like the grass had been whipped out from under her feet. She pressed a hand into the rough wooden shingles next to her, her skin tingling. Was it possible? Were Andres and Kai having sex? Was that why Kai had been so testy when Mandy had tried to talk to her about it?

Omigod, she lied *to us. She stood there the other day, looked at us, and said, "We're all virgins. Every last one of us!"* Here Kai has been acting all concerned about Mandy, like all she wanted was to be a good friend, but meanwhile she has been lying to all of them. And even worse, she was competing against them for a scholarship that she didn't remotely deserve.

The very thought made Mandy sick with anger.

Mandy heard footsteps, and all at once she realized Kai and Andres had stopped talking. She turned and rushed inside.

Mandy had thought she and Kai were going to be close, were *already* close, but the more she learned about her newest friend, the more she realized how different they were. Mandy would never lie to her friends like that.

Except that you have been, she thought shakily.

But that was different, she told herself. Mandy was only lying to protect her family. Kai was lying to protect herself, and she was hurting others in the process—competing for a scholarship she didn't deserve and a club presidency she wasn't even qualified for.

"You wanna get out of here?" Mandy asked Eva, grabbing her jacket from a pile near the side door.

Eva practically flew off the couch. "Yes, please."

Mandy yanked open the door that led to Devon's garage.

"Shouldn't we tell Kai we're going?" Eva asked.

"Kai's a big girl," Mandy said stonily. "She can take care of herself."

fifteen

THE SILENCE WAS INTENSE.

Debbie glared at the back of her father's head as he brought his car to a stop in front of their house. Before he'd even had time to cut the engine, she was out of the backseat, slamming the door as hard as she could.

She hadn't said a word to either of her parents all morning. Not over breakfast, not during the ride to the soup kitchen. When they'd arrived at the temple, she'd volunteered to reorganize the pantry so that she could sequester herself in the large closet all morning, as far away from her father and any other human beings as possible. All morning she had been waiting for her father to come to her and apologize—for him to merely acknowledge the fact that he'd missed her game and that he felt bad about it, but he'd said nothing.

Once inside, Debbie started to stalk upstairs, but she hadn't gotten far when her father walked into the house behind her.

"Deborah Patel, get down here this instant," he said in his scariest voice.

"I want you to explain your attitude to me, young lady," her father said, fuming. Her mother bustled into the house and went straight to the kitchen. No help there. "You have been disrespectful to me and to your mother all morning."

"So what? You're disrespectful to me!" Debbie shot back.

Her father looked like he'd been slapped.

"I am your father and you will not speak to me that way," he said, his eyes bulging.

Debbie breathed in deeply. Breathed out. "Why didn't you come to my game?"

Her father looked toward the ceiling like he was completely fed up by this question, even though she'd never asked it before. "I had *work* to do, Deborah. Work comes before games."

Work comes before me, you mean, Debbie thought, tears stinging at her eyes. She hated herself for being so affected by this. She knew the refrain, had been hearing it all her life. Her father had to provide for the family. *That is my role as the father*, he'd said to her a million times.

"Fine. Whatever," Debbie said finally.

"Now I want you to go to your room and study," her father said. "You have a lot of work to do."

Studying. Apparently that was her role as the daughter.

"Fine," Debbie said again, this time through her teeth.

By the time she got to her room, Debbie was about to explode with pent-up aggravation. She saw the hem of her father's sherwani suit sticking out of her bottom dresser drawer and snapped. She yanked out the silky costume she'd worked so hard on, balled it up, and shoved it in the bottom of her trash can. Then she grabbed her science books and threw them in too. She was just looking around her room to see if there was anything else she could destroy when she caught sight of her phone.

Eva. She grabbed the receiver and dialed her number. Eva would always listen to her vent about her dad and knew exactly what to say to make her feel better.

The phone rang four times before someone picked up. "Hello?"

"Oh, hi, Mrs. Farrell," Debbie said, surprised to hear Eva's mom's voice. The woman was almost never home. "It's Debbie Patel."

"Hi, Debbie," Mrs. Farrell said.

"Is Eva there?"

"No, she's not," Mrs. Farrell replied. "I think she went down to 4-H."

Debbie's heart sank with disappointment. "Oh. Okay. Can you tell her I called?"

"Sure. No problem."

Debbie's call waiting beeped. "Thanks," she said, then hit the flash button.

"Hello?" she said.

"Hey, Deb, it's Riley."

All the anger seemed to rush right out of her at the sound of his voice, even as her embarrassment from the night before came swirling back. "I was going to head over to the library to study," he said. "Wanna come?"

Debbie smiled and glanced at the doodle-covered paper covers on the textbooks sticking out of the top of the trash can. "I'll be there in fifteen minutes."

"Why am I lying to your best friend again?" Eva's mother asked. She hung up the phone and crossed her arms over her pink terry cloth robe. Whenever Eva's mother had a day off, she spent most of the morning lounging around in her pajamas and robe, happy to be away from hospital smells and out of her itchy white uniform.

"I just . . . I don't feel like talking to her right now," Eva said, staring down at the open poetry book on her lap.

And I definitely don't want to hear a play-by-play of

whatever Riley and Debbie did at Devon's last night.

Her imagination was already working overtime. She didn't need actual details. And she really didn't need to hear Debbie's excited voice as she related them.

"Everything okay, hon?" her mother asked, sitting down next to Eva on the couch. "You want to talk about it?"

"Not really," Eva said.

"Okay, then do you want to go catch a movie?" she asked. "I have no idea what's playing, but it's matinee prices until four."

A lump of guilt welled up in Eva's throat. Her mother almost never voluntarily offered to spend money on entertainment, so she must be really concerned. But Eva knew there was no way she would enjoy a movie today. She was just too depressed to concentrate on anything.

"Thanks, but I don't really feel like going out," Eva said. She gazed down at the words in front of her—words that meant nothing even though she'd read them twenty times.

"Well, let me know if you change your mind," her mother said, reaching out and tucking a lock of hair behind Eva's ear. It was too short, and it fell right back out again, tickling her cheekbone. "I'm going to go take a shower."

"Okay," Eva said.

As her mother padded into the bathroom, Eva slapped her book closed, realizing she was never going to get anywhere until she got the image of Debbie and Riley walking upstairs together out of her mind.

Unfortunately, short of a lobotomy, she had no idea how she was going to make that happen.

For all the imagining Mandy had done, it was worse than she expected. She sat in the middle of her freshly made bed, her knees pulled up under her chin, listening to the sounds of the half dozen federal employees tromping around her house. An older man with a kind face had told her to just go about her business but to keep her bedroom door open.

Go about her business. Right. Like that was even possible.

There was a sudden rap on her window and Mandy jumped. *Eric.* She jumped off her bed and ran to open the window. Eric tumbled into the room, his face red and sweaty from the exertion of climbing up her trellis. He'd only tried it once before, and that time he'd ended up with a sprained ankle.

"Eric! What are you doing here?" Mandy asked, relieved and petrified at the same time.

"I came over to talk to you, and this guy downstairs told me to vacate the premises," Eric told her, his eyes wide with worry. "What the hell is going on?"

Mandy's eyes darted to the hallway. The voices that had stayed downstairs all morning seemed to be getting closer. She couldn't stand this. Her home had been taken over by strangers and her own boyfriend was climbing through the window to get to her. She felt like she was living a TV movie. None of this could actually be happening.

"Mandy, please. I'm freaking out," Eric said. "You need to tell me what's going on."

"Okay, come here," Mandy said, grabbing his arm. She pulled him over to her walk-in closet, yanked the cord that turned on the light, and dragged him inside, closing the door behind her.

"Okay . . . okay . . . here's the thing . . . ," Mandy began, keeping one ear trained on the door. Eric crossed his arms over his chest and waited, but Mandy just kept stalling. She shouldn't be doing this. She shouldn't be telling anyone what was actually going on. But what was she supposed to say? Eric had walked in on the search and seizure. There was no way to explain that away.

Just tell him the truth. Tell him!

"My father is being investigated for tax fraud," she blurted, squeezing her eyes shut.

"What!?" Eric said.

"Shhhhh!!!" Mandy told him, grabbing his wrists.

"I'm sorry," he whispered, bending his knees slightly and bringing himself closer to her height. "But *what*?"

Suddenly Mandy found herself spilling the whole story. Once she got started, she couldn't stop. She didn't even know what she was saying. Eric kissed the top of her head. "It's okay, I'm here," he said over and over again until her sobs quieted into tears of relief. "I'm here. . . ."

They were the two most beautiful words in the world.

Eric was here for her. Mandy felt like the poison that had been eating at her insides had been flushed right out of her.

It's okay. I'm not alone anymore.

"Why didn't you tell me all this before?" Eric asked.

"I just couldn't," Mandy said pulling slightly away from him and backing into the hangers full of clothes behind her. "I was embarrassed," she added, ashamed just to admit it. "I mean, how do you tell your boyfriend that your father is a felon?"

"Mandy, you know you can tell me anything," Eric said, holding her arms and looking into her eyes. "I'm not gonna judge you because of something your father *might* have done. I'm not gonna judge you ever. I love you."

"I love you too."

"But you have to trust me."

Mandy looked at him and it all seemed so simple. Of course she trusted Eric. She always had. She didn't have to be alone in this.

"I know," she said. "I do."

Feeling lighter than she had in days, Mandy opened the closet door and led Eric out into her room. They sat down together on the bed and clicked on the TV to some mind-numbing Saturday-morning NBC show. Mandy cuddled up against Eric's side and he locked his arms around her. She didn't care if her parents walked in. She didn't care if the IRS agents walked in. For the first time in days, she felt safe. And she wasn't about to give that up for anything.

sixteen

THERE WAS NOTHING ON EARTH BUT THE SOUND OF her breath, the wind in her ears, the cool autumn breeze mixing with her sweat to cool her over-heated skin. By the time Kai skidded to a stop in her driveway, her mind was made up. She knew what she had to do.

It was time to lay down the law.

She stretched on the front lawn for a few minutes, then headed for the kitchen, where she found Andres sitting at the table, shirtless, eating Cocoa Puffs and flipping through *ESPN The Magazine*. The sun poured in over him from the back window, highlighting his deep tan. Kai cursed the gods for the millionth time for making him so damn beautiful.

Just looking at him reminded her of every huge mistake she'd ever made—trusting him, letting him get close enough to shatter her heart. Mistakes she would never make again.

"Hey," she said. She wanted to sound friendly and neutral. No reason to start out all belligerent.

"Hey," Andres replied in the exact same tone.

Kai opened the refrigerator and stared at the contents, pretending to mull over her choices. She didn't want to look at Andres, because if she did, there was a chance her eyes would wander to his bare chest and then all would be lost. He would undoubtedly notice and he would use it against her. This conversation was all about the upper hand.

"We need to talk," Kai said, picking out a Snapple and popping the top. She took a long swallow, watching Andres out of the corner of her eye. He didn't even flinch.

"About what?" he asked before shoving a huge spoonful of cereal into his mouth.

"About last night," Kai said. She walked over to the counter that separated her from the table and leaned into it. "You can't do that again."

"Do what?" Andres asked, eyes still on the soccer article in front of him.

"You know what. Just . . . show up at a party like that," Kai said, waving her free hand.

"How did you find out about it anyway?" she asked.

"I was at Blockbuster. I heard a couple of people talking about a party and I talked to them. They invited me," Andres said nonchalantly.

"Well, next time say no," Kai told him.

"Fine," Andres said. He turned a page and studied

the headline and photo, his brow furrowing like he was concentrating on a math problem. "I didn't come here to hang out with immature little girls anyway."

"I'm immature?" Kai demanded, her eyes flashing. "You're the one who dropped in here thinking I was just going to throw myself at you!"

Andres looked up at her finally, and there was something hard in his eyes—something Kai had never seen before. Cocky, arrogant, playful, sexy she'd seen on Andres. Hard and cold, never.

"I don't know why I bothered," he said slowly. "As I recall, you were not so good."

Kai felt everything inside her shrink back like her insides had been doused with cold water. He hadn't just said that. There was no way he had just said that. Her hand tightened around the Snapple bottle, and she had a sudden vision of herself hurling it directly at his head.

Luckily for him, the phone rang.

Kai turned to answer it. She was going to kill him. She would kill him in his sleep. Or at the very least, shave his greasy head.

"Hello?" she snapped into the phone.

"Uh . . . Kai?"

"Yeah, who's this?" Kai asked, clomping out of the room. She wanted to get as far away from Andres as possible.

"It's Eric Travers," the voice on the other end replied.

"Oh . . . hey," Kai said. Eric had never called her before. She was surprised he even had her number. A little warning bell went off in her heart. *Mandy.*

"Is everything okay?" she asked.

"Oh, yeah, everything's fine," Eric said brightly. Kai relaxed and walked out to the front lawn with the phone. "I'm just calling about Mandy's birthday. . . ."

"I don't think we should all have to sign something that says we're going to stay virgins forever," Melissa said on Monday afternoon. "It's going to be a personal decision for everyone, right? Some of us will want to wait until we're in love, some of us will want to wait until we're a certain age. . . . I mean, we didn't join this club to give up our free will."

"Yeah. I think it should say something about promising to make good, healthy choices," Liana put in.

"This isn't the Good Healthy Choices Club," Debbie shot back. "What's the point of calling it a V Club if virginity isn't in the honor statement?"

Kai watched as Liana narrowed her eyes at Debbie from across the circle of desks. "Why are you even here?"

Murmuring and chatter erupted across the

classroom, and Kai stuck her fingers into her mouth and whistled to shut them all up. She glanced at Mandy, expecting her to say something, but Mandy was staring into space, just as she had been ever since Madame Kopec left the room with the ballots five minutes ago. They were supposed to be figuring out their honor code while Kopec, the impartial adviser, counted their votes, but so far all they'd done was argue.

"Okay, I have to agree with Debbie on this one. If you don't want to make a commitment to virginity, then you probably shouldn't be in this club," Kai said, ignoring the hot feeling in her stomach. Debbie smiled triumphantly and Mandy let out an audible sigh that sounded somewhat like a scoff.

"So . . . what? We're saying we're gonna stay virgins until when? Marriage?" Becca Rabinowitz asked, pulling a dubious face.

"Why not?" Riley said, eliciting a few giggles.

"How about through high school?" Kai suggested. "It's not like the club rules can bind us after graduation, right? So we'll just say through high school—for as long as we're members of the club."

Melissa and Liana exchanged a look. "That seems fair," Liana said. Melissa doodled something in her notebook, looking deflated. Kai wondered if Melissa was in the same position as she was—if maybe she too was lying about her virgin status and was trying to create herself a loophole.

"So, wait. You're not gonna have sex until you're married?" Marni asked, turning toward Riley.

"Nope," Riley said, lifting his shoulders.

"Not even if you fall totally and completely in love?" Melissa asked.

"If I fall totally and completely in love, then hopefully I'll marry that person," Riley said matter-of-factly.

"Damn," Liana said under her breath. "That's gonna take some willpower."

"How long are you going to wait?" Debbie asked Liana.

"Not that it's any of your business," Liana said. "But I think that if I love someone and really trust them, I'll know it's right."

"Not necessarily," Kai said without even thinking about it. All eyes turned to her. "What? It happens all the time. You think you know someone and you trust them and all that, so in the moment it all feels right, but then later it turns out that person was really just a good actor."

"Why would you say that?" Mandy asked, coming to life for the first time. "You make it sound like all guys will say anything to get you into bed."

"Well . . . not Riley," Eva piped up, then turned beet red.

"Thank you," Riley said.

"Okay, but are you saying Riley is the one and only exception to the rule?" Mandy demanded.

"No. Of course not," Kai said, taken aback by the fire in Mandy's eyes. "It's not like I was talking about you and Eric—"

More giggling. Mandy flushed.

"Then who *were* you talking about?"

"Nobody, specifically! I just . . ." She paused, trying to get her thoughts in order. "It's just, okay, fine, let's take you and Eric as an example."

Mandy crossed her arms over her chest and sank down further in her seat, her skin growing more and more blotchy.

"Just an example!" Kai said. "We're all in high school. Odds are we're not gonna end up spending the rest of our lives with the people we're with now, so odds are you and Eric are going to break up one day. If you guys have sex, that's just gonna make the breakup that much harder. So why not protect yourself from that?"

The room fell silent as everyone took this in. Mandy refused to look at Kai, and Kai knew she had made a misstep in using Mandy and Eric as her hypothetical couple. But Mandy had been jumping all over her and when that happened, Kai tended to speak before she thought.

"You know what I'm wondering?" Mandy said

suddenly, breaking the silence and causing a couple of people to actually jump. She glared at Kai. "How, exactly, do *you* know so much?"

At that moment the classroom door opened. Kai was saved by Madame Kopec's announcement. "I have the results of the election!"

Mandy's heart pounded erratically as Madame Kopec walked to the center of the room. Between the public discussion of her relationship with Eric, her ire toward Kai, and the election, she felt like she was about to shake apart. She took a deep breath and tried to chill, but she couldn't help wondering if something was actually wrong with her heart. She'd been nervous and upset before, but she'd never felt like this. What if she was really sick or something? Could anything else possibly go wrong in her life?

"Hey, may the best woman win," Kai whispered, her tone placating. She looked at Mandy expectantly, so Mandy nodded and smiled a tight smile. But Kai's little statement grated on her nerves. She was too confident. Like she just knew she was going to win.

Mandy felt like she was actually having a heart attack. She waited for that sharp pain in her arm that you always heard about.

"Congratulations to the first V Club president . . ."

Mandy Walters, Mandy Walters, Mandy Walters—

"Kai Parker!"

Everyone around Kai congratulated her, but Mandy couldn't even bring herself to turn her head. She didn't think she could take Kai's elated expression. Instead she got to see Debbie's piteous one. When Kopec dismissed the group a few minutes later, Mandy jumped out of her chair.

Kai was making some presidential-sounding statement about how they would figure out the honor code at the next full meeting, which gave Mandy plenty of time to make her escape.

Her legs were shaking as she made it into the hallway, and her vision was blurring over. She suddenly felt heady and weak, but she kept walking. She didn't pause when she heard her friends calling her name from behind, but at the end of the hall her mind swam and a flash of heat ran up her spine into her head. Mandy stopped and leaned against the cool wall, hoping it would keep her from falling.

She knew she really should eat something. But how was she supposed to do that when her stomach was in constant upheaval? She'd barely been able to choke down a few saltines that morning.

"Hey! Wait up!" Debbie called after her.

Leave me alone, Mandy warned through the fog in her mind. *Leave me alone.*

"Hey . . ." Debbie paused in front of Mandy and made a sympathetic face. "Sorry. I voted for you."

"Thanks a lot," Kai joked, joining them.

"Kopec said it was really close," Eva said, biting her bottom lip and glancing from Mandy to Kai and back again.

"No hard feelings, right?" Kai said with a grin. So condescending.

"Of course not," Mandy said, her mind clearing, the heat dissipating. She stood up straight and focused her eyes on Kai's giddy face. "I mean, you exemplify everything a person could want in a *Virginity* Club president, don't you?"

Kai's mouth dropped open for a split second, and then she rearranged her face before anyone else could notice. But for Mandy, the damage was done.

"Okay, what the heck is going on with you two?" Debbie asked, hands on hips.

Mandy glared triumphantly at Kai as she stepped past her. "Excuse me," she said. "I have to get to practice."

She sauntered off down the hall, head held high, just hoping that the fogginess didn't return. Fainting in the middle of the hallway would really mar her glorious exit.

"All the art supplies go up top," Eva told Riley, proud of her composure under this extreme stress—this extreme stress being defined as her and Riley

183

being alone in an exceedingly cramped space. It was after six, the sun had gone down, and they were reorganizing the day-care supply closet, trying to get things ready for the week ahead.

Riley climbed onto the stepladder and reached up to shove a plastic box full of crayon pieces onto the top shelf. His Ben & Jerry's T-shirt rode up, exposing the tiniest sliver of bare skin, and Eva blushed. Then she blushed even harder recalling her own bared midriff on Friday night, why she'd bared it, and the disappointment the whole debacle had led to.

"So, what the heck happened after the V Club meeting yesterday?" Riley asked, returning to the floor. "You guys looked like you were having some kind of summit talks in the hallway."

"Failed summit talks," Eva said, turning away to organize the glue shelf. "Mandy and Kai are not getting along right now."

"Extracurricular politics are never pretty," Riley joked.

"They've just been competing for a lot of stuff lately," Eva said with a one-shouldered shrug. "I think it's getting to them."

"Competition can be messy among friends," Riley said, more seriously this time. Eva could tell he had sensed her tension and was adjusting his response accordingly. Eva felt herself beginning to smile.

Stop it, she told herself, grabbing up a bunch of scissors and depositing them in their tin can. *He was doing the tonsil tango with Debbie on Friday. You're not allowed to feel anything here.*

Just like that, the sight of him and Debbie walking upstairs at Devon's returned to her mind. Eva sat down hard on a box of paper towels, irritated with herself.

"Hey! What's up?" Riley asked. He pulled over the stepstool and sat down next to her.

"Yeah, I'm just . . . I feel like everything's falling apart," she told him. "My friends mean everything and . . ."

"And what?" Riley asked, leaning his forearms on his thighs and tilting his head to see her better.

"I just feel like we're all about to implode. . . . Mandy and Kai and . . . and me and Debbie . . ."

"What's going on with you and Debbie?" Riley asked.

Eva closed her eyes. She'd said too much. How could she have let herself say that? *We're competing too,* she thought. *For you. Only she doesn't know it, and I always feel like I'm this close to barfing whenever I'm around either one of you.*

"Nothing," she said finally, hating herself for her fear of talking, of opening up, of telling anyone anything ever. Her shoulders slumped and she clasped her hands together between her knees.

Then it happened. Riley put his arm around her. Eva stopped breathing. He put his arm around her and squeezed. She could smell the musky-sweet scent of the soap he used mixing together with the tangy art-supply smells. Eva suddenly knew that whenever she sniffed a crayon for the rest of her life, she would remember this moment.

"It'll be okay," Riley said. "All friends go through crap like this, but you guys really care about each other, so you'll figure it out."

"I know," Eva managed to say. She took a chance and looked up at him. Riley's face was just inches away from hers. She could see every line in his lips, every tiny freckle on his skin. He gazed back at her and his eyes looked somehow heavy.

A chill ran through Eva as realization washed over her. *Omigod! Is he going to* kiss *me!?*

She stood up, kicking over a stack of toilet paper rolls in the process. "Damn," she said. Her face burned as she dropped to the floor to retrieve a roll that had tumbled under the shelving. It came back covered in dust and grime.

"Guess we haven't had a good cleaning in a while," Riley said, standing up and shoving his hands into his back pockets.

He took the roll from her and tossed it toward the garbage can in the day-care room. It hit the rim and bounced right off.

"That was embarrassing," he said.

Please, Eva thought. This boy had no idea what the word meant. How could she have thought he wanted to kiss her? *Her!* He'd recently locked lips with Debbie Patel!

"What are you thinking right now?" Riley asked.

"I was just wondering if you and Debbie made out on Friday night," Eva heard herself say.

Oh my God. I can't believe I just said that.

She stared straight ahead at a row of bottles of Elmer's glue. Time stopped. She held her breath.

"What? No!" Riley said. "Why? Did she tell you we did?"

"No. She didn't. But . . ." Eva glanced over at Riley. He looked shocked and totally confused.

"Why would you think that?" he asked.

"Well . . . you guys . . . you know, you went upstairs," Eva said. It suddenly sounded like the stupidest thing in the world.

"So that means we *made out*?" Riley asked. Then he paused and looked out the closet door. His face suddenly changed. "Yeah, I guess I understand why you might think that, actually."

"But you didn't," Eva said.

"No. She was showing me where the bathroom was," Riley told her. He ran his hands over his blond hair and took a step closer to her. "I mean, I like Debbie," he said. "But just as a friend."

"Oh."

Eva's heart was doing cartwheels. It was running around in circles and jumping up and down with glee. It was hopping on roller coasters and screaming at the top of its lungs.

"So listen . . . I wanted to ask you," Riley said, crouching to pick up some containers of glitter. He glanced up at her and Eva could swear there was a hint of uncertainty in his eyes. "Are you . . . doing anything this Friday night?"

Eva's mouth went dry. This couldn't actually be happening. "Um . . . no," she said. Somewhere in the back of her mind was something she'd read once about being unavailable and coy. She ignored it. "Nothing."

"Do you think you'd want to hang out?" Riley asked. "With me?"

Yes! Yes! Yes! A million times yes!

"Sure," she said, scratching behind her ear. "I mean . . . yeah . . . that sounds . . . good. Hanging out."

Shut up! Shut up! Shut up! A million times shut up!

"Great," Riley said, smiling slowly. "Then we'll do that."

"Cool," Eva said.

And for once her inarticulate awkwardness didn't even faze her.

seventeen

"MINE! MINE!" MANDY SHOUTED AS THE VOLLEYBALL careened in her direction. Kai watched as Mandy reached out her arms to bump it up, then pulled back at the last second.

What is she doing?

"No!" Kai shouted just as the ball slammed into the court, millimeters inside the line. Her heart fell as the Washington High Wolverines cheered and whooped on the other side of the net. The impossibly tall girl who had spiked the ball taunted Mandy and slapped hands with her friends.

"Walters! What're you doing to me?" Coach Davis called out.

"I thought it was out." Mandy hung her head and Kai's heart went out to her. That was the third bad call Mandy had made, and it was only the first game of the match. Everyone had bad games every so often, but this was one for the record books.

"Hey, you're fine," Kai said, slapping Mandy on the back. "You'll get back in there."

Mandy shot Kai an angry look. *So much for that,* Kai thought. After what Mandy had said to her in the hall, Kai thought she was being a pretty big person trying to help her out.

The ball was served again, and once again it was coming right at Mandy. And once again Mandy was staring off into the distance. The ball was coming closer and closer. *Look up, Mandy. Look! Up!* But she was clearly off in her own world, and at the last second Kai dove in. She took the shot and the ball sailed over the net and bounced down between three diving Wolverines.

Kai cheered and slapped hands with her teammates, then Davis blew her whistle.

"Parker, get over here," Davis shouted, causing Kai's heart to plummet. She had a feeling Davis was going to scold her for moving out of position. But what was she supposed to do? Let Mandy lose them the match?

Kai glanced over at Mandy as she bent her ear toward Coach Davis.

"What the hell was that?" Davis asked under her breath. "That was Mandy's shot. Are you thinking she can't handle herself out there?"

"No, Coach," Kai told Davis quietly, her hands on her hips as she fought to control her breathing. "I just . . . I thought I had the better shot."

"I appreciate your diplomacy, Parker, but this is

the state tournament," Coach said. "Get back out there."

Kai felt sick to her stomach, knowing what Coach was about to do. She looked at Mandy, trying to warn her with her eyes before Coach called in the sub, but Mandy was obstinately ignoring Kai's existence.

"Sub!" Davis called out. "Sheridan, you're in. Walters, you're out!"

Mandy glared accusingly at Kai as though somehow it was Kai's fault that she was being taken out. *Unbelievable.* Did Mandy really think she'd be so petty?

Fine, let her believe that, Kai thought, staring right back at Mandy as she trudged to the sidelines. *She can believe whatever the hell she wants.*

"I can't believe they took Mandy out," Eva said, watching her friend from the bleachers across the gym. Mandy was sitting in a chair on the sidelines, looking pale and wan and on the verge of tears.

"She'll be all right," Debbie said, leaning her elbows back on the riser behind her.

"I don't know," Eva said. "She's shooting Kai the look of death."

"What is going *on* with those two lately?" Debbie asked. "They barely said three words to each other at lunch."

"I know. I just wish they would talk about whatever it is," Eva said.

"I think it all started with that V Club thing. I'm sure it'll blow over now that we've had elections. They can't stay mad forever. I mean, it's just a club," Debbie said. On the court Kai slammed the ball over the net and scored the winning point of the first game. She and Eva applauded along with the few other people in the stands as the team gathered at the sideline. "So what's up with you?" she said, turning to Eva. "I feel like I've barely talked to you all week."

Eva blushed slightly and picked at her fingernails. "Not much. I've . . . uh . . . I've been hanging out with Riley at 4-H a lot."

"Omigod, isn't he the sweetest?" Debbie said, grinning. "I've been hanging out with him a lot too. We should all hang out together sometime."

"Yeah." Eva smiled and swallowed back the lump in her throat. Did Debbie really *like* Riley or did she think of him as just another potential frog? Should she tell her what Riley had said yesterday about just thinking of Debbie as a friend? "Yeah. The three of us together, that'd be, um, great."

Should I tell her about our maybe date?

No—I'll just wait until I find out if this is an actual date or if he's thinking this is just a friend thing.

Yes. That seemed like the best plan. That meant

she didn't have to deal with it just now. Later was good. Later was always better.

Mandy walked into the guidance office on Friday at lunchtime and saw Kai sitting there on the couch. *It just figures she'd have her interview exactly when I have my interview,* Mandy thought bitterly. Mandy hadn't spoken to Kai at all since the volleyball match. Mandy hadn't even *looked* at her. And seeing Kai here now just made her feel more ill than she already felt.

"You have your interview now?" Kai asked.

"Masterful powers of deduction," Mandy said sarcastically. Somehow things like that had been coming out of her mouth more and more lately.

"What is your problem?" Kai snapped, drawing stares from a few of the nearby office workers.

"*My* problem?" Mandy shot back, whispering. She sat down on the other end of the couch, her muscles tensing. "I got benched thanks to you!"

"Omigod, I knew it. I *knew* you thought that."

"I only think it because it was *so obviously* true."

"Oh, please. I *so obviously* didn't," Kai hissed back. "Not that I wouldn't have liked to. You couldn't make a shot to save your life."

Mandy felt like she'd been slapped. "Gee, thanks, Miss Goddess of Everything."

"Isn't that *your* title?"

"Girls!" the guidance secretary scolded. "Please! This is an office."

Mandy turned and stared forward, crossing her legs at the knee and locking her arms over her chest. This was just too much. *Kai shouldn't even be here.* "Can I ask you something?" she whispered, turning to look at Kai.

"I'm dying to hear *this*," Kai said.

"Why are you applying for the scholarship when you're not even a virgin?" Mandy demanded, whispering the last word as quietly as humanly possible.

Kai blinked but said nothing. She started to crack the knuckles on her right hand one by one.

"I think you should withdraw your name from consideration," Mandy said.

"Why don't you?" Kai demanded. "It's not like you need it."

"How do *you* know what *I* need!?" Mandy said before she could rethink it. "You have no idea what's going on with me!"

"And why is that again?" Kai snapped. She raised her finger to her cheek and did her fake-thinking pose.

"Well, at least I'm not lying to my friends."

"Oh, and I am?"

"You told us you were a virgin! You told us you couldn't stand Andres! And then I found out that the two of you are hitting the sheets together!"

Kai's jaw dropped. "I don't know how you found out about me and Andres, but it's none of your business."

"Well, maybe there's stuff I'm not telling you because it's none of *your* business," Mandy shot back.

"Fine, then," Kai said, turning her profile to Mandy again.

"Fine."

Mandy's eyes welled up just as the door to the conference room opened and Coach Davis herself stepped out.

"Mandy? You're up next," she said.

Mandy stood up shakily and took a deep breath. This was it. Her future was about to be decided. Before walking into the hostile environment of the waiting room, she'd had a whole list of things to talk about in her head. She'd been prepared, composed—or as composed as she could be under the circumstances.

But now it was all gone. Erased. And all she could concentrate on was not bursting into tears.

eighteen

"IT WAS CAKE," DEBBIE SAID, CLIMBING ONTO THE BIG yellow bus idling in front of Oakridge High School. "Didn't you think it was cake?"

"Keep it down," Riley told her under his breath. He looked around at their classmates with an overly wary expression, rubbing his hand over his scruffy blond hair. "You're gonna get jumped by a hundred disgruntled math geeks," he warned.

Debbie laughed and sauntered to the back of the bus. She knew she had kicked butt on the exam and she was reveling in her post-test high. Against her will she'd gotten all wrapped up in the energy of the day. All the eligible Ardsmore High students had been bused to Oakridge—the county testing site for the Math and Science competition—and on the way there, everyone had been cramming and stressing and debating what would be on the test. The tension in the air in the Oakridge High cafeteria had been infectious, and Debbie had actually felt nervous as the proctor slid the exam in front of her.

But now that it was over, Debbie was feeling fine. Better than fine. She'd aced it and she knew it. If she ever decided that she did want a life in the sciences, it was all hers.

Unfortunately, she still didn't want that life.

Debbie settled into the backseat of the bus, her enthusiasm quickly withering. What was she thinking? Yeah, she'd done well and yeah, she loved to do well, but did she have to do well on *this*? If she won that scholarship, it was a done deal—her parents would be packing her off to Penn State faster than you could say Yaffa blocks. Why hadn't she thrown the test? Was she such an overachiever that she had to ace every little thing?

Oh God, I am *a science geek,* she thought, her heart falling. *It never even occurred to me to purposely fail.*

"Okay, moody," Riley said, sitting down next to her. Even in her distressed state, the brush of his arm against hers sent a pleasant warmth rushing through her. "What happened between the front of the bus and the back of the bus? Did you suddenly realize you forgot to write your name on the test?"

"No," Debbie said, bringing her hand to her head. "I just . . . I can't believe I'm going to spend the rest of my life as Science Girl."

"A whole new brand of superhero," Riley said, sounding like Mr. Moviephone.

"I'm serious!" Debbie said, sliding down in her seat and closing her eyes. A sickening dread settled over her shoulders.

"Hey, you're kind of overconfident there, aren't ya? I mean, you're up against thousands of mega-brains here. Including myself," he added.

"Sorry," Debbie said, sighing. "You're right. What are the chances I'll actually win?"

"We won't know for a few days anyway, so there's no point in stressing out about your impending success now," Riley said, scrunching down in his seat and pressing his knees into the seat back in front of him.

Debbie took a deep breath and pushed herself up a bit. "You're right. What I should be stressing about is my Treemont interview," she said. "I have to go do that when we get back."

"You're kidding," Riley said, his forehead wrinkling. "Long day."

"Tell me about it," Debbie replied.

As the bus rumbled out of the parking lot and onto the nearest highway, Debbie tried to force herself to relax. The interview was the one part of this scholarship thing that she knew she could nail. She was great on paper but fabulous in person. But she wasn't going to be wowing anybody if she had on her morose face.

Debbie glanced over at Riley, who had closed his eyes and was leaning his head back against the seat. He looked so sweet with the sunlight pouring over his face. She could just kiss him right now. She imagined what he would do if he suddenly felt her lips on his. It wasn't like he wouldn't kiss her back, right? There wasn't a guy on earth who wouldn't take advantage of a sudden smooch from a beautiful girl. He'd be surprised at first, sure, but then he would wrap his arms around her and lean her toward the window, kissing her like he'd been waiting for it his entire life.

The bus hit a bump and Riley opened his eyes and caught her staring. Debbie looked away, pretending to be absorbed by some graffiti on the back of the seat. "What's up?" Riley asked.

"I was just wondering, are you doing anything tonight?" Debbie blurted quickly. "I was thinking about seeing a movie, you know, something mindnumbingly dumb to soothe my fried brain."

She grinned and looked over at him, but Riley's expression told her she was about to be let down. Big time.

"Actually, I have plans," he said. Then he cleared his throat and reached out to pick at a piece of frayed vinyl next to him. "With Eva."

"Oh," Debbie said, the smile plastered to her face. Her heart took a nosedive. *Riley* had plans with *Eva*? She was Eva's *best friend*. Why hadn't Eva told her about this?

"But . . . you know . . . maybe some other time," Riley said.

Debbie and Eva had barely talked on the phone at all this past week. . . . In fact, now that she thought about it, she realized she hadn't had one real, extended conversation with Eva in days. And at the game, when she'd asked Eva what was going on with her, she *had* said something about hanging out with Riley. But Debbie was certain Eva had said nothing about a date. A date she would have remembered.

Was *everyone* keeping secrets from her? She didn't like it. Mandy still hadn't explained why she was applying for the Treemont scholarship, Kai had a sexy Spanish guy living under her roof whom Debbie hadn't even met, and now Eva and Riley?

What was going on with her friends?

Bbrrrrrriiiiiiiiiiinnnnnnnnggggg.

The bell rang, signaling the start of history class, and just before the trilling ended, Riley slipped into the room. Eva held her breath. She'd been drowning in nerves for the past five minutes, wondering if he'd make it back from the Math and Science competition in time for class. They hadn't made plans for that night yet, and she had started to fear she wouldn't see him in school today—which would have meant she was in for hours of sitting by the phone, wondering if he'd call. Wondering if they actually *were* going to go out. And although she'd never experienced that particular torture, she was quite sure it would be the worst of them all.

Riley slid into the chair behind Eva's, leaned forward, and whispered a "hey" as Mr. Gilson started his lecture. Eva attempted to not shiver visibly. She shot a smile over her shoulder. About thirty seconds later a piece of folded paper appeared in the corner of her vision. She grabbed it from Riley's fingers, ignoring the curious stares of the people around them. Eva unfolded the note in her lap.

Pick you up at 7 tonight?

She bit her bottom lip, transferred the note to her desk, and wrote under his message.

Sure. What are we doing?

Lowering her hand at her side, Eva reached backward slightly and Riley grabbed the note. She heard his pen scratching behind her. When she saw his response, she almost lost it.

It's a surprise. And I need your address.

A surprise. And he was picking her up. This all sounded very datelike. How was this happening?

Eva quickly scrawled out her address and phone number and handed the note back, then sat forward and attempted to pay attention. But with Riley so close she could feel his every shift, she couldn't help lapsing into her old daydreams. Was there an actual kiss in her future? The thought was as terrifying as it was exciting.

I can handle it, she told herself as Gilson started to write the topics for their next exam on the board. Eva opened her notebook and scribbled them down. *As long as nothing goes wrong, I can handle it.*

Another note suddenly sailed over her shoulder and landed squarely in the center of her desk. Shakily Eva opened the message and learned what it was like to physically melt. All it said was:

I can't wait.

nineteen

RILEY AND EVA . . . RILEY AND EVA . . . RILEY AND EVA . . .

Nope. However she said it, it just didn't seem possible.

Debbie sat in front of the interview panel, her legs crossed tightly and her sling-back shoe hanging off her heel. They had already asked her the basic questions, and she was just waiting as they flipped through some of her paperwork and whispered to each other about who knew what. She wished they would just excuse her already so she could get to this week's lacrosse match and take out her new-found confusion on some unsuspecting opponent.

"We don't seem to have your purity essay here, Debbie," Mr. Simon said, shooting her a quizzical glance.

"Oh, right," Debbie said. "Well, I was spending a lot of time studying for the Math and Science competition, but now that that's over, I'll get right on it."

"The Math and Science competition? That was today, wasn't it?" Mrs. Labella asked.

Debbie took a deep breath. "Yep," she said. "It's been kind of a long day."

A few members of the panel smiled. *Can I go now?* Debbie thought.

"Well, the Math and Science scholarship seems a bit more your speed than the Treemont," Ms. Russo said, shifting through some papers. "We wish you luck with it."

More my speed? *Is she saying what I think she's saying?*

"Thanks," Debbie said tentatively. "But . . . I'm sorry, why would you say the Math and Science scholarship is more my *speed*? Is there something wrong with my application?"

Ms. Russo practically gulped, and a thick tension filled the room. Debbie's heart started to pound. She didn't *want* the Math and Science scholarship to be more her speed. She wanted to take Mrs. Treemont's money and run away to New York and FIT.

"If there's anything I can do to . . . you know . . . improve the application, please tell me," Debbie said, feeling desperate. "Do I need better references or something?"

Ms. Russo exchanged a look with Mr. Simon, and every last member of the panel shifted in their seats.

"No, Debbie, your references are fine," Ms. Russo said finally. "Just make sure you put a lot of thought into your purity essay."

"Yes," Mr. Simon put in. "A *lot* of thought."

Whoa. Wait. Was Debbie imagining things or were five of her teachers actually sitting right in front of her and telling her the Treemont wasn't her *speed* because she was too much of a *slut*? Was she imagining the vibe in the air? And that strange look on Simon's face that seemed to say, *I don't think you'd be capable of writing a good purity essay because you have no clue what purity is?*

She got up from her chair and grabbed her bag. Catty girls she could handle, even moronic boys she could accept. But now her *teachers* were talking about her too? Were they just going to laugh at her the second she was gone?

"Thanks, Debbie!" the vice principal called out.

Debbie closed the door behind her without saying good-bye. It was all she could do to keep from flipping him the bird.

No. Nonononononono.

"Mom. Come on! Isn't there someone else who can pick you up?" Eva pleaded. She checked her watch as she gripped the phone for dear life with her other hand. Riley was supposed to be there in half an hour. He was probably already on his way.

"Look, Cheryl called in sick and Missy was supposed to take me to pick up the car, but her kid called with some emergency. There's no one else," Eva's mother said.

"But Mom, I can't call my friends again. I've already called them too many times. They're not a taxi service," Eva said.

"Eva Marie Farrell, if your overprivileged friends can't help you out every once in a while, then what kind of friends are they?"

Oh, she hated her mother sometimes. She hated her bitterness and her self-righteousness and how sometimes, like right then, she seemed to actually resent Eva for having friends. And now she was going to have to hate her for ruining her first date, what could have potentially turned into her first kiss. The best night of her life.

"Don't forget to bring the checkbook," her mother told her. "We'll have to get the car out of hock."

Eva slammed the phone down, her mind reeling. Unfortunately, there was nothing she could do. She was not going to leave her mother stranded at Urgent Care all night, and she didn't have money to pay for a cab. Besides, her mother needed her to bring the checkbook. So her only option was to go save her mother. Again.

She dialed Mandy's number, pressing the keys so hard she was sure they would break.

"I'll be right there," Mandy said.

"Are you sure I'm not interrupting anything?" Eva asked.

"Eva, please, you have no idea how much I want to get out of here right now."

Her friends seemed to be saying that a lot lately, not that Eva didn't understand. At that moment she would rather have been anywhere but home.

Mandy was at Eva's front door in less than fifteen minutes, breaking all previous records. By the time she opened the door, Eva was near tears and chewing her bottom lip.

"Wow," Mandy said, looking her up and down. "You look amazing."

Eva had put on the same jeans Kai had chosen for her the week before along with an old black T-shirt that used to be loose but was now somewhat formfitting. She'd even managed to style her hair into a reasonable facsimile of the way it was supposed to look and put on eyeliner and mascara. By the time she was done, she'd almost felt like she was dressing up for Halloween. Unfortunately, all the primping was pointless.

"Do you have Riley Marx's phone number in your cell?" Eva begged. Mandy had the home numbers, cell numbers, and e-mail addresses of practically everyone in the senior class because she was involved in so many school activities.

"Uh . . . yeah, I think so," Mandy said, fishing

the green phone out of her jacket pocket. "Why do you need to call him?"

"Because we were supposed to go out tonight and his number's not listed, so I haven't been able to call him and—"

"You were supposed to go out with Riley Marx?" Mandy said, looking up as she scrolled through her phone book. "When did this happen?"

"I'll explain in the car," Eva said, grabbing the phone from Mandy's fingers. As Mandy pulled away from the curb, Eva hit the speed dial button for Riley's cell. The voice mail picked up right away. Eva had to squeeze her eyes closed to keep from crying.

"Riley, I'm so sorry and I really hope you get this message, but I have to cancel tonight," Eva said in a rush. She didn't even know what she was saying, but she hoped it didn't sound idiotic. "Something came up that I have to take care of. I'm really sorry. Um . . . okay . . . uh . . . bye."

Mandy glanced over at Eva. "Are you okay?"

"Sure," Eva said, wiping a mascara-blackened tear away from her eye. Her life was ruined, but other than that she was just peachy.

Mandy leaned back against the side of her VW with Eva, watching through the gas station window as Mrs. Farrell paid for the mechanic. Mandy couldn't even express how sorry she felt for her best friend.

Her first date—and with Riley Marx, no less—and it had been obliterated.

Couldn't anything good happen anymore? To anyone?

"I don't feel like going home," Eva said, staring down at a puddle that was swirled through with multicolored streaks of gas and grease.

"We should go do something," Mandy said.

"Maybe we can call Debbie and Kai and hang out at your house," Eva suggested hopefully. "We haven't had a sleepover in a while."

Mandy winced, her heart heavy. "Actually, Kai and I kind of had a fight this afternoon," she said. "I don't really think she's gonna want to come over."

"You did?" Eva asked, concerned. "What happened?"

"It's kinda hard to explain."

"We're still gonna go to the mall tomorrow, though, right? It's your birthday," Eva said.

Mandy sighed. She, Eva, and Debbie had a tradition of meeting at the mall on the Saturday closest to each of their birthdays to find a gift for the birthday girl. Mandy looked forward to it every year, but this time around she hadn't even thought about it until right then.

"I don't know," she replied. "I don't really think I'm in a shopping mood."

"Okay, *now* I'm scared." Eva forced a laugh, but it came out sounding like a cough.

Eva's mother emerged from the gas-station office and Mandy and Eva both pushed away from the car. Mandy couldn't help noticing how tired and harried Eva's mom looked. *You look like I feel,* she thought wryly. But at least Eva's mom wasn't afraid to let her emotions show. At least she wasn't walking around like some unaffected automaton like Mandy's parents were whenever Mandy was around.

Or whenever they *noticed* she was around.

"Thanks so much, Mandy," Mrs. Farrell said, smoothing her hair back from her face. "I'm glad Eva has such nice friends."

Eva looked away and Mandy smiled. "It's no problem, really."

"I'm gonna go over to Mandy's house," Eva piped in. "I might stay over."

"Okay," her mother said. "Just call me and let me know."

They waited until Eva's mother had driven off before getting into the car. Mandy glanced at the clock. It was already eight. Her parents were attending a benefit tonight, and they were leaving at eight o'clock. That meant the house would be psycho-free, at least for a few hours.

"All right, let's go home," Mandy said, starting the engine. "You can try Riley again from there."

"And we can talk about what happened with you and Kai."

Great, Mandy thought, merging into traffic. *A fun-filled Friday night.*

Both her parents' cars were in the driveway when she pulled up, but that didn't mean anything. Her parents almost always hired a limo when they went to benefits and functions. It wasn't until she and Eva were inside and upstairs that she heard their voices. Mandy froze in her tracks.

"You can use the phone in my room," she told Eva.

Eva hesitated.

"I'm just gonna tell my parents we're here," Mandy told her with a tight smile. *And warn them not to say anything too scary too loudly.*

Eva went into Mandy's room and Mandy walked cautiously toward her parents' bedroom.

"They're going to come tomorrow?" Mandy's mother asked. "So soon? But tomorrow is Mandy's birthday."

"I know what tomorrow is, Shirley."

Heart pounding, Mandy knocked on the open door and her parents both looked up, startled. Her mother was wearing one of her glittering, floor-length sheaths and her father was in his tux sans jacket. His face was as red as a beet and her mother's was pale as milk.

"What's going on?" Mandy asked, frozen on the threshold.

Her mother and father exchanged a look and then her father sighed. "You might as well come in and sit down, pumpkin," he said.

"Why? What's up?" Mandy asked again, petrified.

"Your father has something he needs to tell you," her mother said.

"Um . . . okay, but Eva's in my room. We were going to have a sleepover and—"

"That might not be the best idea," her mother said, walking over and offering Mandy her hands.

Mandy felt like she was in somebody else's body as her mom drew her over to the bed and sat down next to her. Her hand felt like a lump of mush inside her mother's warm and clammy palms. Her father sat down at the dressing table bench and took a long, deep breath.

"Amanda, there's no easy way to say this, so I'm just going to say it." When he lifted his eyes to meet Mandy's, they were warm and sad. "I'm going to prison."

"What?" she said weakly.

"I did what the government said I did, and they've got their proof. They're going to come here tomorrow so that I can surrender myself."

"What did they say you did?" Mandy asked as

her mother's hands tightened around hers. She felt like her voice was coming from somewhere outside her body.

"I've fudged some numbers on our income taxes for a few years," he said. "Put us in a lower bracket so they wouldn't take as much of our money. . . ."

"So they . . . they're coming to *get* you?"

"Mandy, I'm so sorry—"

"So I've been right all along," Mandy said, numb. She stared at the floor but didn't really see it. "All this stuff . . . you guys walking around like nothing was wrong, acting all happy . . . it was all a lie."

"We didn't want you to worry, sweetheart," her mother said.

"God, Mom, I'm not an idiot!" Mandy snapped with such anger that she surprised even herself. "I've *been* worried anyway! Don't you guys think I have a right to know what's going on around here?!"

"Of course you do—"

"Yeah, as long as it doesn't involve telling me that my father is a criminal!" Mandy shouted.

"Now, Mandy—"

"I asked you. I asked you last week and you said everything was fine!"

Her parents exchanged a look.

"You only lied to me to protect yourselves,"

Mandy babbled, tears spilling over. "How could you do this to us, Dad?"

"Now, Mandy. People make mistakes—"

"Not you! Not me! Not Mom!" Mandy said, the anger starting to make its way through her veins and into her very fingertips. "You don't make mistakes. You don't let anyone around you make mistakes. You don't even like it when I get B's in school!"

She was standing now, but she had no recollection of getting to her feet. "You lied to me! And to Mom!" Mandy blurted. "You said you were innocent—that it was all just going to blow over. How could you lie to us? You know what? I'm *glad* you're going to prison! You deserve to go!" Mandy shouted, a tear spilling over and running down to her chin. She hadn't known anything could feel as bad as this—so all-consuming and poisonous. "I don't ever want to see you again."

She turned and ran out of the room and slammed the door. She crashed right into Eva. "What did you hear?" Mandy asked, tears now falling freely.

"I—"

"No. You know what? It doesn't matter," Mandy said, sniffling. "I just need to get out of here."

"Okay. You can sleep at my house," Eva told her. "You want to pack some stuff?"

She wrapped her arm around Mandy, who nodded gratefully as her parents started to fight again from inside their bedroom.

"No, forget it," Mandy said, starting down the hall and struggling not to break into a full-out run. She had to get away from him. From them. From everything. "Let's just go. I just want to go."

twenty

WHEN DEBBIE WOKE UP THE NEXT MORNING, THE first thing she'd remembered was that Eva and Riley had gone out on a date last night.

She had spent the past half hour just sitting at the kitchen table, staring at the back of a box of Special K. Thinking about the fact that Eva and Riley might have kissed last night. Riley might have kissed Eva. It wasn't even so much Eva's liking Riley that upset her. It wasn't even the fact that Eva had kept it a secret. It was the fact that *Riley* liked *Eva* that bothered her the most.

Up until now Debbie had managed to convince herself that she was making headway with Riley. But him going for Eva—the purest of the pure, the girl who had never even been kissed—it was like a statement was being made. I'm *not good enough for him,* Debbie thought, pressing her fist against her mouth. *Riley thinks I'm dirty, just like the rest of the world does.*

She should have seen it coming. Everyone else

would have—or would have if they'd known she'd set her sights on the Boy Scout. Even those teachers on the Treemont panel could have told her. "We think a guy like Danny Brown might be more your speed," she could imagine them saying. "You know, because he's so *fast*."

Debbie heard the phone in her father's study being slammed down, and then a second later he barreled into the room. Her mother followed, wringing her hands with excitement. Suddenly Debbie felt a twinge of foreboding. She knew those looks.

"I just got off the phone with Bob Schneider," her father said. "You won! You won the scholarship!"

Debbie's stomach swallowed her heart.

"We are so proud of you, Deborah," he said.

This was not happening.

Debbie's mother came around the table and kissed the top of her head. She hugged her around the neck. Debbie felt like the life was being squeezed right out of her.

"You see what happens when you listen to your father?" he continued giddily. "Because of my pushing you, because of my belief in you—you now have a bright future, Deborah. You can be anything you want to be!"

Debbie stared at the mush of her soggy cereal.

"No, I can't," she said quietly. So quietly even she could barely even hear herself.

"What was that?" her father asked, still grinning. He'd already picked up the phone and was dialing, probably one of her brothers, to tell him the good news.

"I said *no*, I *can't*," Debbie repeated.

"Debbie," her mother said. Her father stopped dialing.

"What are you saying?" her father asked.

"I'm saying I can't be anything I want to be because I don't want to be a mathematician or a scientist or a doctor," Debbie said. Her heart was pounding, but her courage was mounting with every new word.

"Oh? Well, then, what *do* you want to be?" Her father put the phone back on the cradle. That vein in his forehead was beginning to twitch.

Suddenly Debbie realized she couldn't tell him. Not yet.

"I don't know . . . something else!" she cried out. "Anything else. I hate science! Why do you want me to do something I don't even want to do?"

"See? You don't even know," her father said with a smile that was half relief, half amusement. "You'll go to Penn State and you'll try some things out. You'll find a discipline you love like I did and—"

"No!" Debbie screamed. Her mother jumped

back. "I am not going to Penn State, I am not taking that scholarship, and I am not going to become a physicist!" she shouted. "There's something you've never seemed to understand, Dad! I'm not you!"

Her father's face slackened. "Deborah! You will not talk to me this way!"

"No! You will not talk to *me* this way!" Debbie was afraid of her father, afraid of what she was saying to him, but she was more afraid not to say it. The words had been building up in her for so long she had to get them out. "This is *my* life! What about what I want?"

"So you're not going to go to college? Is that what you want?" her mother asked quietly.

Debbie realized at once that she didn't have an answer for that. After yesterday, she knew the Treemont was out of her grasp, and she hadn't gotten word from FIT and it had been almost two months. If she turned down the Math and Science scholarship, there was a good chance she wouldn't be able to afford to go anywhere.

Her mother was right.

Debbie grabbed her purse and car keys and ran out of the house as fast as she could.

"Come on . . . come on . . . pick up the phone . . ."

Eva twisted the phone cord around and around her finger while anxiously watching the bathroom door. It was 10 A.M. on a Saturday and she knew there was a solid possibility that Kai was out on her morning run, but this was her only chance to call without Mandy knowing.

Finally someone picked up.

"Hello?"

Eva breathed out, relieved to hear her friend's voice. "Hey, Kai . . . it's Eva."

"Oh, hey! What's going on?"

"Um . . . I just wanted to see if you were still coming to the mall this afternoon," Eva whispered.

"Why are you whispering?" Kai asked.

"Just . . . trying to keep it down. Are you in?"

"Uh, actually no," Kai said. "I don't really think Mandy wants me around for her birthday."

"That's not true!" Eva blurted as the water cut off. Even though that was the exact reason she was making this call in secret.

"Look, Eva, I'm sorry. But I just really don't think I should go."

Just then Eva heard the bathroom door opening. "I have a beep," she said quickly. "Um, I'm gonna have to call you back."

She slammed down the phone just as Mandy came out of the bathroom, wrapped in a towel. Eva leaned back against the kitchen cabinets, clutching the edge of the countertop behind her.

"Hey. Who was that?"

"Oh, just my mom," Eva said with a shrug. "She was calling from work to see how you were."

"That was nice of her," Mandy said.

"So . . . how *are* you?" Eva asked.

Mandy paused but didn't turn around. "I'll be fine," she said. "Hey. Thanks for letting me stay over. And thanks for staying up so late talking last night. Just talking about it made it seem . . . made it seem less like I have to deal with this alone." She turned around and gave Eva a small sad grin. "Anyway, I'm going to your room to get dressed."

Once the door closed behind Mandy, Eva reached for the phone and dialed Kai's number again. She picked up after one ring.

"Hello?"

"Kai, listen," Eva said quickly. "Mandy is our friend. She needs us right now and that's all there is to it. I know things have been weird with all of us lately, but none of that matters. Get over it because you're coming. And I don't want to hear another word about it."

"Whoa," Kai said with a laugh. "Did you super-size the coffee this morning or something?"

"You're coming."

"Okay. Okay. Okay. Yes. I'll come. But if it turns into a smack-down, I'm not responsible."

"Got it," Eva told her. "See you later."

*   *   *

"And then Jenny insisted that she wanted to marry Hayden, so we had a whole wedding ceremony in the day-care center and Mesach played the judge," Eva babbled, looking around the food-court table at her nonresponsive friends. "He asked them if they would take each other even if one of them stole the other one's pudding cup. It was so cute."

She stopped for breath and took a sip of her soda. Kai was picking at a plate of french fries. Debbie was flipping through an issue of *Vogue*.

"So . . . um . . . what's up with you guys?" Eva asked. Mandy had yet to broach the subject of her father and Eva wasn't about to force her, but she wished someone would say something already.

Eva shot Kai a do-something look and Kai shrugged. Mandy just stared at her unopened burger like she was waiting for it to reveal to her the meaning of life.

"Mandy . . . do you want to go look for your birthday present?" Eva asked hopefully.

"No thanks." Mandy rested her chin on top of her forearms. "I'm not really in the mood."

"Are you going to tell us what's wrong or what?" Kai asked finally, in an impatient and not-so-friendly tone.

"Oh, right. Like you really care," Mandy said.

"I do care! What makes you think I don't?"

"Oh, I don't know, the fact that you've been lying to me, taking over the volleyball team, stealing the presidency out from under me," Mandy shot back, sitting up. "Yeah. You *really* care about me."

"Um, you guys—," Eva began.

"How many times am I going to have to explain this?" Kai demanded, sitting back in her chair and letting her arms fall at her sides. "I didn't run for club president to hurt you, I did it because I needed an extracurricular. And so what if I lied? It's not like you've been telling us anything!"

"What did you lie about?" Debbie asked.

Eva had no idea what Kai had or hadn't lied about, but she didn't like the way this was going.

"You guys, this isn't exactly what I meant," Eva said. "If everyone could just calm down—"

"Oh, give me a break, Eva," Debbie said, piping in. "Get off your high-and-mighty horse already."

Eva's mouth dropped open and everyone looked at Debbie. "Don't give me that look," Debbie said, still flipping violently through her magazine. "You sit here and you act like you're such a good friend and you just want everyone to get along and meanwhile you're going out on dates with the guy you knew I liked and you didn't even tell anyone. What kind of friend is that?"

Eva suddenly knew what it felt like to get

punched in the stomach. For a second she couldn't even breathe.

"How did you—?"

"Wait a second, *you* like Riley Marx?" Mandy interrupted, staring incredulously at Debbie.

"Oh, so she told *you* about the date?" Debbie demanded. "That's just great. Everyone knew but me."

"Wait a minute, which one's Riley Marx?" Kai asked. Everyone ignored her.

"Debbie, I didn't know you liked him," Eva said, even though she'd had a pretty solid suspicion. "Not for sure, anyway."

"Hold on. Is *that* why you got all decked out for that party?" Kai asked.

"I told you I thought he was delicious. And sweet!" Debbie said, her eyes wide.

"Oh, please. You say that about every guy at our school," Kai put in.

"What do *you* know?" Debbie countered venomously. "Didn't you just move here, like, five seconds ago?"

"Oh, so now you're gonna throw that in my face?" Kai said, rolling her eyes.

"You guys, you guys!" Mandy said, leaning forward. She looked from Debbie to Eva and back, flattening her hands on the table. "You can't let a guy come between you. You've been friends since we were in diapers."

"Oh, no, but a little white lie is enough to obliterate a friendship," Kai said sarcastically.

"It wasn't little *or* white!" Mandy exploded, throwing her hands up.

"Omigod, that's it," Kai said, shoving her chair back noisily as she stood. "I'm out of here."

"Me too," Debbie said, grabbing up her magazine. "Sorry, Mandy," she added as an afterthought. "Happy birthday."

Eva pressed her lips together. Her whole body was trembling. "Well," Eva said quietly. "That went well."

"Yeah," Mandy said, slumping back.

"Are you okay?" Eva asked.

Mandy sighed. "Yeah. I'm fine."

"Come on. Let's shop," Eva said, standing. "Maybe that'll cheer you up. It's your birthday."

"Yeah, sure," Mandy said, pushing herself out of her chair. "Happy birthday to me."

twenty-one

MANDY LOOKED AT HER REFLECTION IN HER BEDROOM mirror. She was wearing her favorite black dress— the one that usually made her feel sexy and cool and *InStyle*-worthy. Today, however, she couldn't help thinking it would be totally appropriate at a funeral. She looked tired and depressed and ready to burst into tears at any second. Still, there was no point in changing. She'd look awful in anything tonight.

Might as well get this over with, she thought. She picked up her purse and headed downstairs to face her parents. The feds, or whatever she was supposed to call them, were going to be here in an hour. Mandy planned to be long gone.

She found them sitting across the table from each other. They each had an untouched cup of coffee in front of them. When she walked in, they both looked up with unabashed hope. A wave of disgust crashed over Mandy. They were so pathetic—practically begging her to forgive them.

Then the wave of disgust was followed by a wave of guilt.

They're your parents! And your dad's about to go to prison! How can you be so heartless?

Mandy had no idea how she'd gotten this way, but she had. "Going out?" her father asked.

"Yeah," Mandy replied. "Eric's making me dinner."

"I think that's a good idea," her mother said. "You don't need to be here when . . ."

"I hope you can forgive me, Amanda," her father said, his voice cracking as he pulled back. "I never meant for this to happen. I never wanted to miss your high school graduation or seeing you off to college."

"I know, Dad," Mandy said, numb.

She leaned down and kissed him quickly on the cheek and he squeezed her hands as if he was trying to remember how they felt in his. Mandy couldn't take it anymore. She turned and ran out of the house, tears streaming down the sides of her face. As she reached her car, her vision suddenly clouded over and she had to grip the door to steady herself.

Her heart pounded as she climbed behind the wheel. That was her worst dizzy spell yet.

She pulled out of the driveway and peeled down the street. Her hands shook as she drove the darkened streets. She was starving, and she felt like she hadn't eaten in days. *You just need to get to Eric's, have something to eat, and forget this day ever happened.*

Mandy pulled up to the top of Eric's driveway, parking in his mom's usual spot, and climbed out of the car. She walked up to the door slowly, an odd weakness in her knees, and took a nice, calming breath before ringing the doorbell.

She was just going to fall right into his arms the second he opened the door. It was all she wanted in the world.

"Hey!" she said as the door swung wide.

"Hey, sweetness," he said with that killer grin. He leaned in to give her a kiss as she stepped over the threshold, and Mandy was just reaching to throw her arms around him when the house exploded with light and noise.

"SURPRISE!!!!!"

"Is this okay? I hope this is okay," Eva said in Mandy's ear as she hugged her in the midst of the mayhem. Everyone was jockeying to get to Mandy, but something about the way she clung to Eva made her want to just whisk her friend out of there and away to safety.

"It's fine," Mandy said. "It's great. Thank you."

"Well, it was all Eric's idea," Eva told her with a smile as she stepped back so the others could get to her. "He wanted to do something to cheer you up."

"Yep. I'm takin' *all* the credit," Eric joked, hugging Mandy from behind. Mandy smiled wanly and touched Eric's face with her hand. Eva could swear her fingers were trembling.

"Are you okay?" she mouthed to Mandy.

"I'm fine," Mandy mouthed back emphatically.

Eva suddenly felt a warm presence next to her and the tingle had already run down her arms before she consciously realized it was Riley. Cool.

But then . . . not cool. She still hadn't talked to him since last night.

"Hey. Can I talk to you?" he whispered in her ear. More tingles.

"Sure," Eva said, her heart slamming around in her chest.

Riley led her through the raucous crowd, past the guys who were fighting over the stereo, and out to the back patio. He closed the sliding glass door behind them, enveloping them in relative silence.

"So," Riley said, putting his hands in the pockets of his baggy khakis. He looked unbelievably cute in a blue button-down shirt and old Converse sneakers.

"So," she replied. She was petrified of saying the wrong thing but knew it was her responsibility to speak first. "I'm really sorry about last night." There. That seemed safe enough.

"Well, like you said on my voice mail, something came up," Riley said with a shrug.

"Yeah. Something did," Eva said, biting her lip. "Actually, a few things did."

"Anything you want to talk about?" Riley asked. Eva felt like he was ten miles away, even though they were only separated by a few varishaped flagstones.

No. But how about the fact that I'm totally and completely in love with you? Wanna talk about that*?*

"Um . . . not really."

"Are you okay?" Riley asked.

"Yeah. A-OK. Peachy keen."

But she wasn't A-OK. In fact, she felt like she was going to burst. Riley kept moving closer to her, and he smelled so good and he was so beautiful, and if he said one more thing to her, she had a feeling she was just going to say something stupid.

Like, "I love you. I've loved you ever since I first saw you."

But would that really be so bad? she thought. *What's the worst that could happen if you just said it?*

Riley blew out some breath and took a couple of steps closer to her. Eva's pulse was pounding in every cell of her body. She could do it. She was going to do it. She didn't even care if he said it back.

But if she didn't say it now, she'd never get up the guts again.

"Eva, I—"

"RileyIreallylikeyou."

Riley's eyes lit up and Eva's heart lit up with them. "Can you say that again slowly?"

Eva flushed. "I kinda don't think so."

Riley laughed. "That's okay. You don't have to." He held his hand over his stomach and took a deep breath. "Wow. And I was just going to ask you to let me down easy."

Eva laughed and looked up at him, her green eyes wide. Inside, someone flicked on a Nelly album and the bass shook the glass door to her right, resounding in Eva's chest.

"You mean that you . . . I mean that we—"

"IreallylikeyoutooEva," Riley said.

"Really?" she said.

For once she didn't even care that she sounded like an idiot. Riley smiled slowly.

"Yes, really," he said.

Eva didn't move as Riley reached up and gently tucked her hair behind one ear. He let his hand linger on the side of her face, a question in his blue-green eyes.

There was something building up inside Eva, but it was not the overwhelming euphoria she'd expected at this moment. It was something not good. Eva's heart started to panic with confusion. She'd imagined this so many times. It couldn't actually be happening. Not to her. Not now. Not possible.

Within seconds her body heat had skyrocketed.

Her heart was sounding an erratic drumroll. As Riley leaned forward, his eyes fluttering closed, Eva went rigid with panic.

Omigod! I can't!

Eva pulled back, even as she wondered what she was doing. Riley's eyes popped open in surprise and all the color ran right out of his face.

Eva felt like crumbling into a ball at his feet. There was no doubt about it. She was a freak. She'd just ruined what could have potentially been the most perfect moment of her life, and it wasn't because of her mother or Debbie or anyone else. She had no one to blame but herself.

"Eva?" Riley said quietly.

But there were no words in her to explain, so she just turned and walked away.

"Okay, why am I here again?" Kai asked, fiddling with the ribbon hanging off one of the dozens of helium balloons that peppered the living room. She watched as Mandy and Eric made their way through the crowd, Mandy doing the gracious, thanks-for-coming thing. "Mandy hates my guts. Or were you not present at the cracking of skulls this afternoon?"

Debbie sighed, pulling a balloon down to face height. She gripped it at the knot and slapped it around with her palm.

"You're here because Mandy is your friend, and one day the two of you are going to make up, and then you're going to regret the fact that you didn't attend her eighteenth birthday party," Debbie said. "Besides, I need someone to keep me company."

"In case you haven't noticed, there are like a hundred people here," Kai said, looking around. "Does Mandy know everyone in this town?"

"Pretty much."

"Deb, you have got to cheer up," Kai told her. "You're even bringing *me* down." She sighed as the front door opened and Danny Brown stepped into the house. "Look! There's Danny. I know *he* can cheer you up."

"Yeah, not likely," Debbie replied.

Kai was about to ask her for the details of what, exactly, was going on with her and Eva and Riley—the strangest love triangle Kai had ever heard of—when Danny turned to usher someone else into the room. Someone very familiar.

Andres.

Before she could even process his presence and what she was going to do about it, Danny was making a beeline for her and Debbie with Andres trailing close behind.

"What's up, Parker?" Danny asked loudly. The stench of alcohol on his breath could have withered a rosebush. "Where the hell you been hiding this guy?" He reached back and hooked his arm around Andres's neck, dragging him forward.

"You two know each other?" Kai asked, arching one eyebrow.

Debbie elbowed Kai in the side. "Andres, Debbie, Debbie, Andres," Kai said flatly. "He was just leaving."

Andres was lifting Debbie's hand to his lips when his eyes went dark. He glared at Kai and Kai glared right back.

"No way, dude! This kid is totally cool!" Danny announced. "He was on my campus tour at Penn State this morning, and did you know that he's actually seen Manchester United play? That's, like, insane!"

"Yes. They are a good team. Not as good as Real Madrid, but good," Andres put in. His eyes were all glassy and his breath reeked. Apparently Danny and Andres had indulged in a little private party before showing up at this one. Typical. Kai grabbed Andres's arm and dragged him over to a corner, leaving Debbie stiff and uncomfortable with Danny.

"What are you doing here?" Kai demanded as Andres tore his arm away.

"You know, the way you're always grabbing me is very much a turn-on," Andres said, leaning toward her and bracing one hand on the wall above her head. "You are sending mixed signals, *bonita*."

"Oh, yeah? How's this for a signal?" Kai pressed both hands into his chest and shoved. Hard. Andres tumbled backward into a group of guys who shoved him right back.

"Excuse me," Andres said to them, clearly embarrassed. He yanked down on his leather jacket and glared at Kai, his nostrils flaring. "I am afraid the little woman is getting testy."

"Ha! Little woman. Bet no one's ever called you that before, eh, Parker?" Devon Randall asked, chuckling as he looked up at her. Devon was the shortest guy in the class, and Kai towered at least six inches over him.

"Stay out of it, Randall," she said.

"Is that the way you always treat men?" Andres asked with a laugh. "It is no wonder you are so frigid."

Kai's face burned as a few more people in the room oohed over Andres's comment. They were drawing an audience, and Kai saw the situation spiraling quickly out of her control.

"So, Deb. It's been a while," Danny said, slipping his hand under the blanket of her hair.

Debbie slapped his arm away and shot him a warning glance. Danny just laughed, tipping his head back and swaying ever so slightly.

"You're drunk," she said.

"So?" Danny said, leaning in toward her like he

was telling a secret. "S'never bothered you before. Come on, baby. You know you want some Danny lovin'."

He reached for her again and Debbie easily moved out of his grasp. God, he was so disgusting. How had she ever fooled around with him before? "You have no idea what I want," she said.

She turned and dove into the crowd. Everyone was always trying to tell her what to do, what she wanted, what she should be. And she was sick of it. She was sick of her father's voice in her head, she was sick of Danny Brown and the rest of the school labeling her a slut. She was even sick of her own brain telling her she wasn't good enough for Riley—that he already belonged to Eva.

What kind of crap was that? Eva had no prior claim to Riley. So what if Eva liked him? Debbie liked him too! For all she knew, she had liked him first! And at least Debbie had said something to Eva about it. If Eva wanted him, she should have told her. What was it with Eva that she couldn't just *tell* people how she felt and what she wanted and who she was? She was like a little child. And Debbie was sick of protecting her. If Eva couldn't handle her life, that wasn't Debbie's problem.

She finally reached the back of the house, grasped the handle of the sliding glass door, and flung it open. Her heart skipped an unexpected beat. Of all the people at the party, the only one sitting in a wrought iron chair on the patio was none other than Riley Marx. Debbie smiled.

It was a sign. It just had to be.

"Hey," he said. He was slumped forward with his head in his hands, but he perked up when he saw her.

"Hey," Debbie replied, shutting the door. "You alone?"

"Looks that way," Riley said.

Debbie sauntered right over to him, fell into his lap, and wrapped her arms around his neck. "Well," she said. "Not anymore."

She pulled Riley's face toward hers and kissed him. At first he didn't move, didn't respond in the slightest. Debbie's heart pounded with trepidation, but she'd started this. She wasn't about to give up now.

"It's just a kiss, Riley," she whispered against his lips, taking his hand and moving it so that it rested on the small of her back. "Don't you want to kiss me?"

Something changed in his eyes and she knew he was hers. He really did want her. She wasn't so very unworthy. She touched his lips with hers again and this time he kissed back. He closed his eyes and Debbie felt her heart sigh with relief as her tongue found his.

She was kissing Riley Marx! Finally! The Boy Scout was hers!

So why did she suddenly feel as dirty as everyone thought she was?

twenty-two

Mandy knew something was wrong when the party started spinning. She was fairly certain that Eric's parents hadn't installed a lazy Susan under the house, so the spinning was definitely not right. People kept coming up to her and hugging her, their congratulatory voices piercing her skull, and it was all she could do to stay steady on her feet. When Liana went to give her a quick hello squeeze, Mandy had to grasp her sleeves for balance.

"If you see Eric, can you tell him I went upstairs?" Mandy said.

"Sure," Liana told her. "Are you okay?"

"Just a little tired," Mandy told her.

She trudged upstairs, suddenly unable to block the thoughts she'd been managing to keep at bay all night. There was one question that kept repeating itself in her mind, hammering away at her nerves, making her feel pathetically sorry for herself.

Why?

Why was all of this happening to her? Why had

her father done it? Why had he lied? And worst of all, why had she been so awful to him?

Mandy made it to Eric's room, figuring she would just burst into tears when she got there, but it turned out she was all out of tears. Instead she just lay facedown on his bed, pulled his pillow to her, and inhaled.

Ah. Eric scent.

The room stopped spinning and Mandy realized how utterly exhausted she was. She closed her eyes and began to drift off.

Somewhere in the back of her mind she heard the sound of the door opening and clicking closed. Footsteps crossed the room toward her and then she felt the warmth of a hand on her back. Mandy smiled slowly and looked up into Eric's eyes. She was somewhere between dreamland and reality and she struggled to hold on, knowing somehow that if she woke all the way up, bad thoughts would flood her mind and heart.

"Hey, sweetness," Eric said. "Everything okay?"

Those two words were all she needed for everything to come rushing back to her. Every time someone asked her if everything was okay, if she was okay, she wanted to scream.

No! No! No! Everything SUCKS!

"Fine," Mandy said groggily.

Eric made a sympathetic face and slid down

until Mandy was cradled in his arms, her cheek resting on the little space between his shoulder and his breastbone. She listened to his heart beating, reveled in the soothing rising and falling of his chest. This was good. This was nice. Now if she could just shut off her brain . . .

"It's gonna be okay," he told her. "Everything's going to be fine."

"I know," she said, even though her heart felt like it had shriveled to the point of no return. She looked into Eric's eyes and kissed him quickly. She didn't just want to be held. She wanted to get lost in him.

She placed her hand on his cheek and turned him to face her, her pulse pounding in her ears. When she kissed him this time, she made sure it was long and hard so that he would get the message. This was what she wanted. She wanted to feel him. Feel something else.

When Eric drew her closer to him, she clung to him like she was afraid to let go. When he started to undress her, she found that all thoughts of her father and her mother and the money and the scholarship and her friends were obliterated. When he produced a condom from under his mattress, all Mandy could hear was the sound of her own breathing and the pounding of her own heart.

Then she heard herself saying yes, heard him

telling her he loved her, and she lay back on his bed, waiting. Waiting to feel that connection she'd been dreaming about. Wanting to feel anything but pain.

Eva spotted Kai in the corner with Andres and wove her way through the crowd toward them, trying to put as much distance between herself and her utter humiliation as possible. She was sure Riley had come back inside by now and was off on the other side of the house, telling people what a psycho tease she was. It was kind of funny, actually. Eva Farrell a tease.

Funny in a totally unfunny, awful kind of way.

"Kai! I need to talk to you," Eva said under her breath when she finally made it to her friend's side.

"I'm going to get myself a drink," Andres announced before loping away.

"I'm not finished with you!" Kai called after him.

"Mixed signals, *bonita*!" Andres called back.

"Ugh!" Kai groaned, clenching her fists. "Okay, what can I do for *you*?" she asked Eva.

"What's wrong?" Eva asked.

"Nothing at all!" Kai shook her head. "What's wrong with you?"

"Um . . . well . . . I think Riley just tried to kiss me and I freaked out and bailed," Eva said, twisting one finger with her other hand.

"You *think* he tried to kiss you, or you *know*?" Kai asked, lowering her chin.

"I know," Eva said, liking the way the words felt on her tongue. "I know he tried to kiss me."

"Eva, can I ask you a question?"

"Yeah," Eva said warily.

"Is Riley your first-kiss-fantasy guy?" Kai asked, crossing her arms over her chest.

"Um . . . yeah."

"And he just tried to kiss you?" Kai said.

"Um . . . yeah," Eva said, reddening.

"Then what the hell is your problem?" Kai asked, throwing her arms out. "It sounds to me like the man has made his decision. The triangle has been flattened into a line. You're at one end, Riley's at the other, so get off your ass and make your move. Grab him by his cute little ears and shove your tongue down his throat already!"

Eva blinked. She straightened her back and smiled at Kai. No matter how indelicate the advice, what Kai said was true. Riley *liked* her. She *liked* him. She could do this! "Okay," she said. "I'm gonna do it. I'm gonna find him and I'm gonna kiss him."

"Yes! You go on with your bad self!" Kai said with a quick nod. She reached out and squeezed Eva's arms, then returned her attention to Andres's every move.

Yeah, Eva thought as she turned around again and started her search for Riley. *Go on with my bad self. That's exactly what I'm gonna do.*

*   *   *

"Mandy, what? What is it? What'd I do?"

Mandy's chest heaved painfully, the sobs racking every bone in her body. She gasped for breath, choked on the air, and kept trying again with the same result. She couldn't breathe or think. She couldn't do anything but bawl her eyes out.

"Did it hurt? Are you hurt?" Eric knelt next to her on the bed, his jeans recently pulled on but still unbuttoned at the waist.

Mandy crossed her legs against the burning sensation that seemed to be growing between her thighs and hugged the bedsheet to her. She wanted to tell Eric that it wasn't him, but she wasn't sure about that. She wasn't sure about anything except that she felt like the whole weight of the world was collapsing in on her.

She had thought that having sex with Eric would make her feel better. She had thought it would feel right and good and pure and that it would take her away from all the confusion and pain. But all it had done was compound everything and brought her already delicate protective walls crashing down.

"Mandy, please talk to me," Eric said, kneeling at her feet now and clasping her hands inside his. He looked so desperate and sad and scared.

"I . . . I . . . I can't," Mandy said between painful gasps. "I can't."

What she meant was that she couldn't stop crying. That she couldn't handle it anymore. That she just couldn't . . . *be*. Not like this. She felt like she couldn't exist anymore with so much heart-wrenching pain.

"You can't talk to me? Why?" Eric asked. "God, Mandy, if you didn't want to, all you had to do was say it."

"Don't be mad," Mandy heard herself say.

"I'm not," Eric said, sounding on the verge of panic. "I'm just . . . I don't understand."

Of course he doesn't understand! You just had sex for the first time and you're having a mental breakdown all over him! Pull yourself together!

But Mandy couldn't calm down. There were too many emotions whirling around inside her. *She* couldn't even understand them.

I'm supposed to be happy. I'm supposed to be ecstatic and in love right now.

It was all too much. There was too much going on in her head. She had to sort it out. Somehow.

"Eric, I just . . . need to be . . . alone—"

"Alone. Of course," Eric said, standing. He quickly buttoned up his jeans and grabbed his shirt from the floor. "That's all you ever want anymore, isn't it? You won't talk to me, you won't tell me what I did. We just made love and you won't even look at me—"

Mandy turned away from him and buried her face in his pillow.

"You know what, fine," Eric said. "You want to be alone, you got it."

The door slammed and Mandy felt it in her chest, as if it were slamming on her heart. Trying to stop crying only made it worse somehow, so she just let herself go.

She knew she should go after Eric and try to explain. They needed to talk. He was right. They'd just had sex . . . made love . . . for the first time. It wasn't supposed to be like this. It was supposed to be special and romantic and sweet and perfect. Not like this, with all the knots in her chest and the tears and the yelling.

No matter what Mandy did lately, she just couldn't seem to get anything right. She was sure there was some proper way to react to her father's being hauled off to prison, but she had messed that up royally. She was certain there was some good way to handle her first big fight with Kai, but she'd tanked on that, too. And now she'd managed to screw up what arguably should have been the most monumental moment of her life and she'd done it with the greatest of ease.

Mandy used to be the girl who did everything right. Now she couldn't seem to avoid getting everything wrong.

twenty-three

KAI HAD LET ANDRES OFF THE LEASH FOR TOO LONG. SHE could tell by the crowd he was starting to draw on the other side of the room. They all looked just a little too intrigued, a little too interested in whatever it was Andres was saying. Kai approached the group and was about five feet away when she heard Andres say, clear as a bell, "President of the V Club? That cannot be right!"

Suddenly Kai had her hand on Andres's arm. She didn't even remember traversing those last few feet.

"Okay, Andres. Time to go home," she said with a dismissive laugh.

"*Bonita!* Did you hear what this girl has said?" Andres asked, his glassy eyes wide. "She has said you are president of some club for the virgins!"

"Yep! That's right! Now you really need to get home and start sleeping this off," she said cheerily. She looked around at Andres's audience, rolled her eyes, and mouthed the words, *"Messy drunk."*

A few of the kids laughed and started to drag Andres away.

"I am confused," he said, pulling away from them and staggering slightly. "You would have to be a virgin to be president of the Virginity Club, yes?"

Suddenly everyone in Kai's immediate vicinity seemed to be salivating like a wild pack of dogs, hungry for this juicy slab of gossip they sensed was about to be tossed their way.

"Andres, don't," Kai said through her teeth, under her breath.

There was a spark in his eyes, though, and Kai knew it was over before he even opened his mouth.

"I do not know what the definition is of virgin in the States, but where I come from, Kai is definitely not one," Andres said, turning back to his new friends and raising his red plastic cup. "I made sure of that two summers ago in the field behind my parents' ranch."

The guys started high-fiving Andres and patting him on the back. The girls looked at her in shock and amusement. Kai shut her eyes and willed them to leave, willed the room to disappear, willed Andres to get sucked directly into hell by a freak Pennsylvanian sinkhole, but none of it happened. When she opened her eyes again, Andres was getting graphic.

"She was much more soft back then," Andres

said now, eyeing her. "Not so tall and athletic."

"Okay!" Kai said, throwing her hands up. "I think they've heard enough, Andres." She clutched both his shoulders and shot the crowd a look as she steered him away. "Hope you all had fun. The eight o'clock and ten o'clock shows are completely different than the early bird."

"*Bonita*, why do you do this?" Andres called out, riling the amused bystanders even more. "Why are you so ashamed that we shared the beautiful act of love? Do you wish you were still a virgin, *bonita*? You can't go back, you know."

"No, Andres," Kai said, turning to him. "I don't wish I was a virgin. I don't regret having had sex. I don't even regret having sex with you—or at least with the person I thought you were at the time."

"What does this mean?"

"It *means*, Andres, that back then I thought you were my friend. I trusted you. And I also thought you were all sophisticated and poetic and deep," she told him. Andres smiled cockily at his spectators and it was all Kai could do to keep from punching him in the face. "But now I realize I was just caught up in the romance of it all. Either that or there's some kind of hallucinogen in the water over there."

A couple of people laughed. Andres glared back at Kai, but his gaze was growing more and more uncertain.

"Now I realize, Andres, that you are a slimy, egotistical, *smelly* liar who used me. Not original, but there it is," Kai said, getting up in his face. "If there's anything I regret, it's the moment . . . the very nanosecond . . . you stepped back into my life."

The crowd around them oohed again and took a step back, itching for Andres's reaction.

Kai watched as Andres's face shut down, and she knew she had gotten the last word. He stared at her, his expression a mixture of anger and hurt so vivid that Kai's heart actually responded with a thump. But she was not going to feel guilty. He'd tried to humiliate her first. All she'd done was return the favor.

Eva slid past Danny Brown and his friends, who were all gathered around the keg in the kitchen, grasped the handle to the sliding glass door, and held her breath. This was it. This was her moment. She was not going to mess it up this time.

She threw open the door, stepped out onto the patio, and turned toward the table and chairs. A huge round of laughter exploded from behind her at the exact moment her heart was ripped free from her veins.

Right there, right in front of her, was the most horrible thing Eva had ever seen. Debbie was sitting on top of Riley, her arms locked around him, her head moving back and forth as she mauled him with her lips. But even worse, Riley's eyes were closed, his hands were on her back, his fingertips pressed into her sweater like they were just itching to get even closer.

Eva told herself to move. She told herself to run and get the hell out of there before someone spotted her. But she was still standing there when Riley's eyes fluttered open. The moment he saw her, he pushed Debbie away from him and then Debbie turned too, her lipstick all smudged and her eyelids all heavy.

"Eva—"

And then Eva ran.

"Eva, wait!" Riley called out.

But there was no way Eva was going to wait. *No way in hell.* Eva tore through the bushes and skidded as she rounded the corner of Eric's house. But Debbie, athlete that she was, caught up with her quickly. Before Eva could get to the front drive, which was a pointless destination anyway since she didn't have a car, Debbie grabbed her arm.

All Eva needed was to feel her touch on her skin and something inside her exploded.

"What is *wrong* with you?" she shouted at the top of her lungs as she whirled around. The tears burst forth along with her words.

Debbie stopped, taken aback, and for a split

second she looked like her five-year-old self getting scolded for eating paste.

"Eva—"

"No! I don't even want to listen to this," Eva said, her feet walking her backward.

"Eva, come on. It's not that big of a deal—"

"Of course it's not! Not to you! To you he's just someone to add to your list!" Eva blurted. "But it *is* a big deal to me."

"Eva, calm down," Debbie said.

"God, Debbie, all you had to do was leave one guy, *one* guy for me," Eva said, bringing her hand to her chest. "Do you have to kiss everybody? Did you have to kiss *him*?"

"Omigod, it's Riley, isn't it?" Debbie said. "Riley's the one. The daydream guy you always used to talk about."

"Yeah, all right, you got me!" Eva said, tears spilling down her cheeks. "Riley's the one. Or he was. Now he's just one of your many. Now he's just one of your frogs."

Then, before Debbie could say anything else, Eva turned and disappeared into the darkness.

Just find Kai, Eva told herself, walking back into Eric's house through the front door. She just wanted to get out of here as quickly as possible. Kai was her only hope for a ride.

Eva stepped into the living room and somehow, right in the midst of all those people, the first eyes she met were Riley's. Her heart plummeted and she turned instantly, ready to head anywhere that was away.

Unfortunately, Eva had no place to go. At the foot of the steps to her left two people were making out like there was no one else in the room. Directly in front of her were four football players, blocking the door to the dining room. If she went right, she was outside again and that was going to get her nowhere. Eva dove into the crowd in the living room and made her way along the wall, looking for Kai. "Come on, Kai," Eva whispered. "Where are you? Where are you?!" It was slow going, however; the party was packed. She had to move quickly or Riley was going to catch up with her any second.

She came to the fireplace, which had a few people in front of it, barring her way. Eva said "excuse me" about ten times, but no one even blinked. Her skin was in the process of turning beet red when a hand closed gently around her arm.

Eva looked directly into Riley's eyes. Her heart was pounding.

"Eva, that wasn't what you think," Riley told her.

"Let me go," Eva whimpered, hating how pathetic she sounded. She knew she must look atrocious and pitiful with the tears drying against her blotchy red skin.

"Not gonna happen."

"I thought you said you liked me," Eva told him.

"I do!!" Riley said vehemently. "I *wanted* to kiss *you!*"

Eva's mouth dropped open. Some part of her wanted to throw herself into his arms just for saying that, but the much larger, logical part of her was beyond offended. "Oh, well, I'm glad Debbie was there as a quick replacement."

"I didn't mean it that way," Riley said. He brought his hand to his head and squeezed his eyes shut. Eva took the opportunity to try to make her getaway. She brushed by Riley and slipped through a sudden space between a gaggle of girls and a gawky boy who was dancing comically for his friends.

Where the hell is Kai? Eva wondered, struggling to keep the tears from welling up again.

"Eva, please just hear me out," Riley said, catching up with her again. Eva's progress was blocked by Hiro Wakasuki, the biggest linebacker in three counties, who was standing with a drink in his hand, retelling the story of his latest, greatest running-back hit.

"Okay . . . what?" she said, surprised by her own harshness. She crossed her arms over her chest, feeling like everyone was watching her.

254

"I . . . I thought . . . when I tried to kiss you and you pulled away . . . I guess I thought . . . I was totally confused. I mean . . . you said you liked me and then . . . I don't know, I thought you were telling me I had no chance," Riley told her. "And I know that doesn't mean I should just go and kiss someone else, but . . . but she kissed me and I was still . . . I don't know . . . confused by what had just happened with you . . . and I . . . I mean—"

As Eva listened to him babble, something inside her started to give. Her shoulders relaxed slightly and her defenses turned to mush. Riley Marx was babbling. He was babbling to her. Mr. Self-assured. A guy she'd never seen with so much as a blush on his face.

Suddenly Eva found herself starting to smile. She didn't understand it, but there it was. She'd never felt so hurt in her life, but somehow he was still making her smile. And then his skin started to flush, growing darker and darker as he went on, his hands gesturing as he tried to explain. He was acting somehow so familiar. He was acting just like her.

Eva felt something warm inside her. Riley Marx was flusterable.

I, Eva Farrell, am causing major fluster!

"God, I'm so pissed at myself I let this happen," Riley said finally. "I'm sorry. Just forget it." He started to turn away and Eva realized that if she didn't do something right now, she was going to regret it for the rest of her natural-born life.

"Riley!" Eva said loudly. Loudly enough that a few people around her *did* turn to look. "Just . . . wait," she said when he faced her again.

He raised his eyebrows, pushing his hands deep into the pockets of his pants and looking almost vulnerable. Eva thought quickly. Could she deal with this? Could she be with somebody who had kissed her best friend? Did she want her first kiss to be with someone who could be labeled Debbie's leftovers?

"It didn't mean anything," Riley told her as if reading her mind. "It's never going to happen again, I swear."

Eva looked down at her hands and swallowed hard against a lump lodged somewhere between her throat and her heart. She still wanted him. She always had and she still did. It didn't matter where his lips had been.

It wasn't about Riley's lips anymore. It was about his heart. Eva wanted his heart. And she had a feeling she had that. All to herself.

"It's okay," she said finally.

Riley's eyes lit up like he'd been sinking in quicksand and she'd just tossed him a rope. "Really?" he asked. Then his brow furrowed. "Wait. What's okay?"

"Um . . . most of it, I guess," Eva said. "I mean, I understand what happened. Kind of."

Riley looked around at the noisy room, gathering himself—still confused. "So does that mean you could . . . that maybe you still . . . you know—"

"I still . . . you know," Eva said with a small smile. "But I'm not gonna kiss you," she added, holding up a hand.

Riley's face fell. "Understood," he said, nodding. "But just so we're clear—are we talking tonight or ever?"

"Tonight," Eva said. "We'll work on ever."

"I can accept that," Riley said, crossing his arms over his chest and looking out at the melee the party was quickly becoming. He stood so close to Eva their shoulders were almost touching. "I'm a very hard worker."

Eva smiled, biting her bottom lip and reveling in the possibilities. Things were about to change. Really change. And it was as if the air around her was dancing with supercharged fireflies. She wasn't afraid. She was, in fact, excited.

As Eva fought to contain her grin, Mandy appeared at the edge of the crowd, unsteady on her feet. Eva knew something was wrong the moment she saw her friend. She started toward Mandy and Mandy practically fell into Eva's side.

"Mandy? What is it? What's wrong?" Eva asked, supporting her weight.

"I really think I need to go home," Mandy said weakly.

Then she stood up on her own, closed her eyes, and went limp. Eva let out a shriek and Riley caught Mandy before she could hit the ground. The crowd that had seemed impermeable just moments before now backed away, forming a little circle of open air around the trio on the floor.

"Mandy?" Eva called out, scared out of her wits. "Mandy, wake up!"

"What happened?" Kai asked, appearing out of nowhere.

Riley looked up, Mandy's head in his lap. "She's unconscious," he said. "I think we need an ambulance."

twenty-four

DEBBIE PATEL WAS POND SCUM. SHE DIDN'T JUST *feel* like pond scum. She *was* pond scum. She'd made mistakes in her life before, there was no doubt about that. But she was not the type of person who knowingly hurt the people she loved. Not her friends. Not her *best* friends. What was *wrong* with her?

She slid open the glass door to the kitchen and pressed her way into the crowd. She hadn't gotten three feet when Danny Brown noticed her.

"Yo, Patel. If you're done with the Boy Scout, let me have at it!" he shouted, rubbing his hands together, causing the entire room to crack up laughing.

"Oh, yeah," some girl said under her breath, eyeing Debbie up and down. "*She's* gonna win the Treemont."

Debbie turned and looked at her reflection in the sliding glass door. Her lipstick was smeared and her skirt was bunched up on one side from the awkward position she'd taken in Riley's lap. Sucking in a deep breath, Debbie straightened her clothes and dragged the back of her hand down her cheek.

"God, she's such a slut," she heard someone whisper.

"I have a question for the room." Debbie asked loudly. This was going to end. Now. "What makes you all think I've had so much sex?" she asked, her voice clear and steady.

More laughter. "Everyone knows it," Melissa Bonny said from her perch on the kitchen counter.

"Yeah, it's, like, a total fact," Melanie Altarescu called out from over by the door.

"Interesting," Debbie said. "So I guess that means that I've had sex with at least one person in this room?" She looked around and saw Danny staring at his feet. Mitch Mascarenhas turned away, suddenly mesmerized by a bag of pretzels on the counter. A couple of other guys avoided her gaze, one of whom she'd never even *talked* to.

They expected her to just drop it. To just walk away. Play the victim. But that wasn't Debbie Patel's style.

"Danny, have we had sex?" Debbie asked.

A bunch of people shifted their weight, looked at each other nervously. She was making them all uncomfortable. Well, good.

Her heart pounded as Danny looked up. "Sure,"

he said with a shrug and a smile. "Lots of times."

He reached over and knocked fists with a couple of buddies. Debbie felt the back of her neck get hot. He was lying about her. Just standing there and lying right to her face.

"And Mitch?" Debbie said. "When, exactly, did we have sex again?"

"We don't need all the gory details," Liana said, tossing her hair. *"Ew."*

"Mitch?" Debbie said through her teeth, staring Liana down.

"After the homecoming party," Mitch told her. "Backseat of my car."

"Riiiiight," Debbie said, nodding as if she were dimly recalling the scenario. "Now tell me, 'cause I'm a little fuzzy on the facts. Who else in this room have I had sex with?"

Slowly, guiltily, a few other guys raised their hands. "Great . . . good," Debbie said, taking a moment to savor the bomb she was about to drop. "Okay, so if I've had so much sex with all of you, maybe one of you can tell me what the tattoo is that I have right here."

Debbie pointed to the spot just to the right of her hip bone. No one said anything.

"Come on, Danny," Debbie said, crossing her arms over her chest, feeling more and more confident by the second. "We've had sex *lots* of times, so you've seen me naked *lots* of times, right? You must know what the tattoo is."

"Yeah," Danny said, recovering himself. "Yeah . . . right. Right."

He swallowed hard and looked into Debbie's eyes with desperation. He was asking her to bail him out.

For a split second Debbie faltered.

But she needed to put these assholes in their place.

"It's a heart!" Danny said finally, raising his cup and looking triumphant. "Of course it's a heart!"

"Yeah!" Mitch agreed, nodding cockily. "Nice one, Deb. Nice try." Quickly all the other guys agreed, jumping on the bandwagon. A heart. A red one. Small. Simple.

Debbie smirked. She unbuttoned the top button of her black denim skirt, slowly, deliberately, even sexily. Then she opened the second, then the third, causing hoots and howls to go up all over the room. Melissa was so offended she grabbed her purse and stalked out to the living room, but Debbie just kept going. She lowered the waistband on her red panties, looked up, and waited.

All eyes focused on her yellow honeybee with the pink, yellow, and purple streaks of movement swirling around it. A design that could never be mistaken for a simple heart. Danny looked like he was about to throw up. Once again the room fell silent. Debbie glared at all the guys, waiting for someone to say something. For someone to admit they were wrong and apologize. But then she realized their silence was enough. They were snagged. They knew it, she knew it, and all the girls in the room knew it.

Debbie had just broken the tattoo rule in front of a couple dozen people and it was totally, completely worth it.

She reached down to button up her skirt, feeling suddenly invincible. Like maybe she could even find Eva and apologize—maybe even beg for forgiveness. But before she got to the top button, Kai ran into the kitchen, her face ashen.

Her eyes found Debbie's and Debbie's heart constricted before Kai even spoke.

"What?" Debbie asked.

"It's Mandy," Kai said. "We have to go."

In the hospital emergency room waiting area, Eva looked down at her hand, which at some point had found its way into Riley's. She was holding hands with a boy for the first time and she barely even noticed it. This wasn't the way these things were supposed to happen.

"We should have seen this coming," Debbie said for the hundredth time. "Has anyone seen the girl eat in the last week?"

"Try the last two weeks," Kai said, walking back and forth in front of her friends, gnawing on her thumbnail. "And we did notice it, remember? We tried to talk to her—"

"Well, we should have made her listen," Debbie put in, sounding nearly hysterical.

"You can't make people listen to you," Eva said quietly. "People only hear what they want to hear."

She looked from Kai to Debbie, then back at her shoes.

Riley's grip tightened on Eva's hand and a shot of warmth radiated through her.

Please just let Mandy be okay, Eva thought, watching the second hand on the clock across the room slide around and around. *That's all that really matters.*

The curtain behind the counter slid open and Eric walked out. Eva thought he looked older than he had that morning. More like a man than just a guy. He was in charge here, and they all felt it.

Debbie stood up and Eva and Riley sat forward in their seats as Eric approached, wiping his hands on the back of his jeans.

"She's gonna be fine," he told them, causing a universal whoosh of relief. "It was just . . . her blood sugar was really low, so they've got her hooked up to an IV."

"Can we see her?" Kai asked, surprising Eva by being the first one to ask it.

"The doctor says not tonight. He says she needs to rest," Eric said. "But you can come see her tomorrow."

"What about her mom?" Eva asked.

"She's on her way. I talked to her," Eric said. "She sounded freaked."

"Obviously," Debbie said under her breath.

"So what do we do now?" Eva asked, looking around at them.

"Go home, I guess," Kai told her.

For a moment nobody moved and Eva had a feeling they were all sensing the same thing she was. This wasn't enough. It was anticlimactic somehow. Something was missing.

Riley stood and picked up Eva's jacket. "Want me to drive you home?" he asked.

Eva looked at Debbie, whose face was unreadable, then at Kai. "We'll see you tomorrow," Kai told her.

"'Kay," Eva said.

Then they all hugged Eric, one by one, and left the ER, heading off in separate directions.

twenty-five

THE SKY WAS RAPIDLY LIGHTENING AS DEBBIE FINISHED off the last seam on her father's sherwani suit on Sunday morning. Her eyes stung from strain and her fingers shook as she pulled the needle through the soft, silky fabric. She tied off the thread, sat back in her chair, and sighed.

It was beautiful. The silk shantung draped perfectly, and the gold piping around the collar, sleeves, and cuffs of the legs contrasted perfectly with the burgundy fabric. It was regal. And her father would love it, that much she knew. When it came to the rest of her questions, she'd just have to wait and see.

Debbie pulled out a piece of the personalized stationery her parents had given her for her sweet sixteen—ivory colored, with her name written in purple across the top—and wrote a note to her father. No need to get into all the details of her internal arguments and stresses. After what had happened with first Eva and then Mandy last night, Debbie felt a huge desire to just keep it simple.

> *Dear Dad,*
>   *I made this for you for Nirav's wedding. This is what I want to do with my life. I want to design clothes. I'm good at it. And I want you to be happy with my decision, but if you're not, that's okay. It's my decision. But no matter what, I love you.*
>
>   *Love,*
>   *Deborah*

Debbie placed the suit on a padded hanger and pinned the note to the collar. She tiptoed downstairs to her father's study and hung the hanger over the drapery bar on the window by his desk. She stepped back once more to admire her work. There was no going back now. Once her father got up, he would know everything.

It was going to be a fight to the finish. Right there in the Patel living room.

And Debbie could accept that. She was even ready for it. But if she was going to be killed in battle in a few short hours, there were two things she had to do first. She headed back to her room and pulled her kiss list out of her bedside drawer. She hadn't added Riley to the list and she wasn't going to. For the first time in her life, she respected a guy too much to make notes about him.

Debbie pulled an old boot box out of the back of her closet and pulled off the rubber bands that held the top down. Inside was every note she'd ever gotten from her friends and from various guys, every letter Mandy had ever sent her from summer camp, and every issue of the Ardsmore High literary magazine with Eva's poems earmarked. Debbie dug down to the bottom of the box and shoved the kiss list under all the other papers, then stashed the box back on its shelf.

She didn't need the kiss list anymore. It was fresh start time.

Debbie sighed. Just one more thing to do. She grabbed her bag and keys from the floor where she'd dropped them on returning from the hospital and headed out. She knew she was going to wake Riley up, but this couldn't wait. She had something she needed to tell him and he needed to hear it—as soon as possible.

Mandy woke up in the hospital on Sunday to find that her mother had fallen asleep with Mandy's hands in hers, her head down next to Mandy's legs. The sight of her mother resting, holding her, made Mandy smile. She lay there awake for half an hour without moving so she wouldn't disturb her mother's slumber.

The second visiting hours began, the door opened and Eric walked in, struggling with a balloon bouquet that was far too big for the door. The commotion woke up Mandy's mother and they both watched him, giggling until he finally made it inside.

"Hey," Eric said, flushed. "You're awake."

"How could I not be?" Mandy asked.

"Oh . . . sorry." Eric tied the balloons to the bottom of her bed. They were a combination of Get Well Soon designs and Happy Birthday designs and a couple of Snoopy characters thrown in for good measure. Flashes of bright blue, yellow, white, purple, green, pink, and gold lit up the bare room.

"Well. I am going to go get some coffee," Mandy's mother said, smoothing her hair down on one side. "I'll see when they're bringing you breakfast, sweetie," she told Mandy before sweeping from the room.

The second she was gone, an uncomfortable silence fell over the room. Eric rolled back and forth on the balls of his feet and Mandy looked down at the IV tube running into her arm. She felt better this morning, rested, not so hungry, a little less weak. But she still had no idea what to say to Eric about what had happened the night before.

Too bad they didn't have an IV that could feed her the right words.

"How are you feeling?" Eric asked finally.

"Okay . . . better," Mandy said. "You can sit."

Eric looked relieved. He sat down on the edge of her bed and reached for her free hand. His touch sent a skitter of warmth up Mandy's arm and she smiled.

"What?" Eric asked.

"I just . . ." She looked up into his eyes for the first time since he'd entered the room. "I just love you."

"OhthankGod," Eric said as if it was all one word. He brought his free hand to his forehead. "I thought you were going to hate me forever."

"Why?" Mandy asked, her brow furrowing. She moved her head to the right on her pillow so she could see him better.

Eric stared down at their hands, his shoulders hunched as he spoke. "Come on, I mean, after what happened last night . . . and then we fought and then you ended up here. . . ."

"Eric, I'm not here because of you!" Mandy said simply.

"I know," he said quickly, glancing at her. "I mean, I guess . . . I don't know."

"Eric, come on, look at me," Mandy said. Eric tipped his head back, shaking his bangs away from his eyes, and did, finally, look right at her. "I haven't been able to eat for two weeks. That's why I'm in here."

Taking a deep breath, Eric struggled to maintain eye contact with her. Mandy felt his pain and confusion in her own heart.

"I just handled everything wrong," Eric admitted. "I'm so sorry."

"It's okay," Mandy told him.

"And I don't want you to regret last night," he said, sending another shiver through her. "I don't know what I would do if—"

"I don't," she told him. "I don't regret what we did. . . ."

She trailed off, trying to find the words she wanted to say—determined to say them. She was sick of hiding things. Sick of telling half-truths and full-out lies. Mandy wanted to lay her cards on the table for once and see how it felt.

"But you do regret something," Eric said slowly.

"I regret . . . I regret that I did it for the wrong reasons," Mandy told him. "I was just . . . I was miserable last night, you know? I was fighting with Kai and I had just seen my dad right before he was going to turn himself in. . . . It was like the number-one sucky birthday on the list of all-time sucky birthdays. . . . I mean, thank you for the party and everything. But I don't know if I was quite in the party mood."

Eric snorted a laugh and played with her fingers, touching the tip of each one by one.

"I guess I just thought that being with you would make it all better," Mandy concluded.

"But it didn't," Eric said.

"It didn't," Mandy said. "It just made me ridiculously emotional." She smiled and squeezed his hand. "You'd think they would have warned us about *that* in health class." This time Mandy laughed. "So . . . I think we should wait awhile before we do it again."

Eric took a deep breath, leaned down, and pressed his lips to her forehead. "I love you, sweetness," he told her in a whisper. "I don't even care about any of this. I just want you to get better and get the hell out of here."

"I'm with you on that one," Mandy replied, closing her eyes and inhaling his comforting scent.

"Breakfast is served!" A blue-clad nurse walked in, carrying a tray full of steaming food, and Eric stood up to make room for her. She set the food on the rolling table and swung it over until it was right in front of Mandy. The very sight of the scrambled eggs, the toast, the butter made her stomach turn, but she knew she had to at least try to eat.

"You need help with this?" the nurse asked, ripping the wrap from the plastic cutlery. Mandy shot Eric a look and he jumped up.

"I got it," he said, pulling a chair up next to Mandy's elbow.

"You make sure she eats," the nurse told him firmly. "We're not letting her out of here until she eats."

"Oh, don't worry," Eric told her, spooning some eggs up onto a fork and looking Mandy in the eye. "I'll take care of her."

Mandy and Eric shared a smile, and Mandy knew that he meant it. She knew it all the way down to her toes. Suddenly she felt like a heavy blanket was being lifted off her and everything was going to be all right. She had a lot to deal with. A *lot*. But with Eric and her mom and her friends to help her, she knew she'd be okay. Her face broke into a big, broad grin.

"I've never seen someone so happy about hospital food before," Eric said.

"You know how I love reconstructed eggs!"

The nurse disappeared and Eric held the full fork up in front of Mandy's face.

"Don't make me do the airplane thing," he deadpanned.

Mandy opened her mouth, took the bite, and made herself swallow. Things were going to get better. Starting now.

Kai ran upstairs on Sunday morning, irritated with herself for sleeping hours longer than she'd intended. She'd wanted to get to the hospital early so she could talk to Mandy before anyone else got there, but she had a feeling she'd already missed out on that. Miss Popularity was going to be inundated with visitors all day, but maybe Kai could somehow request a little alone time.

Kai shoved open the door at the top of the stairs and saw Andres's backpack and suitcase, stuffed to the gills, sitting by the front door. She paused with one hand on the doorknob and one on the doorjamb, not sure what to think of this new development. When Andres appeared at the end of the hall, rolling his new Penn State shirt over his hand, she was still standing there.

Andres paused momentarily at the sight of her, then continued past her over to his bags, shoving the shirt in among his other things.

"You're leaving?" Kai asked, closing the basement door and leaning back against it. She crossed her arms over her chest as he stood in front of her.

"Yes. It is what you want," he told her.

"It's what I've wanted for two weeks. Why leave now?" Kai asked, following Andres into the kitchen.

Andres walked around to the other side of the island in the middle of the room, laid his hands on top of the tile, and sighed. When he raised his head again, his eyes were soft and apologetic. This was new.

"It was what you said last night at the party," he told her. "I was drunk. I was not right to say what I did. But you . . . you were not drunk, yes?"

"Yes. I mean . . . no. I was not drunk," Kai said, her skin growing warm as she recalled all the things that had come flying out of her mouth at the party.

"So you meant what you said," Andres stated. No question in his tone. "Kai, there is something you should know. You make it sound like I wanted to hurt you. You said I used you. But this is not the case."

A sudden lump formed in Kai's throat and for once, she had no comeback. Somewhere in the back of her mind she realized she'd been waiting two years to hear him say something just like this.

Just don't let him screw it up, she thought.

"We *were* friends, Kai. We were," Andres continued. "Don't you remember the rope swing by the river . . . that time we lost annoying Tina Torres in the woods and we hid inside that log for hours. . . ."

Kai felt her heart softening. "Yeah. I remember."

"We *were* friends. But that is why I should never have tried to make it anything more. I was just a dumb boy. It is not a good excuse, but I am sorry. I never wanted to hurt you."

"Okay, stop!" Kai said, holding up a hand. "I don't do mushy."

She was going to cry if he kept talking, and that was just *not* acceptable.

"I am also sorry about what I said the other day here. It was just . . . you were hurtful to me, so I was hurtful to you. It was stupid."

Sounds familiar, Kai thought. She'd done the exact same thing the night before.

Andres looked down. "I never meant to make you hate me."

"I don't hate you," Kai said, surprising both of them.

"Then you sure fooled me," Andres told her.

"I don't," Kai said, realizing it was true even as she said it. "I did. A couple of years ago I definitely did. But now I just . . ."

I just what? she thought. Andres had just said all the right things. After all this time, that was all she needed—acknowledgment that what he'd done was wrong. And now she wasn't angry or upset anymore. She didn't even feel attracted to him. Somewhere between last night's tirade and this apology, she'd gotten Andres Cortez out of her system.

"I just want to forget the last two weeks ever happened," Kai told him finally. Both of them had been immature and hurtful, and she found herself wishing she could take it all back. Unfortunately, that wasn't possible.

The reality was that she and Andres had a history and that was never going to change, but she could decide if they were going to have a future. And what kind of future that might be.

"I would like that, *bonita*," Andres said with a smile.

"Eh! None of that!" Kai said, holding up a finger. "If we're going to be friends, you can't call me *bonita* anymore. And no more coming on to me. I know it'll be hard. . . ."

"We're going to be friends again?" Andres asked, raising his eyebrows hopefully.

"I'll take pity on you," Kai told him with a shrug. "I think we both equally humiliated each other last night, so maybe we should just call it a draw and start over."

Andres nodded slowly, drumming his fingers on the countertop. "Start over," he said. "I like it."

"Yeah," Kai said, smiling at him. "I do too."

Kai walked into the hospital room on Sunday afternoon just as the nurse was helping Mandy out of bed. Mandy's eyes locked with Kai's over the nurse's shoulder.

"Hey," Kai said, hands in the back pockets of her jeans.

"Hey," Mandy said.

Nurse Rose turned to look at Kai and stood up

straight. "You a friend of hers?" she asked Kai.

Kai looked at Mandy tentatively, as if unsure of how to answer that.

"Yeah. She is," Mandy told the nurse, sliding to the edge of the bed.

"Do you want her to walk with you instead?" Nurse Rose asked Mandy. "She looks sturdy. She can catch you if you fall," she joked with a wry smile.

"I'm on it," Kai told the nurse.

She walked over to the bed and bent at the knee so that Mandy could grip her arm and haul herself up. The second she was on her feet, Mandy got a head rush of epic proportions and squeezed her eyes closed until it passed.

"You okay?" Kai asked her.

"Fine," Mandy said finally. "Let's go."

The nurse held the door open for them and Mandy walked slowly into the hall, Kai at her side. Mandy couldn't believe how shaky and weak her legs felt. Like walking was this whole new thing. Each hospital room they passed held another patient, some old, some young, some sleeping alone, others surrounded by kids and family and bustling friends. "So . . . there's something you should know about me," Kai said, stepping around a cart in the middle of the hallway and holding her arm out slightly as if she were guarding Mandy from it. "I've never been good with apologies."

"Okay," Mandy said, shuffling along.

"But you should know that I am . . . sorry," Kai told her. "About, well, about a lot of things."

"I know," Mandy said.

"I think I have a problem with letting people . . . you know . . ."

"Letting people in?" Mandy suggested.

"Yeah."

"I'm with you there," Mandy said. "I was so pissed at my parents for not telling me what was going on and pretending like everything was fine, but I was doing the same thing to you guys."

"Kind of. So it's in your genes?" Kai asked, raising her eyebrows.

"Apparently."

"Bummer," Kai lamented, cracking a smile.

"Yep. I'm doomed." Mandy grinned back. But then her stomach growled audibly and she suddenly felt nauseous. "I need to stop," she said, leaning back against the cool wall.

"Should I get someone?" Kai asked.

"No, just hold on a sec," Mandy said, breathing in and out. "Keep talking. I need to concentrate on something else."

"Uh . . . okay, something else you should know about me?" Kai said, leaning back next to her. "I've never had friends. I think it's a symptom of the whole not-letting-people-in thing."

Mandy snorted a laugh. "Yeah, right."

"Don't get me wrong, people like me," Kai said jokingly. "I mean, I'm highly entertaining."

Mandy smirked and lifted her head, the nausea passing. She looked at Kai and could see that whatever she was trying to say, it wasn't easy for her to say it. Mandy knew that feeling—she'd been experiencing it every day since her parents' first argument. Surprisingly, her heart went out to Kai, and everything they'd been arguing over lately just seemed . . . stupid.

Who cared about volleyball or the presidency of the V Club—a post neither one of them was qualified to hold anymore? What really mattered was that Kai had tried to be there for her, she'd tried to keep Mandy from ending up here, in the damn hospital.

"It's just I've never lived in any one place for very long," Kai told her. "So I've never really bothered with friends. Not *real* ones. Not ones who I'm totally honest with. Not ones who I really talk to about real stuff. You know what I mean?"

"I think so," Mandy told her.

"So I was thinking, if you want, you know . . . maybe you could be my first," Kai said as they started walking again.

"Your first real friend?" Mandy asked, pausing.

Kai reddened slightly and looked at their feet

before meeting Mandy's eye. "Yeah," she said with a shrug.

"All right," Mandy told her with a nod. "I'll give it a shot."

Kai grinned. "Cool."

"Okay, now get me back to my room before I collapse," Mandy said, flinging her arm around Kai's shoulders.

"No problem," Kai replied, supporting her as they walked. "Just don't ask me to clean out any bedpans and we're all good."

They both laughed and Mandy leaned her head on Kai's shoulder. Somehow, in the midst of all the crap, some things had actually changed for the better.

twenty-six

WHEN THE DOORBELL RANG ON SUNDAY EVENING, EVA experienced the sensation of being sucked out of an alternate plane back into reality. Or at least, what she assumed that experience might feel like. The events of the last few days had opened the floodgates within her and she had spent most of the afternoon scrawling out ideas, lines, poems, and pieces of poems in her creative-writing notebook. She was so involved that she wasn't even entirely certain the bell had rung until it rang again.

Eva slapped her notebook closed and trudged over to the door, figuring her mother had gotten off work early and didn't feel like trolling for her keys in the bottom of her bag. She opened the door to find Riley standing there, holding forth a huge bouquet of giant sunflowers.

"Hi," Riley said.

"Hi." This was just too bizarre, seeing the guy she'd been dreaming about for over a year standing in the middle of her reality.

"I'm taking you out," Riley said, stepping past her and walking into the kitchen.

Eva slammed the door and followed him, watching helplessly as he went through the cabinets until he found an old glass vase. He filled the vase with water, unwrapped the flowers, and stuck the whole arrangement in the center of the table. Eva quickly took out her hair rubber band, ran her hands through her hair, whipped off her frumpy cardigan, and smoothed down her T-shirt.

"Um . . . you are?" she asked when he finished.

"Yeah," Riley said with a grin. "Unless you have a problem with that."

Eva glanced at the phone, her heart seizing up in her chest, knowing it was going to ring any second and ruin yet another chance.

"No," she told him, grabbing his wrist and yanking him out the door. "Let's go." She slid her keys from the counter and slammed the door, then sprinted down the stairs, trying to get out of earshot of the ringer as quickly as possible.

"Don't you even want to know where we're going?" Riley asked with a laugh.

"Nope," Eva told him, grinning. "Let's just go."

Twenty minutes later she and Riley were sitting on a blanket on the edge of Huff Lake, the tall, old-fashioned streetlamps that lined the running path glowing in the darkness. Eva wore Riley's leather jacket to guard against the cold and watched as he lit tiny votive candles in the center of the blanket. He pulled his backpack over and unzipped it, revealing a stack of Tupperware, each one filled with a different food.

"What is all that?" Eva asked as Riley pried one of the containers open.

"I forgot to tell you another interesting thing about myself," Riley said, rubbing his hands together. "My mother always makes too much food. But that's not really about me, is it?"

Soon there was an entire meal laid out in front of them. Cold fried chicken, salad, bread, pasta with some heavy-looking Italian sauce. Riley pulled out a bottle of Sprite and filled up two plastic champagne glasses. Eva blushed as he handed one to her. The picnic, the lake, champagne. This was it. This was her perfect first kiss.

"Riley, can I ask you a question?" Eva said as he scooted closer to her. She grew impossibly warm as his arm leaned against hers.

"Shoot," he said.

"What are we doing here?"

"Well, I had a visit from one of your friends this morning," Riley told her. "She was under the impression that I liked you but that I might need a little help, you know . . . with the wooing."

"The wooing?" Eva repeated, cracking up.

"Yes, the wooing," Riley deadpanned. "So she gave me a few tips about what Eva Farrell might like in an evening of romance."

"Wow. You just lay it right out there, don't you?" Eva asked, her heart skipping around.

Riley took a deep breath. "You may not believe it after last night, but I'm an honest person, Eva," he told her, staring at her profile. "I don't mind if you need me to prove that to you, but it's the truth."

Eva's heart thumped and she pulled her knees up under her chin and hugged them to her, holding her champagne glass in front of her shins. "It was Debbie, wasn't it?" she asked, hazarding a glance at him. "Debbie told you to bring me here."

"We both know we messed up," Riley said. "But you should have heard her talking about you. She's, like, president of the Eva Farrell fan club."

Eva's heart warmed and she smiled slightly, touched.

"She's a good friend," Riley said. "She cares a lot about you."

"Yeah, I know," Eva said. "I mean, she is a good friend."

Riley smiled. It was the kind of smile you smile when you really admire someone. When you're tucking away something they've said or done because you want to always remember it.

"Eva, there's something I have to tell you and I don't want you to freak out," Riley said, turning to face her. He placed his champagne glass aside and looked down at his hands.

Oh God. This can't be good, Eva thought. She felt sick to her stomach, but she didn't run. She didn't look away. Pressing her hands into the blanket, she turned to face him as well, their knees touching as they sat Indian style.

"Okay," Eva said finally. "What?"

Riley looked up at her then, his Caribbean blue eyes twinkling in the soft light. Suddenly Eva felt it. That same sensation of anticipation that she'd felt hundreds of times in her daydreams. The hair on her arms stood up, tickling her skin. This time there was nothing panicky about it.

"I told you I liked you last night, but that wasn't exactly true."

Oh God.

"Eva, I think I'm falling in love with you," Riley said.

"Wow." The word escaped her lips with a sigh. A relieved, ecstatic, perfect sigh.

"I take it that's a good wow?" Riley said tentatively.

"Oh, yeah," Eva said, nodding. "It's a good wow."

Riley scooted over to sit next to her, cupped her face with both hands, and pulled her to him. Just before their lips met, Eva saw it, exactly the way she'd always pictured it.

In that moment Eva Farrell learned what it meant to have a dream come true.

"Deborah."

Oh, that was not good. That tone was never good. Debbie stopped with her foot on the bottom stair and turned slowly to face her father. She lifted her chin and tried not to look like her heart was trying to beat its way out of her chest. He stood in the doorway of his study, holding his glasses in his hand, down by his side. How was it possible that he seemed to be twice the size he had been yesterday?

"Come in here, please," he said.

On unsteady ankles, Debbie followed her father into his office. The sherwani suit still hung over the window, blocking the light from the street-lamps, but the note was gone. Her father had read the note.

For once in her life, Debbie wished she had paid attention when her mother was teaching her all those prayers to Buddha.

"There is something I need to give you," Debbie's father said, his back to her as he walked behind his desk. From a stack of papers he pulled out a large, white envelope. Before handing it to her, he looked down at the address and sighed, but when he reached out to give it to Debbie, there was a small smile on his creased face.

Debbie's mouth went dry when she saw the return address. The package was from FIT. And it was very thick.

"Where did this come from?" Debbie asked.

"It came in the mail yesterday," her father told her, sitting down in his leather chair. "About five minutes after your dramatic exit."

Hands shaking, Debbie turned over the envelope and ripped it open. Catalogs and pamphlets and paperwork and a subway map clattered to the floor, but Debbie held in her hand the only thing she needed. The letter.

Dear Ms. Patel,

We are pleased to inform you that you have been awarded a full scholarship and placement in the Fashion Institute of Technology class of . . .

"I got in," Debbie said, under her breath. She looked up at her father, clutching the page. "I got in."

"I see that," her father said, looking down at the mess on his floor. "FIT. That's a fashion design school, I believe."

Debbie had never felt such elation and unadulterated fear at the same time. She wasn't sure her body could handle such contradicting emotions. She had a sudden vision of herself fainting to the ground just as Mandy had the night before. Or exploding into a million tiny pieces.

"Yeah," she said. "Yeah, Dad, it is."

Her father nodded slowly, looking again at the floor. An eternity seemed to pass before he looked up at her again. She had no idea what he was thinking.

"Well, then, I think that's exactly where you should be."

Debbie's heart thumped once as if to punctuate his words.

"Are you serious?" she said.

"Am I ever not serious?" he asked, smiling.

Debbie screeched and jumped into her father's arms before he even had time to stand up.

"Are you sure you're okay with this?" Debbie asked, pulling back from him.

Her father turned and plucked his suit from the drapery bar. He laid it reverently down on top of his desk and fingered the fabric, rubbing it between his thumb and forefinger.

"You may be good at the sciences, Deborah, but this. . ." He looked up at her, his eyes gleaming with pride the way Debbie had been longing to see them. But this time it was even better. This time they were shining over something *she* was proud of too. Something she wanted to do.

Her father reached out his free arm and hugged her to his side. "This," he said, "is art."

*　　　*　　　*

As soon as Mandy's mother walked into her hospital room on Monday afternoon, Mandy instantly noticed the change. There was some color in her mother's face, and something about the way she was carrying herself was different. She looked a little more together, a little more energetic than she had for the past couple of weeks.

"Hey, sweetie," her mother said, leaning over to kiss her cheek. Mandy had adjusted the electric bed into a seated position for lunch and was still propped up. Her mother leaned back and inspected her quickly. "You look much better."

"I was just thinking the same thing about you," Mandy told her. "What's up?"

Her mom put her purse on the floor and sat down on the edge of Mandy's bed. "I have some good news," she said, beaming at her daughter.

"You're kidding," Mandy joked. "What's that again?"

"I know. It's practically a miracle," Mandy's mother told her. Mandy smiled. It was nice to joke with her mother again. It would have been an almost normal moment if she hadn't been sitting there in her pj's with a tube in her arm. "I spoke to Jim Morrow this morning, your father's accountant?"

"Yeah . . . ," Mandy said.

"He called to tell me that your college account

is completely protected," her mother said. "Your father put it solely in your name, so the IRS can't touch it. As of your eighteenth birthday, it's all yours to do whatever you want with it."

Mandy could barely allow herself to believe what she was hearing. "But I turned eighteen on Saturday."

"Exactly," her mother said with a smile. "Jim said he'll be happy to meet with you as soon as you're feeling better so you can sign the paperwork."

"You're kidding," Mandy said, sitting forward. "Wait . . . so I can still go to Princeton?"

"Yes, you can still go to Princeton," her mother said, beaming.

Mandy reached out and hugged her mother, laughing and crying at the same time. Her mother gripped her back tightly and rocked her back and forth. But Mandy was only able to revel in the moment temporarily. She pulled away from her mother abruptly and looked into her eyes.

"But wait, aren't we going to need that money?" Mandy asked. "I mean, are we going to have to move? What if we need it to pay for a place to live?"

"That's not your responsibility," Mandy's mother said. "Let your father and me worry about that."

"But Mom—"

"Mandy, all your father and I have ever wanted was for you to have the future you dreamed of," her mother said, tears in her eyes. "You're going to have it. That money is yours and we want you to use it for school."

Mandy's eyes welled up and she looked down at her mother's hands, which covered hers. Her mom's diamond rings were gone and Mandy wondered what she'd done with them, but she didn't ask. Her mother and father still wanted to protect her and for the moment, Mandy didn't mind being protected a bit. She'd had enough reality in the past few weeks to last her a lifetime.

She'd do what her parents wanted her to do. She'd go to Princeton and ace everything and graduate a star. Then she could start protecting them.

"Okay," Mandy said, sighing blithely. "If you want me to go to Princeton, I guess I'll go to Princeton." Like it was such a chore.

Mandy's mother laughed and hugged her again. "That's my girl." She leaned back and pushed Mandy's hair behind her ears. "And when you're ready, you can go visit your father and tell him that."

Slowly Mandy nodded. The very thought of seeing her father behind bars hollowed her out inside, but she knew she would do it. Whatever her father had done, he still cared about her. He still loved her. And she loved him. If there was one thing

Mandy had learned over the past couple of weeks, it was that people made mistakes. Lots of them. She couldn't go through life if she couldn't forgive.

"Okay," Mandy said with a nod and a smile. "I will."

twenty-seven

KAI STOOD IN THE GUIDANCE OFFICE WAITING ROOM on Monday afternoon, watching the clock as the scholarship panel finished up their last interview. Her pulse was racing with excitement and determination. She knew her friends would think she was crazy for doing what she was about to do, but she had to do it. If she didn't say something now, it would be too late.

The second Marni Raab walked out of the conference room, Kai grabbed the door and barged right in. The five teachers and administrators were packing up their things and looked up, surprised to find Kai standing before them with a clear sense of purpose on her face.

"Kai! Here to give us your purity essay?" Mr. Simon asked.

"No," Kai said, standing in the center of the room before their long table. "No, I'm not."

Ms. Russo and Mrs. Labella exchanged a look. "Ms. Parker, is everything all right?" Ms. Russo asked, her forehead wrinkling.

"No, it's not," Kai said, taking a deep breath. "I've got something to say to you people and I'd appreciate it if you'd just give me a few minutes of your time."

For once Mr. Simon didn't laugh. He sat back in his seat with the rest of the panel and they all watched her expectantly. Kai hesitated for a moment. And then she jumped right in.

"All right, here's the thing—I don't think it's right for you guys to make us prove to you how pure we are," Kai told them. "What we do in our personal lives, that's our business. And you know what? Our definitions of purity are our own business too. This Treemont lady, she was clearly out of her mind. I mean, where does she get off putting something like that in as a requirement for a scholarship? What is she saying? If we've had sex, we're unworthy of succeeding in life? Well, that's bull and we all know it!"

Kai paused, waiting for someone to interject, but the teachers just looked back at her. In all the scenarios she'd imagined coming out of this speech, she'd never thought she'd be met with silence.

"Do you people have any idea what you've put us all through with this thing?" Kai continued. "You've got friends lying to friends, you've got people regretting decisions that were made years ago that can't be taken back. Everybody's totally stressed out, rethinking this and questioning that. Everybody's completely confused because of this stupid scholarship."

Mr. Simon leaned forward and rested his elbows on the table. "I hear you, Kai, but don't you think that this is a good thing?"

"That what's a good thing?" Kai asked.

"That this scholarship has got people thinking . . . questioning, as you say. I happen to think people *should* be confused about this topic. It's not a simple thing."

Okay. Kai swallowed hard as she considered this. *He's got me there.*

"Okay, yeah, but I still think it shouldn't be a requirement for a scholarship," she finished, feeling lame.

Coach Davis took a deep breath and leaned forward, her hands clasped on the table in front of her. "The truth is, Kai, we happen to agree with you."

Kai's heart took a little leap. "You do?"

"Yes, we do," Mr. Simon told her. "Unfortunately there's nothing we can do about it. We have to award the scholarship based on Mrs. Treemont's specifications."

Kai deflated slightly. "I understand," she said. "But in that case, I'd like to withdraw my name from consideration."

"Are you sure about that?" Coach Davis asked.

"I am," Kai said, nodding. She'd made this decision and she was going to stick by it. She didn't want to participate in a scholarship that had turned her and all her friends into secret-keeping, back-stabbing, confused crazy idiots.

"Well, good," Coach Davis said.

"Good?" Kai asked.

"I was going to practice in a few minutes to tell you that there were some scouts at the game last week and they're coming back to see you play in the finals," Coach Davis told her. "You play as well as you did in the semis and I don't think you'll have any problems getting financing next year."

Okay, this she *definitely* hadn't expected.

"Really?" Kai asked, her voice jumping about two octaves. A volleyball scholarship? She could play volleyball next year and get paid for it? She'd known she was good, but not *that* good.

"Really," Coach told her, standing up.

Then Kai narrowed her eyes. "Wait a minute, which schools?"

Mr. Simon laughed, and the panel continued packing up their stuff. Coach Davis came around the table and hooked her arm around Kai's neck, leading her out of the room.

"We'll talk about it after practice," she told Kai.

"No, wait a minute, which schools?" Kai asked as

she stumbled along next to her coach, hoping these places were in close proximity to the slopes or the beach. Or both. "'Cause I have some very strict requirements about where I wanna be next year. . . ."

Debbie dimmed the lights in Mandy's hospital room, Kai lit the candles, and Eva placed the cake on the table that swung over Mandy's bed. Mandy grinned, her eyes glowing in the candlelight as her friends whisper-sang the "Happy Birthday" song to her so as not to attract any attention to the complete fire code violation.

"Okay. Make a wish," Eva told her, grinning.

Mandy closed her eyes. There were so many things to wish for, choosing seemed like bad luck, so she decided to take her chances and just blew out the candles.

Her friends applauded and Debbie flicked on the lights as Eva took the cake away to cut it.

"So when the hell are they springing you from this place?" Kai asked, plopping onto the bed and causing Mandy to bounce up and down slightly.

"Tomorrow. But I'm not coming back to school until next week," Mandy told them.

"Lucky," Debbie said.

"You're gonna miss states," Kai told her.

"I know," Mandy said. "So you're gonna have to kick a little ass in my name."

"Not a problem," Kai told her, crooking her arm behind her head to stretch her triceps muscle. "I am a volleyball goddess."

Mandy rolled her eyes as Debbie handed her a piece of cake and a plastic fork. They all gathered around the bed and dug in. Mandy smiled, knowing the others were just as happy to see them all back together as she was.

"I have news," Debbie told them, licking icing from her fork. "I got into FIT."

"You're kidding!" Eva blurted, probably the first words she'd said to Debbie since Saturday.

Debbie flushed as she looked at Eva.

"I knew it!" Mandy said brightly. "Didn't I tell you?"

"Yeah, but the question is, is she *going* to FIT?" Kai put in, her fork poised above her plate. They all gazed at Debbie, waiting for the answer.

"Yep," she said giddily. "I'm going."

Eva and Kai jumped up and hugged Debbie, knocking a slice or two of cake onto the floor. Debbie sat in her chair, cringing as they smothered her but smiling as well.

"That's amazing, Debbie," Eva told her as she pulled away. "I guess I have news too," Eva said, bending to clean up the mess. Her skin darkened from her forehead down to her neck. "Riley and I kissed," she told the floor.

"What?" Mandy said above her. "When? Where? How?"

"Um . . . last night," Eva told her, standing up with her hands full of messy paper plates. "And then again after school today . . . and then out in his car when he dropped me off here . . ."

"Omigod! You little vixen!" Kai said.

"I know," Eva said, tossing the plates in the garbage can. "I'm a wanton woman."

"I'm really happy for you," Debbie told her as Eva sat back down on the other side of Mandy's bed.

"We all are," Kai said. "Sheesh. It was about time."

"I know," Eva said, smiling. "I mean, I know you're happy for me. And it was *so* about time."

"Well, as long as we're spilling, I have something to tell you guys that you already probably know," Kai said, slapping her hands on her thighs. "I am going to resign as president of the V Club because I am not, in fact, a virgin," she announced, looking right at Mandy.

"Andres?" Eva asked.

"Andres," Kai said with a nod.

"Lucky shit," Debbie said, shaking her head in awe at Kai.

"Yeah, that's all relative," Kai told them. "But anyway, this means Mandy can take over as president," she added, reaching out and rubbing Mandy's knee through the blanket.

Mandy took a deep breath and laid her half-eaten piece of cake on the table next to her bed. She pushed her hands into the mattress and sat up straighter, looking from Debbie to Eva to Kai.

"Actually, I don't think that's the best idea," she said.

"Why not?" Debbie asked.

Mandy smiled, her heart pounding, and shook her head. "Because if actual virginity is the prerequisite for a V Club president, then I don't really qualify anymore."

There was a prolonged moment of silence as this statement sank in, and then the room exploded.

"Omigod! You guys *did* it?" Debbie screeched, jumping up from her chair. "*When?* Why didn't you *tell* us?"

"I can't believe it," Eva said. "Where? What was it like?"

"We are just dropping like flies," Kai lamented, shaking her head.

Mandy's friends gathered around her as she told the story—the true and somewhat heartbreaking story of her first time. It hadn't been perfect, but she knew now that imperfection was okay—part of life, even. And for the first time in her life, Mandy Walters was realizing that she could live with imperfection.

But as her friends sat and listened and lamented

and laughed and hugged and comforted and cajoled and hoped, Mandy realized that even with all that imperfection, there were still perfect moments.

And this was one of them.

twenty-eight

"Dude, Pennsylvania is, like, arctic," Kai said, kicking back in the booth at the Ardsmore Diner, her bare leg hanging out into the aisle.

"Well, maybe if you didn't wear *shorts* in *November*," Debbie pointed out, rolling her eyes.

"Hey, I didn't need fashion advice from you last year, and I don't need it now, even if you're FIT's star pupil," Kai deadpanned. "Besides, these things are everywhere in L.A.," she added, admiring her cargo cutoffs.

"Right. And it's also about fifty degrees warmer there," Mandy said, munching on a french fry.

Kai was staying with Mandy and her mom in their new, smaller, but still nice house for the Thanksgiving break while Kai's parents were in Australia for a few months. Ever since she'd stepped off the plane from L.A. that afternoon, Kai had been shivering, but she still insisted on dressing like she'd never left the beach.

"Don't remind me," Kai lamented. "When can I go back?"

"Hello? We just got here!" Eva told her, shoving Kai with her elbow.

"Ow!" Kai rubbed at the spot dramatically. "Since when did you get loud and violent?" she joked.

"Wesleyan is having a positive effect on me," she said with a shrug.

"It's having some kind of effect, but I don't know if it's good," Kai said. She was smiling.

"Oh, no, it's good," Eva said with a grin. "Would you guys believe that yesterday I actually raised my hand in class?"

"No!" her friends said in unison, their mouths dropping open.

"Yuh-huh!" Eva said, preening. "I didn't get called on and I almost wet my pants, but I have high hopes for the future."

Mandy and Debbie laughed, shaking their heads, and Kai flung her arm over Eva's shoulders. "Our little overachiever."

"What about you?" Mandy said to Kai. "Our volleyball coach can't stop talking about UCLA's freshman wonder."

"Yeah. I'm famous," Kai said with a shrug, then she took a huge bite of her burger. "Don't worry, though. I won't forget you guys when I'm on the Olympic team."

"And I won't forget you guys when I go to Paris for the fall runway shows," Debbie put in.

"And I won't forget you guys when I'm elected the first female president," Mandy told them.

"How does Eric feel about being the first husband?" Kai asked. "Or the first man? Or . . . how would that even work?"

"I don't know," Mandy said with a laugh, blushing over the mere mention of him. "Maybe we'll let him make up his own title."

She was supposed to head over to Eric's after seeing her friends, and she couldn't wait to get her hands on him. It had been two whole weeks since his last trip from Villanova to Princeton and Mandy was suffering from withdrawal, both physical and emotional. Her second sexual encounter with Eric had gone *much* better than the first and since then, whenever they got around each other, well, let's just say they made up for lost time.

Mandy had never thought she was capable of becoming a sex goddess, but she kind of was. Not that she'd ever tell anyone that.

"So what about you?" Debbie said to Eva. "We all said we wouldn't forget you. What are you going to do and then not forget us?"

At that moment Riley walked through the front door and grinned when he saw Eva and her friends. Eva's heart did a few backflips.

"I don't know," Eva said giddily. "Get married?"

"*What!?*" her friends blurted. Debbie dropped her hand on the table and sent a fork careening across the restaurant.

"Well, you guys . . . we love each other, and we know we want to be together, so . . . yeah. We're engaged," Eva said, grinning so wide it hurt. Riley approached, his giddy expression matching her own. Neither one of them had been able to stop smiling since he'd officially popped the question that morning.

"Shut *up!*" Mandy said loudly, slapping Eva's hand from across the table.

"Omigod, I am going to be the last one of us to have sex," Debbie said, slumping down in her seat.

If she had thought Ardsmore was devoid of worthy men, FIT was a veritable wasteland. There were plenty of great guys on campus, but unfortunately they were, for the most part, same-sex oriented. Debbie and her friends had recently taken to hanging out at all the NYU watering holes to meet people, but so far she'd yet to find anyone worthy of rebreaking the tattoo rule. And this time she was sticking to it. No pitter-patter of the heart, no sweaty palms, no true love equalled no tattoo.

"Don't worry, Deb. We're gonna wait till we graduate, so you have three and a half years to get *someone* to sleep with you," Eva said archly.

"Ha, ha," Debbie shot back.

"Me-ow!" Kai said.

"See? I'm like a whole new person," Eva joked.

"Hey, guys," Riley said, arriving at the end of their table.

"Riley! You're taking the plunge, huh?!" Kai said, standing so that Eva could get up and throw her arms around Riley's neck. He kissed her right there in the middle of the diner like he hadn't seen her just a few hours ago when he'd dropped her off at her apartment. He'd driven from Yale to Wesleyan to pick her up, and all they had talked about on the long drive was their engagement and Riley's vow to wait until he was married and how Eva's existence was making that vow deliciously hard to keep.

"Um, you guys? You're gonna make me heave," Debbie told them.

"Yeah, *God*," Mandy added with a smile. "What would Mrs. Treemont say?"

Eva pulled away from Riley and they both grinned down at her friends.

"I think she'd say that the panel split her money on the two most deserving candidates," Riley told them.

"The two most deserving candidates with the greatest willpower she's ever seen," Eva added, lacing her fingers through Riley's.

"If you guys are really going to wait three and a half years, then I agree with that assessment," Kai said, dunking a fry in her ketchup. "No one deserved that scholarship more than you."

"All right, enough sex talk," Debbie said, sitting up straight. She snapped her fingers as the waiter walked by. "Garçon! A round of chocolate milk shakes to celebrate our friends' engagement!" she said haughtily.

"Coming right up," the cute waiter answered with a lopsided smile.

A few minutes later the five friends were seated around the table, clinking glasses and giving themselves chocolate mustaches as Riley retold the story of his proposal. Mandy daydreamed of the day when Eric might do the same, Kai tried to envision a scenario in which she would ever say yes to spending the rest of her life with a guy, and Debbie quietly, surreptitiously got the waiter's phone number.

Eva smiled as she looked around the table at each of her closest friends. There was no going back to high school, no going back to sharing every little thing and that kind of close friendship that blossomed when people saw each other every single day.

But that was okay. Eva still loved her friends and she knew they loved her. They were just moving forward. Changing. And change was good.

"To Eva and Riley!" Debbie said, holding up her half-empty glass once Riley's story was finished.

Everyone knocked their glasses together, their cheers filling Eva's heart with a happy warmth she would cherish forever.

"To Eva and Riley!"

Kate Brian is the author of the popular *The Princess & the Pauper* and *Lucky T.* She has written many young adult novels under a different name. She lives outside of New York City. We're not telling you if she's in the club or not.

Here's a sneak peek at
Kate Brian's next book,
Lucky T

When Carrie saw Jason standing on her
doorstep that evening, she understood first-
hand the meaning of the phrase "a sight for
sore eyes." Hers were definitely sore from
crying away half the afternoon, and just
looking at him in his American Eagle rugby
shirt and rugged FCUK denim jacket, his
light brown hair perfectly tousled and his
blue eyes all soulful, made her feel instantly,
if not totally, better.

"I'm so glad to see you," she said, step-
ping out and closing the door behind her.
It was pouring now, which meant that
Carrie had to cuddle close to him under the

awning in order to stay dry. Not that she minded. Being next to Jason's warm athlete's body always made her feel tingly all over.

Jason squirmed a bit. "Actually, I was thinking maybe I'd come in for a while."

"Would you mind if we went somewhere else? I've had such a bad day and I'd really like to shake it off," Carrie said. She didn't even bother waiting for a response. Instead Carrie pulled the hood on her rain jacket up over her face and ran down the stairs. The rain pounded against the vinyl around her ears and she ducked quickly into his Jeep, which was double-parked in front of the gate.

Jason climbed in a second later, shook his head, and groaned. "I hate rain."

"You hate it? My hair's been a frizz ball ever since it started," Carrie grumbled. If she had her T-shirt, it might not be sunny and dry, but she'd definitely look perfect right about now. "I must look awful, huh?"

She waited for him to tell her that she was crazy and that she looked amazing, but he didn't even glance in her direction.

Unbelievable. Wasn't that standard boyfriend protocol? She started to feel a rumbling in her stomach—a telltale sign that she was getting real anxious. Carrie tried to push her concern aside and forced a smile.

"So, where're we going?" she asked, hoping he'd planned a fun evening for them. Thankfully, it was their anniversary. She needed a major distraction. She needed romantic candlelight. She needed some big-time lovin'.

"Carrie, I'm sorry you've had a bad day . . . but I was hoping we could talk," Jason said, running his hand along the steering wheel, down, up, down, up. He was obviously nervous. Carrie could see a little bit of sweat gleaming on his forehead.

"Okay . . ." Carrie said apprehensively. "Talk about what?"

"About . . . us," Jason said, hazarding a weak glance in her direction.

Okay, bad sign. Jason wasn't a talker to begin with and tonight Carrie was planning on cracking him open and seeing what was inside. But from the look on his face, which was pretty panic-stricken, she had a strong feeling that whatever was happening in his mind was not good at all. Her emotions already raw, she felt her breath start to quicken and began wringing her hands.

"What about us?" she asked.

"I just . . . I don't know if it's . . . working out," Jason mumbled while staring out at the droplets popping against the windshield.

Oh my God, this is not happening, Carrie thought.

"What's not working out?" she asked, accessing her emergency calm reserve as quickly as possible. "I don't understand."

He opened his hands and then curled them into fists and pressed them together. "It's just . . . we've been together a year, you know?"

"It's our anniversary," Carrie replied.

"Well, that's the thing," he said. "There's this party over at Doug's—all the guys are there watching basketball right now. I mean, it's the *finals*. And I have to do this anniversary thing—"

"Have to?" Carrie blurted, her heart

palpitating out of control. "I thought you wanted to be with me, not that you *had* to."

"I do . . . I mean . . . I just . . . This is all coming out wrong," Jason said, looking at her with a pleading expression.

Carrie stared back at him. What did he want her to do, make it easier for him to break up with her? Well, that wasn't going to happen. For a few moments the only sounds were the splatters of raindrops as they battered the car.

"Look," Jason said, searching for the right words. "I just want to be able to hang out with my friends. It's not that I don't like you, it's just—"

"You don't like me enough," Carrie said as she felt tears well up in her eyes again. She blinked them back angrily. She'd thought she was all cried out, but that was back when she had believed she was going out with her cute-as-hell boyfriend to have an incredible time and get her mind off The Day It All Changed to Crap, Part I. But the reality was clear. She was experiencing her first breakup and her first horrible moment after the loss of her lucky T. If only Piper were here. She'd finally be able to convince her best friend of the simple truth: life with lucky T = good; life without lucky T = bad.

"Carrie, I feel terrible about this," Jason said when he noticed the tears.

The tender tone of his voice was pushing Carrie over the edge into an alternate universe her mom liked to call The Temper Zone. Ever since she was little, she had the tendency to fly off the handle when things weren't going her way, and Carrie had a feeling that was going to be happening a lot more often now. Even so, she tried really hard to be graceful under pressure.

"Well, Jason, you certainly know how to show a girl a good time," Carrie said snidely. "Woo-hoo! Happy anniversary!"

She fumbled her way out of the car and slammed the door behind her. She raced back up to the house, taking the many rain-slicked steps two at a time. She couldn't believe this was happening. Everyone always said they were the perfect couple. That's exactly how Carrie saw her and Jason too.

She was secretly hoping that they had something that would last forever or at least until their first year of college. How could he dump her on their anniversary? Did Jason have an iceberg for a heart or what?

"Carrie!" Jason shouted behind her, causing her heart to leap. Maybe he'd realized he made a mistake. Maybe he was coming after her. Carrie turned around under the awning and saw him leaning over the passenger side seat, peering out the opened window so he could face her.

"Yeah?" she said loudly.

"So, we're broken up, right?" he asked.

What?! she yelled, not quite able to believe what she'd just heard.

"I mean, I just want to be clear," he said. "We're not together anymore."

She wanted to hurl something at him. Something big and very, very heavy. She was now entering . . . The Temper Zone.

Carrie took long strides back toward Jason and his precious Jeep that always smelled of Barbecue Lays, which at one point she really liked, but now the thought of it made her sick. The rain was pummel-ing her, yet Carrie didn't care how soaked she got. She and Jason were going to have words, all right. She was about to tell him everything that was on her mind and it wasn't going to be pretty. She was going to tell him that after he worked out and he took off his sneakers, the odor was so nasty it had killed every plant in her room. She was going to recommend that he invest in Proactiv because chronic back acne is not exactly a bonus. She was seconds away from revealing that she would have waved him on to third base if he didn't royally suck in the making-out department, which wasn't really true, but who cared? Carrie wanted to hit below the belt and make Jason feel as horrible as she did.

But when she approached his side of the window, all riled up and ready to rip, Jason's car pulled away and drove through a large collection of puddles down the street, then around the corner until he was out of sight.

There was nothing else Carrie could do but walk inside.

Carrie sneaked upstairs, avoiding her mom, who was watching TV in the living room. She only felt like talking with one person right now, and that was Piper. Carrie went into her bedroom, and the first thing she did before grabbing a big towel was dig out her cell from her purse and dial Piper's number.

As she listened to the phone ring, Carrie's thoughts kept going back to Jason. God, what was *wrong* with him? True, he wasn't a genius, and he never really had anything important to say except for, "Man, *The Matrix* rules." But they had lots of fun together, and Carrie thought she was safe with Jason. She had hoped that he was going to stick around for a long time, unlike the other major male figure in her life. She thought she was about to learn all these interesting things about him, but when he finally opened up, it was to push her away. Carrie's world was crumbling before her very eyes, and just then she wanted to speak with Piper even more than she wanted her lucky T back.

The line rang four times and the voice mail picked up. She could feel a steady stream of tears flowing down her flushed cheeks. Carrie sniffled hard and left a message.

"P, it's me. I really need to talk. You're never going to believe what Jason did. Call me back as soon as you get this."

Then she hung up the phone, lay face-down on her bed, pulled the comforter over her cold, shivering body, and sobbed as much as she did the morning her parents sat her down and said, "Mommy and Daddy aren't going to live together anymore."

When her cell phone rang an hour later, Carrie snapped out of her emotional-exhaustion-induced slumber and lunged for it.

"Hello?"

"Carrie, I just heard. Are you okay?" Piper asked.

"I am so not okay," Carrie replied, relieved beyond belief to be talking with Piper. She sat up straight on her bed for the first time since she'd walked back into the house. "Let's just say Jason Miller is total scum."

There was a sudden loud and raucous cheer on the other end of the line and Carrie held the phone away from her ear.

"Where the heck are you?" she asked Piper.

Fumbling noises were followed by the sound of a door closing. A couple of muffled whispers and for a moment everything was silent.

"I told you earlier, remember? My brother is throwing this NBA party. Everyone is over here watching the Blazers game," Piper said.

There was a thud inside Carrie's chest like she'd never felt before. "Wait a minute, is *Jason* there?"

Piper sighed. "Yeah, he is. And he told me what happened. He—"

"So you didn't even listen to my message?" Carrie asked, swallowing hard.

"Well, I didn't hear the phone, Carrie. It's kind of noisy in here. Fifteen guys. Lots of testosterone. You know how it is."

Carrie was on her feet now, pacing back and forth next to her bed. She clutched the phone for dear life. "Wait a minute, wait a minute. How long has he been there?"

"I don't know . . . half an hour, maybe?" Piper said.

He broke up with me and went straight to the party, Carrie thought, half seething, half drowning in humiliation. *He's hanging out with my best friend while I sit here alone crying my eyes dry.*

"So when did you decide it was right to call me? During the halftime show or when Doug and his friends went out to recruit bums to buy beer for them at the Shop-N-Go?" Carrie asked mockingly.

The betrayal was almost too much to handle. Piper was supposed to be there for her in times like this. But instead she had missed her call for help because she was watching basketball with the very guy who had broken her heart.

"Listen, I know you're really pissed off," Piper said, trying to console her.

"Why don't you tell me what happened?"

"It sounds like you already know what happened," Carrie said flatly.

"Carrie, obviously I didn't know he was coming," Piper said. "I thought you guys were going to be out all night."

Carrie's heart ached even more, thinking about the romantic night she should have had. "Yeah, so did I."

"Look, Carrie, I know it's hard right now, but it's gonna be okay," Piper said. "Sometimes people just grow apart."

Carrie wrapped her free arm around herself and held on tight. "Is that what he told you?"

"Yeah. And he feels really bad about the whole thing. He actually said he hoped you guys could still be friends."

This was unbelievable. Piper was pleading Jason's case! She was supposed to listen to Carrie's story and be appalled and righteously indignant and was supposed to vow never to talk to Jason again for the rest of her life. But instead Jason had gotten to her first and told her some watered-down version of the story, which for some reason Piper believed without hearing Carrie's point of view. This was so out of whack and hurtful to Carrie that she couldn't help but visit The Zone again.

"This is complete BS," Carrie snapped. "I can't believe you're taking his side."

"I'm not taking anyone's side," Piper said.

"Yes, you are!" Carrie shouted. "I thought we were best friends, Piper. I thought I could count on you. But on the night my boyfriend callously dumps me, you're telling me I should still be his friend? He's probably sitting there watching you talk to me."

The silence on the other end of the line said it all.

"Oh my God! He is! He's sitting right there!" Carrie cried. The very thought of Jason listening in their conversation, watching Piper for signs of how things were going, made Carrie want to hurl. She had never felt so wronged.

"Carrie, you guys are both my friends," Piper said. "I didn't know what to do. I'm sorry, but—"

"I'm sorry too, Piper," Carrie interrupted. "Sorry that I trusted you."

She turned off the phone without allowing Piper to explain herself or make any more excuses. Then, hands trembling, she turned around and ripped the cord of her landline out of the wall. Afterward she burst into another crying fit that she assumed would last for days.

Three weeks later Carrie rubbed her rabbit's foot under the table in biology class as Mr. Dumas handed back the final exams. She had bought the trinket the day after losing her T, hoping to get some of her luck back, but so far it hadn't done much but be fuzzy and hang off her key chain. Today her stomach was tied in dozens of tight little knots. She had a bad feeling about this.

On the morning of the test not one but two black cats had run right by her as she locked up her bike in front of the school. That really did not bode well, especially with her lucky T on a whole other continent and the fabric of her life viciously unraveling yard by yard. Not even a rabbit's foot could combat that.

The last three weeks had been long, miserable, and lonely. Carrie had avoided Piper as much as possible at school, changed lunch tables, and given her the cold shoulder until Piper finally stopped trying to talk to her. Jason hadn't even bothered to try, which fueled her anger and kept her from mourning him too much. Still, every day was a struggle. Carrie had to concentrate to remember the new routes to class that would help her avoid both Piper and Jason. She had to keep her eyes peeled in the hallways so that she could spot them first and avoid eye contact. It was exhausting to the point that she hadn't been sleeping well or able to concentrate on studying.

But there was hope on the horizon. By this time next week the school year would be over. Then she wouldn't even have to get up in the morning. A depressing fact, but true nonetheless.

Mr. Dumas placed Marni Markenson's test on the table in front of her. Carrie sneaked a peek. Marni had gotten a B+. If Marni had pulled off a B+, that meant Carrie had to have gotten at least a—

D?

Carrie stared down at the paper that had just been dropped in front of her. There were red marks *everywhere*. It was as if Mr. Dumas's main heart artery had hemorrhaged while he was grading her test. The D had been circled and underlined and had arrows pointing to it, apparently indicating that her work was beyond *dismal* and *disappointing* and other negative adjectives beginning with the fourth letter in the alphabet. Carrie was absolutely shocked. She had never gotten a D in her life!

"See me after class," Mr. Dumas said before walking away.

Carrie slumped in her seat, tossing the rabbit's foot and her attached keys into her backpack in disgust. She should have known this would happen. The lucky T was shining its light somewhere else, and obviously the straight-A Carrie Fitzgerald was history.

❀ WANTED ❀

Single Teen Reader in search of a FUN romantic comedy read!

How Not to Spend Your Senior Year
BY CAMERON DOKEY

Royally Jacked
BY NIKI BURNHAM

Ripped at the Seams
BY NANCY KRULIK

Cupidity
BY CAROLINE GOODE

Spin Control
BY NIKI BURNHAM

South Beach Sizzle
BY SUZANNE WEYN & DIANA GONZALEZ

She's Got the Beat
BY NANCY KRULIK

30 Guys in 30 Days
BY MICOL OSTOW

Available from Simon Pulse ★ Published by Simon & Schuster

♥ ❀ ♥ ❖ ♥ ❖ ♥ ❖ ♥ ❀ ♥ ❖